"It's going to be all right," Lucas murmured against her ear.

Nicolette raised her head to gaze up at him, and all he knew was that she looked as if she needed to be kissed…badly.

Following instincts alone, he lowered his lips to hers, stunned when she tightened her grip around his neck and pressed closer against him.

She opened her mouth to allow him to deepen what he'd intended simply to be a kiss of compassion, of support. The kiss became so much more complicated than that. It stole his breath away. *You've got to stop*, a little voice whispered inside his head. Finally he broke the kiss.

It was as if she heard the little voice. She suddenly stepped back from him, her green eyes glowing and her breathing labored.

Before he could mutter an apology or say anything she grabbed his hand  "Come to my room, to me."

It never entered his r real cowboy never tu

'It's going to be all right,' Lucas
murmured against her ear...

...

Reluctantly, he made up his mind to deny her. After all, a
real ... had never turned down a lady's request.

A REAL COWBOY

BY
CARLA CASSIDY

MILLS
BOON

Published in Great Britain 2015
by Mills & Boon, an imprint of Harlequin (UK) Limited,
Eton House, 18-24 Paradise Road, Richmond, Surrey, TW9 1SR

© 2015 Carla Bracale

ISBN: 978-0-263-25406-8

18-0315

Harlequin (UK) Limited's policy is to use papers that are natural, renewable and recyclable products and made from wood grown in sustainable forests. The logging and manufacturing processes conform to the legal environmental regulations of the country of origin.

Printed and bound in Spain
by CPI, Barcelona

Carla Cassidy is a *New York Times* bestselling and award-winning author who has written more than one hundred books for Mills & Boon. In 1995 she won an *RT Book Reviews* award for *Anything for Danny*. In 1998 she won a Career Achievement Award for Best Innovative Series, also from *RT Book Reviews*.

Carla believes the only thing better than curling up with a good book to read is sitting down at the computer with a good story to write. She's looking forward to writing many more books and bringing hours of pleasure to readers.

Chapter 1

Even two weeks after the tornado that had ripped through the area of Bitterroot, Oklahoma—and in particular Cass Holiday's large ranch—the damage was still evident in the topless shed, the broken trees and in the very heart and souls of the twelve men who had worked as Cass's ranch hands.

The tornado had not only damaged outbuildings and felled trees, it had also taken the life of Cass Holiday, the tough, sixty-eight-year-old owner who had been like a mother to the cowboys she'd raised.

As dusk swept the area, Lucas Taylor leaned against the two-story house's porch railing. It was Saturday night and the rest of the cowboys had gone into town to drink away their sorrow and to commiserate with other people in town who had lost property or loved ones to the massive spring storm.

Lucas had never been much of a drinker and had volunteered to stay behind, knowing from the lawyer that Cass's niece and beneficiary was due to arrive sometime during the evening hours.

Lucas wanted to get a look, a feel for the woman who would now be their boss. From what he'd heard about her, he wasn't inclined to be overly impressed.

According to what they'd all been told, Cassandra Peterson was a struggling artist who co-owned a clothing boutique in the Soho area of New York City. She'd probably never seen a cow in her life, and Lucas had a feeling that she wouldn't stick around long.

No doubt, she'd have the cowboys work to put the place back to right and then she'd sell it. She'd make enough money to never struggle again and could go back to her life in the big city. Unfortunately, that meant Cass's dream and all of her hard work here would die.

The cowboys would eventually find jobs on other ranches, in other places, but the sense of community, the special bond of family they had shared here for so long, would be lost forever.

Pain shot through him. He remembered all too well what it was like to be alone, to be lost. He'd found a home here with eleven "brothers" and Cass years ago. Now at thirty-one years old, he didn't want to have to start all over again.

Hopefully he was wrong. Maybe Cassandra would be thrilled with the inheritance of the ranch and want to work it as her aunt had and continue to build on Cass's dreams.

It would be great if that happened, if she wanted to keep the ranch, live here and work it with the men who had helped to build it into the success it was now.

He straightened as he saw the faint dust rising up on the long dirt lane that led to the ranch. A dark sedan slowly approached, and Lucas's gut tightened when he realized it probably held the new boss.

The car turned into the ornate black gates with the overhead sign that read The Holiday Ranch. As the car got closer, Lucas could see that there was more than one person in it.

The vehicle, a rental car, pulled up in front of the house and came to a halt. He could see the blonde behind the wheel and realized there wasn't just another person in the passenger seat, but what looked like a kid in the backseat.

Maybe she wouldn't be in such a hurry to sell the place after all. Maybe she intended to stay and raise her kid here in the wide-open space of the ranch and the nearby small town of Bitterroot.

The driver door opened, and the minute he caught sight of the bright red high heel that hit the ground, he knew there was no way she would stay. A woman who wore those kinds of la-di-da shoes would never be happy on a big ranch in the middle of nowhere.

The high heel belonged to a short, slender woman who had the same blond hair and bright blue eyes as Cass, but that was the only characteristic she shared with her aunt. She was a pretty thing, but looked fragile and nervous.

Lucas made no move to greet her until the passenger stepped out of the car, along with a little dark-haired boy about six years old. The taller dark-haired woman with eyes the color of new spring grass smiled at him, and an instant wave of heat suffused him.

Cassandra Peterson might be pretty, but the woman

she'd brought with her was the stuff of Lucas's dreams. Long dark hair waved and curled loosely down her shoulders and framed a heart-shaped face with delicate features and those amazing green eyes.

"Mr. Benson?" Cassandra asked.

"No, Adam went into town this evening," Lucas replied.

"Oh, I understood that he was the foreman here," she said.

"He is, but all the men went into town and I volunteered to stay behind and get you settled in. I'm Lucas Taylor." He didn't bother to attempt to shake her hand, but he did tip his hat. "And you must be Cassandra Peterson."

"I am." She turned to the woman and little boy who had joined her. "And this is my friend Nicolette Kendall and her son, Sammy."

"Nice to meet you all," Lucas said. He might find Nicolette hot as hell, but she had the slick of the big city on her, too.

The little boy, Sammy, left his mother's side and stepped up in front of Lucas with a suspicious stare. "Are you a real cowboy?" he asked.

Lucas smiled down at him. "I'm a real cowboy," he replied.

Sammy looked him over from his head to his toe, and then met Lucas's gaze with a faint disdain. "My mommy says real cowboys spit and smell like cow poop and never take baths."

"Is that a fact?" Lucas shot a quick glance at Nicolette, whose cheeks flamed with color. If he had any question about how the two women would fare on the ranch, Sammy's words confirmed that they were clueless about real cowboys and working ranches.

"The only time I spit is if I get a bug in my mouth, and as far as I know I've never smelled like cow poop. But cowboys do only have to take a bath once a week." Lucas felt a sense of satisfaction wing through him as he watched Sammy slowly process what he'd said.

"Mom, did you hear that?" He ran back to his mother's side. "Cowboys only take baths once a week. I think I want to be a cowboy."

"Maybe we should get unloaded and settled in before it gets too dark," Cassandra suggested. She leaned into the driver door and popped the trunk open.

Although Lucas would have liked to see the two women struggle inside by carrying the mounds of suitcases and tote bags without his help, he knew that would only confirm their misconceptions. Besides, Cass would turn over in her grave if he didn't do the gentlemanly thing.

He moved to the trunk and grabbed two massive suitcases. "If you'll follow me, I'll show you around the house." They each grabbed a duffle bag and Sammy carried a smaller overnight case and together the four of them walked up the porch stairs and into a small formal living room.

"This room is where Cass would talk to one of us if we did something she didn't like," he said. "She didn't use it for much of anything else." He dropped the suitcases at the foot of the staircase that led up to the bedrooms and then guided them on through and into the huge great room with the attached large and airy kitchen.

"It's much nicer than I thought it would be," Cassandra said.

"Yeah, we've even got running water," he replied drily. He returned to the foot of the stairs and once again picked up the two suitcases. Without waiting to see if they followed, he headed up the stairs.

He heard their footsteps behind him and when he reached the first of the four bedrooms, he turned and immediately found himself face-to-face with Nicolette.

Up close she was even prettier than he'd initially thought, and she smelled like a flowery orchard of apples and pears and a touch of spice that made him want to taste her.

Instead he took two steps backward and motioned toward the bedroom. "This is the smallest and has the two twins. There are two more bedrooms with queen-size beds and the master that has a king. Two baths up here and two downstairs."

He dropped the suitcases, figuring they could decide bed assignments without his help. "The house was cleaned yesterday and all the bedding is fresh. The kitchen is fully stocked, and now I guess I'll leave you all to get settled."

"Mr. Taylor? The other cowboys? When would be a good chance for me to meet with all of them?" Cassandra asked.

"If you step out the back door and look in the distance, you'll see a building that looks something like a small motel. That's our bunks and at the back of the building is a dining-room area. That's usually where Cass talked to us if she had something specific to say. We eat breakfast around six each morning."

Cassandra blinked, as if she'd had no idea that there were two six o'clocks in a day. "Even on Sundays?"

"Even on Sundays," he replied.

"Then would you let them know that I intend to meet with them in the morning?"

Lucas nodded. "I'll let them all know. And now I'll just tell you all good-night."

The scent of Nicolette seemed to chase him down the stairs and finally dissipated from his senses as he stepped out into the now darkening night.

As he headed to the bunkhouses in the distance, he tried to shove all thoughts of Nicolette Kendall out of his head. The last thing he needed was to entertain any thoughts about a woman who held such low opinions of cowboys.

In any case, Lucas had no desire for any lasting relationship in his life. There were a couple of women in town he saw occasionally, women who knew he was not in it for the long term and were just fine with that.

Knowing it would be some time before the men started straggling in from town, Lucas headed for his own unit. When Cass had built the bunkhouse, she'd made it work like a motel. Each cowboy had his own room with a bed, a dresser and a bath.

It was their private space to decorate as they pleased and to entertain whomever they wanted. For Lucas it was just a place to be alone.

The dining area behind the private rooms held not only tables and benches for eating, but also a stone fireplace, two sofas, a couple of easy chairs and a television that was rarely turned on. The meals were prepared by an old cowhand nicknamed Cookie who had worked as the ranch cook for all of the nearly fifteen years that Lucas had been at Cass's place.

Lucas unlocked the door to his unit and stepped inside. He sat on the edge of the double-sized bed. Other than the clothes that hung on a small rod and the toiletries beneath the small sink, the room held nothing else personal.

He stretched out on his back and stared up at the ceiling and wondered what Cassandra would have to say to the men the next morning. Was this the beginning of a new era or was she the beginning of their end?

He'd had a faint sick feeling in his stomach since the moment he'd seen that red high heel step out of the car. He'd already lost the woman who had transformed his life. Now he feared that they were all about to lose their jobs and the place that had been, for some, their only real home.

It would be the end of family, the end of life as they all knew it. Cass's death had already been a devastating blow to them all, and he had a feeling the bad times weren't over yet.

Nicolette sat across from her best friend and business partner at the round wooden table in the kitchen. Sammy was upstairs, unpacking his things in the small room with the twin beds.

"I didn't expect the ranch to be so big," Cassie said as she wrapped her fingers around a hot mug of coffee. "I mean, I knew on paper how much acreage there was, but I didn't really grasp it."

"That's because the concept of big to us is an apartment with three bedrooms," Nicolette replied.

Cassie smiled, but only briefly. "I also didn't expect to see all the damage."

Nicolette nodded. "You hear about tornadoes and the damage they do on the news, but you don't really get a clear picture unless you actually see it with your own eyes."

As they'd driven past the small town of Bitterroot on their way to the ranch, they'd witnessed the devastation in the area that the massive storm cell had left behind.

"I feel so bad that it's hard for me to mourn a woman I scarcely knew. I mean, I only saw Aunt Cass a couple of times when I was young and then after my parents died we kept up through occasional letters, but we weren't exactly close," Cassie said. "We lived in such different worlds. I never dreamed that if anything happened to her I'd inherit her ranch."

"Have you definitely decided what you're going to do?" Nicolette asked Cassie. She knew how stunned Cassie had been to learn that her aunt Cass had died and left her as sole beneficiary to a working ranch with over a dozen employees.

Cassie sat back in the kitchen chair and looked around the large kitchen. Her friend was probably thinking of how different this kitchen was from the one they shared in their tiny Manhattan apartment.

"I'm still thinking that the best option is to get the damage cleaned up as quickly as possible and then sell the place. I'd make enough money from the sale that we could move into a bigger apartment and get a larger storefront to sell both my artwork and your clothing line."

Nicolette grinned ruefully. "Right now my clothing line is just a bunch of sketches in a book."

"But, if I sell this place we could make it all a reality," Cassie replied. "We could even afford to actually hire some help so that we aren't spending all our time at the store."

"What about the people who work here?" Nicolette's head instantly filled with a vision of the tall handsome cowboy who had greeted them.

Cassie waved a hand as if to dismiss the hired help. "I imagine the new owner would probably want to keep most of them." A grin lit her face and a small laugh escaped her lips. "I can't believe Sammy told that man what you said about cowboys."

Warmth leaped into Nicolette's cheeks. "I just wanted the ground to swallow me whole. I've never been so embarrassed."

Cassie laughed again. "At least he appeared to take it all in good humor."

"I guess, although he seemed pretty brusque after that when he showed us around the house." She looked at her watch. "It's getting late. I need to get Sammy into a bath and to bed."

"Yeah, and I should probably go to bed pretty soon if I'm going to be up by six to meet with all the cowboys. You will come with me, won't you?" Cassie looked at her hopefully.

"Are you going to tell them tomorrow that you intend to sell the place?" Nicolette asked.

Her friend frowned thoughtfully. "I think I'll just keep that to myself for right now and if anyone asks you, you don't know what my plans are."

"Are you sure you want to play it that way?" Nicolette asked, and got up from the table. "Maybe it would be better if you'd just be up-front with everyone."

Cassie's frown deepened. "I'm afraid if they know I'm planning on selling out, they'll all quit and find other jobs before the work here gets done. They certainly don't owe me any loyalty. Besides, at this moment I have no idea for sure what I intend to do. Just please tell me you'll be there with me in the morning when I face them all." Cassie got up from the table, a look of pleading on her pretty face.

Nicolette released a deep mock sigh. "You know that means that I'll have to wake up my six-year-old son to come to the bunkhouse with us, but you also know I'll do it because I owe you so much."

"Nonsense, you don't owe me anything." Together they put their cups in the sink and then headed for the stairs.

Nicolette told Cassie good-night as she veered into the first bedroom, where her son had unpacked his suitcase and was now seated on the bed clad in his pajamas with his handheld game system in play.

"Whoa, what are you doing in your pajamas already?" Nicolette asked. "You know it's always bath time before bedtime."

Sammy didn't look up from his game. "I took a bath last night, Mom. That means I don't have to take a bath until next Friday night. I told you that I've decided I'm going to be a cowboy."

"Sammy, I'm not going to argue with you about this. Now, get into the bathroom and into the tub."

He finally looked up at her, his blue eyes filled with innocence. "But, we're on a ranch and I just told you I'm a cowboy like Cowboy Lucas and he told me cowboys only take a bath once a week." His chin jutted out in a show of stubbornness.

"Cowboy Lucas was just joking," Nicolette replied, knowing that it was her own words and Lucas's response that had prompted this ridiculous problem.

Normally Sammy was a good, obedient child, but on the rare occasion he got that chin-jutting going on he became a monster child who could throw a tantrum as big as the entire state of Oklahoma.

"He wasn't joking. He didn't even smile when he told me cowboys took baths once a week," Sammy replied and folded his arms across his chest.

A rising irritation began to build in Nicolette, not because of the child on the bed, but rather toward the man who had filled his head with such nonsense.

"If Cowboy Lucas tells you he was just joking with you, then will you be a good boy and get into the bath?" Nicolette asked.

Sammy looked at her suspiciously. "I gotta hear it from him. You can't just pretend that you talked to him and then tell me that he said I had to take a bath. I gotta hear it from the cowboy's mouth."

Nicolette stared at her son in dismay. She knew she could do one of two things—she could demand that her son obey her, resulting in tension and tears and a battle she was too weary to endure, or she could go get that handsome cowboy and straighten this out once and for all.

"You wait right here," she said, and then left his room and walked down the hallway to the master suite. The door was open and Cassie had already changed from her clothes into her nightshirt. "Cassie, could you do me a favor and keep an eye on Sammy while I go chase down a cowboy?"

Cassie raised a blond eyebrow and gave her a teasing grin. "I never took you for the pushy type, but I have to admit he was rather hot."

"Aren't you a funny one," Nicolette said drily. "I need to make Cowboy Lucas talk to Sammy and tell him that cowboys bathe every night, not just once a week."

"Uh-oh, sounds like our ideas about cowboys have come back to bite our backsides," Cassie said. She grabbed Nicolette by the arm and they headed back to Sammy's bedroom.

"I'll read him a story. You'd better find a flashlight if you have to go all the way to the bunkhouse. You don't want to step in any cow poop." Cassie grinned and then gave Nicolette a quick hug. "I can't thank you enough for taking this journey with me. Now, go find your cowboy."

"He's not my cowboy," Nicolette muttered darkly as she headed down the stairs. She went into the kitchen to look in the cabinet under the sink, which seemed a likely place to store a flashlight.

"Bingo." She grabbed the big yellow-handled light and headed for the door in the kitchen that would take her outside and in the direction of the bunkhouse.

She just wanted this night to be over. The past week had been frenzied with them closing up the store indefinitely, packing and preparing for their trip here. The day had been particularly long as their plane had been delayed twice in a layover in Chicago. Then there was the task of obtaining a rental car and taking the forty-minute drive from Oklahoma City to Bitterroot and the ranch.

She shone the flashlight beam on the ground before her as she made her way toward the building in the distance. Thank goodness she was also aided by the light of a full moon overhead.

In truth, she'd rather eat dirt than ask Lucas for his help, but he owed it to her considering he was the one who had told Sammy cowboys bathed only once a week.

Well, if she was perfectly truthful with herself, she was the one who had first told Sammy that, but that had been before she'd actually met a cowboy. She'd never dreamed she would be on a ranch with real cowboys, and she marveled now at all the paths she'd walked so far in her relatively short life.

She'd gone from wife to a wealthy man, to near poverty and single parenthood in what felt like the blink of an eye. What little money she'd had when she'd left her husband she'd invested in the store, but that venture was barely making money. New York was a brutal city if you didn't have money.

She looked ahead to the structure looming close. Lucas had been right; it did look like a twelve-unit motel. It was easy to see which one was Lucas's, as it was the only unit that had lights shining out the window.

Her stomach tensed as she approached the door. Even though she'd told Sammy first about cowboys not taking baths, Lucas should have told him different. It was his fault that this whole mess had happened with Sammy.

With more than a touch of irritation rising inside her, she knocked briskly. He opened the door and her breath caught just a bit. Without his hat, his dark, slightly shaggy dark hair gleamed in the light. His intense blue eyes widened before he raised a hand in front of his face.

"Turn off that flashlight," he exclaimed.

Warmth leaped into her cheeks as she realized she'd had the light shining directly on his handsome, chiseled features. She quickly clicked it off. "Sorry about that."

He stepped outside and looked around. "What are you doing out here all by yourself in the dark?"

"You told my son that cowboys only bathe once a week and now Sammy won't get into the bathtub."

By the light of the room spilling out where they stood, she saw his amusement curve his lips upward. "Is that a fact," he replied. "Sounds like a personal problem to me."

"It's all your fault," she said, at the same time trying not to notice the wonder of his broad shoulders, the slim hips that wore his jeans so well.

He raised a dark eyebrow. "The way I see it, you started it." He turned his head and spit to one side. "Oh, sorry about that. I'm just doing what cowboys do."

This time the heat that filled her cheeks was a new wave of pure embarrassment. "Look, I'm sorry. When I told my son those things, I'd never really met a cowboy before. The only cowboy I've ever even seen in my entire life is the naked singing cowboy in Times Square."

This time both his dark brows rose in surprise. "There's a naked cowboy who sings?"

"Well, he's not really naked. He wears a pair of briefs." She shook her head in frustration. "But that's not the point. I now have a little boy who refuses to take a bath because he's decided he wants to be a cowboy and you said he only had to take one once a week. Can you please come back to the house with me and tell him differently?"

Lucas leaned back on his boot heels. "Little boys can get pretty sweaty just sitting around and doing nothing," he mused. "Your son must be pretty headstrong for you to resort to coming all the way down here for my help."

"He's usually a good boy, but it's been a long day and he's a bit out of sorts and he told me the only way he'd get into the tub was if Cowboy Lucas told him to."

Amusement once again danced in his eyes as he gave her a smile that made her feel just a little bit breathless. "Basically you've come to say you're sorry about your preconceived notions about cowboys, because I think it would be nice if you apologized before asking for my help about anything."

"You're right. I am sorry," she replied, wondering if he wanted her to get down on her knees before him and grovel, as well.

"Okay then, let's go." He pulled the door of his unit closed behind him and fell into step next to her.

"A naked, singing cowboy...and you New Yorkers think we're strange." He laughed, a low, deep rumble that she found far too pleasant.

She realized at that moment that she wasn't afraid of cows or horses, that she wasn't worried about falling into the mud or getting her hands dirty.

The real danger came from the attraction she felt for the man who walked next to her, a man whose laughter warmed her and who smelled like spring wind and leather.

She didn't want to get too friendly with anyone on the ranch. She definitely didn't want to feel attracted to any cowboy who worked here. She knew Cassie's plan to sell the place and get back to New York City.

All she needed from Lucas was for him to straighten

out bath time for Sammy and, before she knew it, she and her son and Cassie would be back on a plane headed back to their real life in New York.

Chapter 2

Nobody was surprised when six o'clock rolled around and there was no new boss in the building. Lucas sat at one of the long picnic tables sipping coffee as most of the other cowboys finished up their breakfasts.

Sunday morning breakfast was usually the quietest of the week, as lack of sleep and hangovers were invisible, unwelcomed guests. This morning the crew was a bit livelier than usual as they anticipated meeting their new boss.

"Think she'll be here by noon?" Clay Madison asked Lucas drily.

"Big-city folk probably never see a sunrise," Jerod Steen said from his seat down the table.

"I think maybe we should all cut her a little bit of slack. It's the first morning and they're now on central time, not eastern time," Lucas replied.

He was perfectly content to sip his coffee and wait

until Cassandra Peterson showed up for her official coronation as the new leader of the pack. He only hoped his fellow "brothers" wouldn't tear her to bits on the very first morning.

At that moment Cassandra came through the door, followed by both Nicolette and Sammy. Sammy's gaze tracked around the room, and when it landed on Lucas he gave him a big smile and an enthusiastic wave before he and Nicolette sat down on the picnic table bench closest to the door.

Cassandra stood just inside the door and cleared her throat, obviously nervous as she faced the dozen cowboys, who had all fallen silent. Cookie, the ranch-hand cook, made a baker's dozen and now stood in the doorway between the dining area and the kitchen.

By the faint tremor in her voice and her forced smile, it was clear that Cassandra was uneasy. Lucas knew his attention should be focused on the woman who held his future in her trembling hands, but instead he found his gaze shifting to Nicolette.

Both she and Cassandra were clad in skinny jeans that probably cost more than Lucas's entire wardrobe. Cassandra wore a tailored white blouse, the jeans and a pair of heels, but Nicolette had on a pair of gold sandals and a green form-fitting spring lightweight sweater. And the form it was fitting was slamming hot.

Unlike last night when her hair had hung freely beyond her shoulders, this morning it was neatly tamed and clasped in a green-and-blue little beaded tie at the nape of her neck.

Although he'd liked her hair the way it had been the night before, slightly wild with a touch of curl, this morning with it pulled back it gave him a perfect view of her long neck and delicate jawline.

He was vaguely aware of Cassandra talking to them about repairing the damage from the tornado and getting the ranch back up to normal.

Sammy turned his head and gave him a quick thumbs-up. Lucas nodded to the boy, whom he had found both bright and a bit precocious the night before. He'd had little interaction with Nicolette as he'd told her son that actually real cowboys bathed every night.

He wondered where the kid's father was and if he was in the boy's life. Lucas knew all about growing up without a father. Hell, he knew all about growing up without much of a mother, too.

The absence or not of a father in Sammy's life is not your problem, he told himself and directed his attention back to Cassandra, who had introduced herself as Cassie. As long as she didn't call herself Cass, he thought.

They were all Cass's cowboys, and Cassandra Peterson had a lot to prove before any of them would even begin to consider themselves Cassie's cowboys.

He turned his attention back to Cassie, as she appeared to be winding down. "I know it's going to take a while for us all to get comfortable with each other. I also know that I'm asking a lot in hoping that you all will continue to do whatever you do as daily chores and get the property repairs finished as soon as possible."

She turned her gaze to Adam, who worked as foreman. "If you could come up to the house with me, I'd like to have a chat with you about exactly how things run around here."

Adam rose, looking none too happy, and he, Cassie, Nicolette and Sammy disappeared out the door.

"Guess that's a wrap," Dusty Crawford said, and grabbed his hat from the bench next to him.

"They won't last a week here," Brady Booth replied. He got up from the table and grasped his hat. "She looked so nervous, like she half expected us to rope and hog-tie her and send her back to New York."

Dusty flashed dimples in a grin. "I wouldn't mind roping her, but I might have something else in mind rather than sending her back to the big city. I wouldn't mind having her as a bunk mate. She's just my type, blonde and small and sexy."

Lucas stood and tipped Dusty's hat so it nearly covered his face. "Big talk from the baby in the group." At twenty-six Dusty was the youngest of all the men. Truthfully, Lucas was just glad that as they all left the dining room the talk was about Cassandra and not Nicolette.

Not that he cared about the dark-haired beauty. He didn't know anything about her and in any case didn't need to know anything. She was just his boss's friend, nothing more, nothing less.

He followed the rest of the men out into the early May morning and headed for the stables. The daily tasks were rotated, and today was Lucas's day to ride the fence line and look for any breeches or issues.

Thank God he'd mucked the stalls the day before and wouldn't have to do that nasty task again for another eleven days. It was one of the jobs that had to be done that nobody particularly liked to do.

This morning it was just his horse, Lucky, and him and the wide-open pasture. He strode toward the stables, breathing deeply of the clean air and enjoying the warmth of the sunshine on his shoulders.

The stables held twenty stalls, ten on each side. All the ranch hand horses were housed here as well as several other horses that Cass had for herself and guests. When Lucas walked in, several of the men were saddling up their mounts for the morning chores.

Some of them would be heading out to the pasture to check on the cattle, to make sure none appeared ill and there were no signs of prey that had bothered the herd overnight.

Dusty had disappeared into the tack room, where he would spend most of the morning cleaning and oiling the saddles and harnesses that weren't in use.

The ranch worked like a well-oiled engine. Everyone knew what they were supposed to do each day. Cass had believed in structure and routine, and all of the men had thrived beneath her rigid system.

It took only minutes for him to saddle up and head out, the sun warm and the smell of sweet spring grass filling his head. Lucky was a strong, fast mount who danced his feet as if eager to go for a run.

Sawyer Quincy opened the gate that led to the pasture for Lucas, and when Lucas had ridden through Sawyer closed the gate once again. Although it was rare for the cattle to come this close to the stables and other outbuildings, it wasn't unheard of.

Somebody checked the fence line every day, but since the storm that had ravaged the area, trees and large limbs had fallen and continued to fall, sometimes causing a new break in the fencing.

He rode at a slow pace, keeping an eye on the fence

while enjoying the freedom and sense of pride he always felt when on the back of his horse and working.

There had been a time in his past when he was certain his future held only two outcomes, jail or death. Cass had changed all that and now she was gone.

Sorrow squeezed his heart as he thought of the sixty-eight-year-old woman who had saved them all. Cass Holiday had been tough, but loving. She'd been fair and had instilled a sense of pride, of belonging and of self-esteem in all of the cowboys who'd served her. He shoved away thoughts of the woman they had buried in the family plot not far from where he rode.

Instead a vision of Nicolette leaped into his head. He'd never felt the kind of instant attraction that he'd felt for her for any other woman in his life. The moment she'd gotten out of the car the night before, something inside him had sizzled with an unusual heat.

He thought of the little nest egg he'd saved up over the years. He'd always known that this life with Cass wouldn't last forever, and there was a small ranch on the other side of Bitterroot that had been for sale for the past year.

He'd often thought about buying it and beginning to build what Cass had here, but his loyalty to Cass had stopped him from any action in that direction.

Now with Cass gone and the future of the ranch up in the air, maybe it was time for him to go his own way. Still, the idea of leaving the men he'd thought of as his brothers, of walking away from here before he knew what Cassie intended to do, now made the thought of going elsewhere painful.

In his deepest fantasies, when he made his move he hoped there would be a woman by his side, a woman

who wanted to build something lasting and meaningful with him. Although he told himself that was his
heart's hope, his head told him not to believe that fantasy, never to trust any woman again and to never give
his heart away.

If and when he decided to build a life away from
Cass's ranch, he would be alone, as he'd been for so
many years.

Besides, the only woman who had captured his attention for more than a minute recently was definitely
a woman who would prefer champagne to cold beer,
chiffon to flannel and city lights to the starry Oklahoma skies.

It was almost noon when he finally finished his sur-
vey, finding no issues with the fence line. He got off his
horse to open the gate and from there he walked Lucky
toward the stables.

He'd almost made it to the building when he saw
Sammy running toward him, his dark hair gleaming
in the sun and a happy smile on his face.

Lucas had a feeling his mother wouldn't be wearing a happy smile when she saw the filthy condition of
what had once been white sneakers on the boy's feet.

"What are you doing out here?" Lucas asked. He
guided Lucky into the stables with Sammy close on
his heels.

"Waiting for you." Sammy watched as Lucas unsad-
dled Lucky and hung the saddle over a sawhorse, where
several others also hung, waiting to be oiled and polished by Dusty. "I was hoping maybe I could eat lunch
at the bunkhouse with all you cowboys."

"Does your mom know you're out here?" Lucas
asked.

Sammy hesitated a moment, giving Lucas his answer. "She and Cassie were making a big salad for lunch and talking about Cassie's painting and clothes." He wrinkled up his nose. "They're boring. I want to be out here with you and learn everything about being a cowboy."

His blue eyes shone with an eagerness that Lucas remembered feeling the first day he'd arrived here at the ranch. Still, the last thing Lucas wanted was to be pulled into the life of some kid who would certainly be around for only a short period of time.

"Where's your dad?" Lucas asked, more gruffly than he intended.

Sammy shrugged. "Probably he's on his yacht. He's a very busy man. I haven't seen him since we divorced him two years ago and I didn't see him much before then." Again Lucas's heartstrings were plucked. "So, can I eat lunch at the bunkhouse with you?" Sammy asked eagerly.

Lucas put Lucky into his stall before replying. He stepped outside the stables with Sammy at his side. He was about to tell the kid that he needed to talk to his mother, but at that moment he saw Nicolette hurrying toward them...and she looked like a mad bull who had just seen red.

Nicolette's heart felt as if it might beat right out of her chest. For the past fifteen minutes she'd run through the house, calling her son's name without hearing any response.

Unsure where her son might have wandered, but knowing how vast the ranch was and how unknowledgeable he was about the dangers, she'd become frantic with worry.

Now that she saw him safe and sound with Lucas, her worry turned to anger. "Samuel Ray Kendall," she yelled as she drew closer to the two.

"Uh-oh," Sammy said and winced.

Her boy understood that when she called him by his full name he was in big trouble. As he should be, she thought, fully steamed. "Don't ever leave the house again without telling me," she exclaimed when she finally reached him. "I've been frantic, searching everywhere in the house for you."

"We were just about to come and find you," Lucas said. "I found him just a minute ago by the stables."

Nicolette gazed at her son. "You can't just run wild around here. You don't know how dangerous it might be."

"I just wanted to find Cowboy Lucas and see if I could eat at the bunkhouse dining room," Sammy replied, looking down at his feet. "I'd rather eat a cowboy lunch than a girlie lunch."

"If you don't mind, he can eat lunch with me," Lucas said.

Sammy begged her with his eyes. "Please, Mom?"

The last thing Nicolette wanted was for her son to forge any real bonds with the cowboys here. She didn't want his heart broken when they eventually left…and they would leave as soon as Cassie decided it was time to go. But, surely a lunch wouldn't hurt and she hated to disappoint her son, who had already had a lifetime of disappointments.

"I suppose it would be okay as long as you come

right back to the house when you're finished eating," she relented.

Lucas touched Sammy on the shoulder. "Why don't you run ahead and tell Cookie that I said to set an extra plate."

"Cool," Sammy replied and took off running toward the building in the distance.

"I don't want him to be a bother," she said to Lucas once Sammy was far enough away not to hear her.

"I'll let you know if he becomes a bother," Lucas replied. "I asked him where his father was and he told me he was probably on a yacht, that he is a very busy man." Lucas's blue eyes gazed at her not just with curiosity, but also with the heat of an interest in her as a woman.

Nicolette felt her cheeks warm. "I divorced my husband two years ago and he probably is on his yacht, or in his penthouse or someplace that is party conducive, because that's what he likes to do."

Lucas tilted his head, the cast of the sun and the brim of his hat momentarily hiding his eyes. "You don't sound bitter about it."

She smiled and shook her head. "I'm not bitter. It's a long story and lunch is waiting. Sammy was the best thing that came out of my marriage and he's all I wanted when I walked away. Samuel got to keep his yacht, his trust fund and whatever else he owned, and I got Sammy, definitely the best part of the deal."

Lucas leaned his head forward so that she once again got a look at his beautiful blue eyes, and they appeared to be filled with a longing and an admiration that she wasn't sure she understood.

It unsettled her and she smiled again and took a step backward. "I'm keeping you from lunch."

He nodded. "I'll see to it that Sammy gets safely back to the house after eating."

"Thanks, I appreciate it." She turned and hurried away, feeling the heat of his gaze lingering on her. She hadn't been so attracted to a man since nine years ago when she'd first met Samuel Kendall, and never had two men been more different from each other.

She'd been a naive twenty-one-year-old when she'd met Samuel. He'd been elegant, airbrushed and hair sprayed, but he'd managed to sweep her off her feet with sweet talk and empty promises.

She had a feeling that Lucas Taylor had never made a promise to anyone that he hadn't kept and that the wind-and-sun scent he carried was just as evocative as the expensive cologne that Samuel had worn.

"I see you found him," Cassie said as Nicolette stepped up on the porch.

"He wants to eat lunch with Lucas at the bunkhouse."

"Why is it that every time you say that cowboy's name your cheeks get pink and your eyes sparkle just a little bit brighter?" Cassie asked.

"Don't be ridiculous," Nicolette scoffed and pushed open the door to enter the house. She walked through to the kitchen, where she and Cassie had prepared a chicken Caesar salad for lunch.

She sat at the round oak table and Cassie took the seat opposite her. "You know it would be crazy to get attached to any of the men here," Cassie said.

"I know that." Nicolette filled her plate with the salad. "I have no intention of getting close to anyone. How did things go this morning with you and Adam?" she asked in an effort to get the conversation off Lucas.

Cassie groaned. "There's so much to learn. Thankfully Adam pretty much knows everything and can keep things going smoothly. He told me in the last couple of years Aunt Cass had depended on him more and more. I won't be here long enough to learn all there is to know. I told him I wanted the repair work to be a priority."

"Do you think he knows you want to sell as soon as possible?"

"I don't think so. I told him I wanted him to teach me about the bookkeeping and the ordering process and whatever else I should know. Oh, and the big bell that hangs off the front porch? If we ever need help or anything, we ring it and the cowboys will all come running."

Nicolette raised a brow. "That's good to know, and it sounds like you and Adam are going to be spending a lot of time together. Adam isn't too hard to look at, either."

Cassie took a bite of her salad and washed it down with a sip of iced tea. "You don't have to worry about me going crazy about any man here. I know where we belong, and this definitely isn't the place."

Nicolette stared out the window absently. Her problem was that since her divorce from Samuel, she wasn't sure where she and Sammy belonged. As much as she loved Cassie, sharing her tiny apartment certainly wasn't what she wanted for herself and her son forever.

"We need to take the rental car back tomorrow." Cassie interrupted her thoughts. "I guess we'll have to have somebody follow us into Bitterroot and bring us back here. Adam told me Aunt Cass has a car here, so we can use it to go back and forth to town once we get rid of the rental."

"Did you ask Adam if he could follow us tomorrow?" Nicolette asked.

Cassie shook her head, her pale blond hair glistening in the noon sunshine that drifted in through the windows. "I didn't want to ask him because I think he needs to be here to supervise things. We'll snag one of the other men in the morning to take care of it."

Nicolette nodded and focused on her salad. She wondered what Sammy was eating with the cowboys. She hoped none of them took offense to his being there, although she was certain that he was in good hands with Lucas.

Funny how she'd known the tall, handsome cowboy for only fewer than twenty-four hours and yet she trusted him without question with the safety of her son. She hadn't ever trusted Samuel completely with their son's safety.

There was just something strong, something solid about Lucas Taylor that invited trust. She didn't want to think about the other qualities he possessed that had instantly sparked a physical desire.

As they ate, Cassie talked about new plans for the store, trying her hand at painting landscapes instead of cityscapes and the idea of a new apartment where the three of them could comfortably cohabitate when they returned to New York City.

Nicolette didn't want to live with her best friend for the rest of her life. She knew she had to somehow figure out a plan of action that would gain her enough money to support herself and her son.

She also knew that there would probably never be a clothing line with her name on it. The idea that she could be a fashion designer with her own label had been born when she'd been the bored, neglected wife of a wealthy man.

Cassie had nurtured the idea because it worked with the idea of her store and her identity as a creative artist who surrounded herself with other creative people. The problem was since her divorce Nicolette hadn't managed to figure out exactly what she wanted to do and where exactly she belonged.

After lunch Cassie disappeared into her bedroom and Nicolette sat on the back porch to watch for Sammy. A faint breeze blew the scent of grass and hay that was both novel and pleasant. In the distance she could see cows in the pasture, and she heard the rustle of leaves in the trees.

For a few minutes she felt completely at peace. Her thoughts didn't linger on the painful past, or jump ahead to worry about the future. She was just in the moment, enjoying the lack of traffic noise and the press of people at a stoplight, the feeling that you were always one step behind everyone else in the world.

She sat up straighter upon seeing Sammy in the distance, Lucas by his side. She watched as the two of them headed in her direction and she tried not to admire the confidence and easy roll of Lucas's hips with each step.

She couldn't help but notice that Sammy appeared taller, more grown up, as he tried to match Lucas stride for stride.

They got halfway to the house and then Lucas stopped and raised a hand to her. Sammy broke into a run and Nicolette felt a faint disappointment as she realized Lucas didn't intend to escort him all the way home.

And why should he? she chided herself. He probably had afternoon chores to get done and he'd already gone out of his way to allow Sammy to eat with them.

Sammy's face was lit with a smile that flew happiness through her. "It was great, Mom," he exclaimed as he plopped down next to her on the stoop. "I met all of the cowboys. There's Dusty and Mac, and Tony and Brody and Clay…"

"Whoa." Nicolette laughed. "I won't be able to remember all those names. What did you have to eat?"

"A big bowl of beef stew and corn bread. It was awesome. And they all said I could be the mascot of the ranch and eat lunch there every day if you let me, and Lucas said he'd start teaching me about being a cowboy. You'll let me, right, Mom?"

Oh, those blue eyes of his held such wonder and excitement, things she hadn't seen in him for a very long time. "I think we can work it out that you can have lunch there occasionally as long as the men don't mind. As far as Lucas teaching you to be a cowboy, we'll have to make sure he has time for that."

"He already told me he'd do it in the evenings after all his chores are done for the day," Sammy replied. "Maybe when we go to town we could get me a cowboy hat."

"We'll see," Nicolette replied.

Sammy jumped to his feet. "I'm going to find Cassie. I got to tell her all about her cowboys." Before Nicolette could reply, Sammy disappeared through the screen door and into the house.

Hours later Nicolette once again found herself sitting on the porch step, gazing upward at the thousands of stars that glittered like diamonds in the sky.

Sammy was in bed asleep, Cassie had retired to her room, but Nicolette had been too restless to settle in for the night. She was pleased with her decision to sit out here, the starlit sky an unexpected surprise.

In New York their apartment windows looked out on other apartment windows. Even standing outside, the bright lights of the city obscured the glimpse of most of the stars.

"Bored to tears?"

The deep voice so close to her made her jump. She turned to see Lucas standing nearby, his features hidden in night shadows. "You scared me half to death," she replied.

"Sorry, I didn't mean to scare you." He stepped up on the porch and then took his hat off and sat down next to her. Instantly she was surrounded by his slightly wild, wonderful scent. "And no, I'm not bored. I was just enjoying the beauty of the night skies."

He tilted his head and looked up, then gazed back at her. "It is pretty, isn't it?"

She nodded. "And as alien to me as the cows in the pasture. We don't get many stargazing nights in New York City. I hope Sammy wasn't too big of a pain today."

He smiled, his teeth flashing white in the semidarkness of the porch. "The men all easily took to him. He seems to be a good kid."

"He is, but you don't have to teach him how to be a cowboy. I'm sure you have other, more important things to do in your spare time." She could feel a faint heat wafting from him, a heat that flowed through her veins and curled into a pool inside her stomach.

"Don't have a wife, don't have a girlfriend, I've got plenty of time on my hands and I can't think of any way I'd rather spend it right now than with a kid eager to learn." He hesitated a moment and then continued, "What about you? You have a boyfriend anxiously awaiting your return to the big city?"

She laughed and shook her head. "In the last two years I've only had two priorities in my life, Sammy and the store I co-own with Cassie, and they don't leave any time for dating. Besides, I'm not looking for a romance right now. Since my divorce two years ago I'm just trying to figure out my life."

She was far too conscious of his nearness, of the scent of him, the heat of him and the allure of his beautiful eyes. Once again she looked up at the stars as they both fell silent.

There were so many things she wanted to ask him, such as how he'd come to work for Cass Holiday and where he had come from. Did he have a close family who lived in the area? And yet she knew Cassie was right—she'd be a fool to get close to anyone here.

"I guess you haven't had a chance to get into Bitterroot yet," he said, finally breaking the silence that had become more uncomfortable by the second.

"Actually we need to go there tomorrow to return the rental car. We were going to ask one of you to follow us so that we'd have a ride home."

"I'd be glad to do it," he replied instantly. "I've got a king cab pickup so there would be plenty of room for everyone. Maybe you all would like to go a little early, have some lunch at the Bitterroot Café and take some time to soak up some of the local color."

"That sounds like a good idea. I'll talk to Cassie in the morning and see if we can make plans to go around eleven or so. Sammy wants a cowboy hat, so before lunch we could get that. We could arrange for a time for you to come back and pick us up so that you aren't cooling your heels while we do a little exploring of the town." She was babbling and she knew it, but seemed unable to help herself.

He stood and held out a hand to help her up from the porch stoop. "Why don't we plan on eleven."

She hesitated only a moment and then held out her hand to grasp his. Warm and big and slightly calloused, his hand engulfed hers. She stood, half-breathless by the simple contact.

"Okay, then I guess I'll see you in the morning around eleven," she replied.

Only then did he release her hand. With another of his gorgeous smiles, he grabbed his hat, put it on his head and then turned and disappeared into the darkness of the night.

Nicolette released a deep breathless sigh and went inside the house. She locked the door behind her, wondering how on earth she was going to sleep with the smell of him filling her head, with her fingers tingling from the contact with his and the thought of those slightly calloused hands moving all over her body.

Chapter 3

Sammy danced along the back porch with the excitement of new adventures to come. Nicolette stood at the back door, a different kind of excitement stirring in her as she watched for Lucas's truck in the distance to follow them into town.

It was ridiculous how long she'd tossed and turned the night before with visions of the handsome cowboy dancing in her head. Cassie was at the kitchen table, reading the Monday morning edition of the Bitterroot newspaper that Adam had brought to her earlier that morning.

"There isn't much here as far as hard news," Cassie called out. "Although there is a report of a missing woman who worked as a waitress at the café. Her name is Wendy Bailey and she hasn't been seen or heard from for over a week. Other than that, I can tell you that there's a big sale at the discount store and Jerry and

Wanda Swaggart celebrated their fiftieth wedding anniversary yesterday with a reception at the Methodist church."

"That's nice," Nicolette replied. She'd once thought she and Samuel would be married for fifty years or more. When she'd married him she'd believed in a happily-ever-after, but her happy had really lasted for only about a year.

She shoved aside thoughts of her broken marriage as she saw a black pickup driving up from the large building that housed the vehicles.

"He's coming," she said to Cassie. "Come on, Sammy. We'll meet him out front by the rental car."

By the time the three of them got to the front door, Lucas had pulled his truck up next to the car. "Good morning," he said.

"I really appreciate this," Cassie said to him. "We were told there was a place in Bitterroot to return the car."

"Gus's Gas Station," Lucas replied. "Gus dabbles in a little bit of everything, including rental cars. His place is right on Main Street. You can't miss it as it's the only gas station in town."

"Can I ride with Lucas?" Sammy asked Nicolette.

"Oh, I don't think…" she began.

"I wouldn't mind his company." Lucas cut to the chase.

Nicolette shrugged helplessly as Sammy raced to the passenger door of the truck and climbed up inside. "We'll see you in town," he called to her and gave her a beaming smile.

Minutes later they were on the road, following the

big black pickup. "Sammy seems to have taken a real shine to Lucas," Cassie said.

"I know. He seems to be a nice man and he's already spent more time with Sammy than Samuel ever did."

"Doesn't it worry you a bit? I mean, we aren't going to be here that long…maybe a couple of months at the most, and that's it. We'll want to be back in New York before the school year begins in September."

Nicolette stared out the side window, where the rural landscape was beautiful in its vastness. Of course, spring in New York held its own special kind of beauty.

She finally turned back to gaze at Cassie. "I want Sammy to enjoy every minute of his life, and that includes his time here. He needs a man's presence around him even if it's a cowboy and even if it's only temporary. He'll be better for this experience when we get back to the city."

"I just don't want to see him hurt," Cassie said. "You know I love that kid like he is my own."

Nicolette smiled. "I know and I appreciate it. I don't know what Sammy and I would have done when I left Samuel if not for you." She hesitated a moment and then added, "But you know we can't live with you forever. I've got to figure out a path that has me earning enough money so that Sammy and I can make our own way."

"Just wait. Once I sell the ranch and invest the money into our store, you'll be making plenty of money." There was a confidence in Cassie's voice that Nicolette wished she felt.

Although Cassie painted beautiful paintings, she did so in a city where talent was on every street corner and in hundreds of galleries. She was attempting to sell her work out of a store that also carried clothes, purses and shoes that Nicolette chose to go on the racks and displays.

So far their joint venture could scarcely be called a huge success. While they made enough each month to cover the bills, there was rarely any money left over for anything else.

There had been a time when Nicolette had met Samuel that she'd dreamed of being a teacher. She'd been working as a dress saleswoman in an upscale store and taking night classes when she'd first met the man she would marry.

After their marriage, he'd insisted she stop going to school because being his wife was a 24/7 kind of job and it didn't look right for a woman who had married as well as she had to be taking classes to become a teacher.

She cast aside all thoughts of the past as they drove by the sign that indicated they'd entered the city limits of Bitterroot, Oklahoma. They had driven past the town on the highway when coming in from Oklahoma City, so this would be her first real glimpse of the town that would be a part of their lives until they left here.

Main Street consisted of three blocks of businesses. Nicolette sat up straighter in her seat as they crawled along behind Lucas's pickup.

They passed the Bitterroot Café with its bright yellow awnings. The police station, a one-story brick building, was next door. She spied a shop that sold Western wear and knew that was probably where they'd find the hat for Sammy.

There were the usual businesses you would expect to find in any town, a post office, a bank and a hardware store. There was a grocery store, a feed store and even a little boutique and a tearoom that looked interesting.

Gus's Gas Station was at the end of the business district, a small two-pump station with signs advertising the rental of everything from cars to wedding champagne fountains.

Lucas pulled up in front of the building and Cassie parked next to him. Sammy jumped down from the passenger seat as Lucas leaned out the window.

"You want me to wait for you to get the car checked in and then take you to the café?" he asked.

"No, thanks. We'll just walk back," Cassie replied. "If you need to head back to the ranch, then I can call Adam to come and get us later."

"Actually, I've got some shopping to do myself. Cookie gave me a huge list of supplies he needs and so I'll probably still be in town when you all finish up. I'll park in front of the post office and we can meet up there later."

He backed away and Sammy, Cassie and Nicolette headed into Gus's business to return the rental. Gus was a character, with wiry white hair growing everywhere but on the bald dome of his head. Hairs sprouted out of his ears, his eyebrows were forests and a pure white mustache covered his upper lip and drooped down on the sides to his chin.

He flirted with both women, teased Sammy and took care of the business efficiently. Within minutes they were leisurely walking toward the center of town.

"I suppose the first thing we should do is get this little cowboy a hat," Nicolette said, and was rewarded by the huge smile from her son.

"A black hat just like Lucas's," he said.

"I thought all the good guys wore white hats," Cassie said.

Sammy looked at her with a touch of indignation.

"Now, it would be just plain silly to wear a white hat when you're working outside and doing all kinds of ranch stuff."

Cassie exchanged an amused glance with Nicolette. "Well, excuse me for not knowing about such cowboy things."

Sammy giggled and swaggered just ahead of them, as if he already wore a big hat and had spurs on his heels. If nothing else this break from the city was good for him, Nicolette thought. It was good for him to know that there was something different in the world besides concrete sidewalks and throngs of people.

It was just after noon when they entered the Bitterroot Café. They'd had a fun morning walking down the sidewalks and peeking into different stores. They had all laughed as Sammy had tried on a variety of black hats, some sitting low on the tips of his ears and others perched atop his head like a little black bird. They finally found one that fit him perfectly, and his swagger became even more pronounced.

The Bitterroot Café was what Nicolette had assumed any small-town café would be like—worn yellow vinyl booths against the walls, tables in the center and a long counter with stools.

"I can feel the calories finding my hips right now," Cassie said.

Nicolette smiled, knowing she was talking about the sinful scents of fried food, homemade pies and yeasty breads. "I'm not even going to think about a diet during this meal," she replied. "I intend to completely indulge myself."

They were greeted by a brassy redhead who introduced herself as Daisy, the owner of the café. As she led them to a booth toward the back of the establishment, Nicolette was aware of the curious gazes that shot their way from the other diners.

She was grateful to arrive at the booth, where she and Cassie sat on one side and Sammy and his hat sat across from them. Daisy handed them menus with the promise to return.

"I already know what I want," Sammy said and shoved his menu aside. "I want grilled cheese, French fries and a glass of chocolate milk."

"Sounds like a hearty cowboy lunch to me," Nicolette replied. She tried to ignore those gazes and the whispers of the other people in the café, especially the gazes from several rough-looking men who sat at the counter.

They were obviously ranch hands, although she knew they didn't work at Cassie's ranch. The glances they slid in Cassie and her direction were both slightly salacious yet filled with a touch of derision.

When Daisy returned to take their orders, she must have seen Nicolette looking at the men, who were now laughing among themselves. "Don't pay no mind to them. I'm assuming you all are from Cass's place." She looked at Cassie. "You have your aunt's eyes and coloring. Those men at the counter are just knuckleheads who were never big fans of Cass's or her cowboys. Now, welcome to Bitterroot, and what can I get you?"

Sammy ordered his meal and then Cassie and Nicolette both went for broke and ordered the daily special of chicken fried steak, mashed potatoes, gravy and a roll.

"Be back in a shake with your drink orders," Daisy said as she once again swished away from their table.

"She seems nice enough," Cassie said once she'd left.

"Hopefully we'll meet a lot of nice people while we're here," Nicolette replied. "Although I'm not sure how many of them are in the café right now."

"All I feel right now is animosity radiating from those men," Cassie said in a half whisper. "I wonder why they didn't like my aunt Cass."

"Who knows?" Nicolette replied. "Maybe before we leave here we'll have it figured out. In the meantime I'm not going to let them ruin my lunch."

By the time Daisy delivered their drinks and their meals, Nicolette and Cassie were deep in a discussion about what little Cassie had learned so far about the ranch.

"We have a big herd of black Angus cattle," Cassie explained. "Adam said they are one hundred percent naturally grown with just grazing and no growth hormones or anything added to their diet. Each fall we sell half the herd to a beef company who then cuts and packages the meat and advertises it as all-natural. It's a big contract and Adam said the company wants to continue to work with me."

Nicolette took a bite of her yummy chicken fried steak, wondering how long it would take before her friend would confess to Adam or any of the others that she had no intention of staying.

Would a new owner ensure all the hands a job? If not, then what would happen to Adam...to Lucas? She was disturbed by the fact that just thinking about Lucas created a tension in the pit of her stomach, a tension that wasn't exactly unpleasant.

Of course, she was set up to think kindly of anyone who took any time at all with Sammy. She knew her son was hungry for a male in his life. Samuel had certainly been a nonpresence from the moment Sammy had been born.

Surely all she felt toward Lucas was gratitude for the way he had taken Sammy under his wing. It couldn't be anything more than that. She scarcely knew the man.

She knew so little about him, just that his eyes were a deep blue that could easily pull her in and that the touch of his hand on hers had sparked an instant electricity she'd never felt before.

"This is the best grilled cheese sandwich I've ever had," Sammy said.

"Hey!" Nicolette gave him a mock look of hurt. "After all the grilled cheese sandwiches I've made for you in your life?"

Sammy giggled and shrugged. "What can I tell you, Mom? A cowboy only speaks the truth."

"Did you get that out of a fortune cookie?" Cassie asked teasingly.

Sammy frowned thoughtfully. "I don't think they have fortune cookies in the Wild West."

They had just about finished up their meal when one of the cowboys at the counter began to walk past their table, apparently headed to the restrooms in the back.

As he reached the side of their booth, Sammy accidentally knocked his glass of chocolate milk with an elbow. The glass flew off the table and landed at the cowboy's feet. Some of the chocolate milk splattered the bottom of his jeans.

"Oh, we're so sorry," Nicolette said as she quickly jumped up to right Sammy's glass.

"Stupid city-boy brat," the man spat.

Nicolette reacted impulsively and tossed the last of her iced tea at the man. "And I'm the stupid city-boy

brat's mother," she said angrily. "His spill was an accident, but mine was on purpose because you're a jerk."

For a brief heartbeat she feared the man was going to
punch her, and then Daisy was between them. "Let's all
just calm down," she said. "Lloyd, go on and take care
of your business and leave the kid and the ladies alone."

The man she called Lloyd gave Nicolette a glare that
chilled her to her very bones and then headed on to the
back. "Don't pay him no mind," Daisy said and patted
Sammy's shoulder as he began to cry, his face buried
in his hands. "He's just a cranky old man."

"It…it was an accident," he said between sobs. "I
didn't mean to do it."

"We know it was an accident. How about I bring you
one of my special chocolate chip cookies with some
ice cream for dessert?" Daisy asked with a wink at Nicolette. "I've never known a little cowboy who didn't
love my cookies."

Sammy swiped his tears and looked up at the red-
headed owner. "That would be really nice. Thank you."

As Daisy left to get the dessert, Nicolette reached
across the table for her son's hand. "It's really okay,
Sammy. Accidents happen and he was not nice at all."
She squeezed his hand and then released it, knowing
Sammy would be embarrassed if anyone saw him hold-
ing his mother's hand.

By the time Daisy delivered the goodies to Sammy,
Lloyd and his buddies had left the café and Nicolette
breathed a sigh of relief.

They finished their meals without further incident
and left the café to find Lucas's truck. The minute Nicolette spied the black pickup with Lucas seated on the

tailgate, his hat low over his face, her heart began that crazy beat that was definitely not normal.

He sat up as he saw their approach and bumped his hat back, a frown crossing his forehead. He must have noticed the soberness of the group.

"How was lunch?" he asked as he stood.

"An experience," Nicolette replied, hoping he could read her eyes to know she didn't want to discuss it at the moment. The last thing she wanted was for Sammy to get upset all over again.

He turned to the back of the pickup, which held a variety of grocery bags, and grabbed a big shoe box. He bent down so that he was eye to eye with Sammy. "I see you got your hat, but I have a feeling you'll be needing these, too."

Sammy took the lid off and his entire face lit up at the sight of the black polished cowboy boots. "Really? For me?" he asked.

Lucas laughed. "They sure aren't my size. Why don't you pull them on and take a little stroll down the sidewalk to make sure they fit."

Sammy sat on the tailgate and quickly shucked his tennis shoes and then pulled on each boot. When he took off walking down the sidewalk, Nicolette turned to Lucas. "Just tell me how much they were and I'll pay you."

"Don't offend me," he replied. "This is a gift from me to Sammy and has nothing to do with you." He smiled at her, tiny lines radiating out from the corners of his eyes. "Besides, if he's going to be one of the ranch hands, he needs a good pair of boots. Those white tennis shoes won't last a week in the pasture."

"Then I guess I'll just say thank you," she replied.

Sammy ran back to them. "They fit perfect. I love them. Thank you, Cowboy Lucas."

"You're welcome, partner. Now, let's get in the truck and head back to the ranch."

Nicolette and Sammy rode in the small seats behind Lucas and Cassie as they headed back home. The conversation was neutral, focused on the weather and the passing landscape. Lucas pointed out other ranches they passed and mentioned who owned them, but Nicolette paid little attention.

The gift of the boots had obviously erased the trauma of the spilled milk for Sammy, and Nicolette was grateful to see her son dancing his feet against the floorboard and adjusting and readjusting his hat on his head.

Despite her desire to the contrary, Lucas Taylor was definitely getting under her skin. If the way to a man's heart was through his stomach, the way to Nicolette's heart was through Sammy.

When they got to the house, Lucas dropped them off and then drove on toward the bunkhouse in the distance. Nicolette knew he had supplies to drop off and then probably afternoon chores to take care of.

Sammy went up to his room, Cassie disappeared into her bedroom and Nicolette wandered the downstairs restlessly. She tried to keep her mind off the lunch debacle and the way Lloyd's glare had made her feel.

He'd frightened her more than just a little bit. For just a moment she'd thought he was going to pick up Sammy by the scruff of his neck and slam him against a wall. There had been that kind of wild meanness in his eyes. She'd believed he was going to punch her in the face. She didn't want to think about what might have happened if Daisy hadn't intervened.

It was almost nine that night when she tucked a happy and exhausted Sammy into bed. She kissed him on the cheek, but before she could leave he grabbed her hand and indicated he wanted her to sit next to him.

She sat on the edge of the mattress, wondering if he wanted to talk about what had happened at lunch. "I want to stay here forever," he said. "I don't ever want to go back to New York. I like it here."

She looked at him in surprise. "Honey, you know we can't stay here forever. This is Cassie's home, not ours, and she isn't planning on staying long. We have our home in New York."

He sat up. "We don't have our own home in New York. We have Cassie's apartment. Why couldn't you and me get a home someplace around here where we could visit with Cowboy Lucas all the time and I could always be a cowboy?"

"Sammy, honey. My work is in New York. I have the shop to work in. I can't just pick up and move here. This isn't where we belong."

Sammy flopped back down on his back. "I think we could belong here if we wanted to."

She leaned over and kissed him on the forehead and then stood. "Just enjoy being here now, Sammy. Besides, Cassie hasn't made up her mind yet about what the future holds. Who knows what might happen. Good night, my sweet cowboy."

"Good night, my sweet mom," he replied, and she left the room to the music of his soft laughter.

"Got the little bug tucked in?" Cassie asked from the sofa when Nicolette entered the great room.

Nicolette collapsed into the comfort of a big easy chair. "He wants to stay here forever."

"It didn't take long to get the city out of him. I wonder how long it will take to get the country out of him when we go back home," Cassie said.

"I have a feeling he'll have to outgrow those boots before he willingly stops wearing them," Nicolette said.

"How did Lucas know what size to buy?" Cassie mused. "He got it right on the money."

"No idea how he did that. I imagine he and the salesman just made a lucky guess."

"I sure didn't feel any welcome from anyone around town today," Cassie said. "We're definitely the outsiders."

"Daisy was nice," Nicolette said.

"Daisy is probably a smart business owner. She has to be nice to everyone who comes into the café."

Nicolette gazed at her friend thoughtfully. "You should be glad that nobody was particularly friendly. You're the one who said we shouldn't get friendly with people since we aren't sticking around."

"I know. I'm just feeling perverse. It would have been nice if somebody acted like they wanted to meet the new owner of the ranch." She curled her slender legs up beneath her. "Adam told me Cass was something of a legend around here. I have a feeling that even if I decided to stay on, I'd never be able to live up to her in the eyes of everyone here."

"You don't have to live up to anyone, Cassie, and you're stronger than you think you are. But thank goodness you don't have to make any decisions at the moment. There's still plenty of work to do around here before you make a final decision about selling or staying."

Cassie nodded. "Adam told me that tomorrow most

of the men are going to work on cutting up the trees the tornado blew down. He said the wood would be stacked both here at the house and at the bunkhouse for the fireplaces in the winter."

She yawned and then continued. "You know that missing woman I mentioned that was in the paper? I guess one of the ranch hands here, Nick Coleman, was seeing her before she disappeared."

"What have the police said about it?" Nicolette asked.

"They think it's possible she just left town. Apparently she'd only been in town a couple of months. Adam said there's no way he believes that Nick had anything to do with her disappearance."

"Sounds like you and Adam are getting quite cozy," Nicolette said.

"Strictly business," Cassie replied. "Tomorrow he's going to take me on a tour of the entire ranch so I can make notes on what I think needs to be done, and to explain more about the everyday operations." She yawned again. "And on that note, I think it's time for me to head to bed. I'm exhausted."

"It's all this fresh air and sunshine." Nicolette grinned. Cassie got up from the sofa, and with goodnights exchanged, she went upstairs.

Nicolette thought about going out on the porch and sitting for a little while, but when she realized that part of her reason for doing so was in hopes that Lucas might show up and share part of the night with her, she dismissed the idea.

They'd been here for only two days and one evening and already she was spending far too much of her time thinking about Lucas Taylor. She should be focusing on what her future would look like when they returned to New York.

Although she hadn't mentioned it to Cassie, Nicolette was considering having Cassie buy out her half of the business, and that would give Nicolette enough money for her and Sammy to get their own place. Nicolette could finish her schooling and get a teaching job.

Of course, it all depended on what Cassie decided to do, and while she knew Cassie's initial decision had been to sell the ranch, who knew how her friend would feel in two or three months from now? By then the cowboys wouldn't be just names on paper, they'd be real people, and that might make it more difficult for Cassie to just walk away.

Realizing she was more tired than she'd thought, she decided to head upstairs. She turned off all the lights and climbed the staircase, trying not to worry about the future or think about Lucas.

As always as she passed Sammy's bedroom, she paused to peek in at her sleeping son…and saw a person with a ski mask on at his window.

For the space of a heartbeat she froze, her brain not understanding how a man could be at the second-floor window. His glittering gaze caught hers, and it was at that moment she screamed.

Chapter 4

Lucas jumped off his bed at the sound of the big dinner bell ringing through the night, adrenaline instantly exploding inside him. He pulled on his jeans and grabbed his holster and quickly buckled it, the weight of his gun familiar on his hip as he opened his bunk door.

Other men were coming outside, as well. "What's going on?" Dusty asked.

"Maybe one of them wants one of us to make a cappuccino run," somebody else replied.

Lucas didn't pay attention to anyone. He ran, his heart racing, vaguely aware of the sound of running feet behind him. He knew something was wrong… somebody was in trouble. Otherwise that bell would have never been rung.

All he could think about was that the house held two defenseless women and one young boy and something bad had happened or was happening.

The distance between the bunkhouse and the main house had never seemed so far. When he was halfway there the bell stopped ringing, the sudden silence creating even more anxiety in his chest.

He didn't bother with the back door, but rather ran around the house to the front where the big bell hung. His gun was in his hand as he reached the front door.

Cassie opened it for him. "Thank God," she exclaimed. He released a deep sigh of relief when he saw Sammy in his mother's arms on the sofa.

Adam came in just behind him, along with most of the other dozen cowboys, all of them armed and ready to protect their own.

"There was a man," Nicolette said, her voice trembling with fear and her eyes simmering a deep green. "He…he was at Sammy's window."

A couple of the cowboys left the house, and Lucas knew they'd be checking it out and scouting around the area for anyone who didn't belong.

"The police are on their way, but I rang the bell after Nicolette screamed and grabbed Sammy out of bed. We knew you could get here quicker than law enforcement," Cassie explained.

Nicolette's eyes were huge, as were Sammy's, and a swift sense of protectiveness rose up inside him. What in the hell had somebody been doing looking into a second-floor window? There was nothing he wanted more than to find the person who had put such fear in Nicolette's and Sammy's eyes.

Instead he holstered his gun and walked over to where they were cuddled together. "You both okay?"

Nick Coleman came back in from outside. "There's

a ladder against the house. We didn't touch anything, but it's definitely not one of ours."

"Spread out all the men and see if you can find who was on that ladder," Adam said. "He can't have gotten too far. Lucas and I will stay in here to wait for Chief Bowie and his men to arrive."

As if to punctuate his sentence, a siren became audible in the distance. Lucas remained next to the sofa, and despite the circumstances he couldn't help but notice the evocative scent of Nicolette mingling with the minty soap scent of a freshly bathed little cowboy.

Who would have been at the window? Was somebody trying to harm Sammy, or had his window just been an accidental choice for a break-in? And if it was a break-in attempt, why not come through the front or back door instead of trying to gain entry on the second level, where the culprit had to have known they would all be sleeping.

Maybe the perp had seen lights on downstairs and had just assumed nobody would be in bed already. It still seemed a stretch to believe that somebody wanting to rob the place had decided to come and go from a ladder at a second-floor window. What did he intend to carry out?

These thoughts created a tighter, more powerful knot in Lucas's chest as he wondered what the real motive of the person might have been.

He was glad to see Chief of Police Dillon Bowie walk through the door. Lucas and Dillon had become friends throughout the years, and there were few people Lucas trusted as much as he did the tall, broad-shouldered, dark-haired keeper of the law in Bitterroot.

Adam made the introductions and Dillon took

Cassie's hand in his. "I've been meaning to stop by to meet Cass's niece before now. I'm sorry we have to meet under such circumstances. Now, tell me exactly what happened."

Lucas listened intently as Nicolette talked about going up to bed and peeking in on her son, only to see a person with a ski mask at the window.

Two of Dillon's men entered the room. Officer Juan Ramirez nodded to everyone and then looked at his boss. "There is a ladder against the house going up to the bedroom window. All the ranch hands say it isn't one of their ladders."

"Print the whole thing, although I imagine since whoever it was had on a ski mask, he probably had on gloves, as well," Dillon replied.

He motioned Cassie into the nearest chair and then he pulled a pad and pen from his pocket. "It's possible that whoever tried to get into the house knew that you all were city folks and it might be easy pickings for a robbery. Or it could be some local kids out for a little mischief who didn't realize you all had arrived in town yet. I can't imagine that you've been in town long enough to make any enemies."

"Actually, we did have a little incident today at the café," Nicolette said.

Lucas looked at her in surprise. "What kind of an incident?" he asked before Dillon got a chance.

She tightened her arms around Sammy. "Sammy accidentally spilled his milk and it splashed on a man's jeans. He went off, calling Sammy a spoiled city brat and then…" She paused and then continued. "And then I threw my iced tea at him."

"He was sitting at the counter with a bunch of other

men and they all gave us the evil eye when we came in," Cassie added.

Lucas's stomach tightened at the thought of any man accosting Nicolette and Sammy. And he was oddly pleased that she had enough mama bear in her that she'd added to the milk insult by tossing her tea at whoever it was.

"Did you get a name?" Dillon asked.

"Lloyd. Daisy called him Lloyd," Nicolette replied, the tremor back in her voice.

"That has to be Lloyd Green. He's the only Lloyd around," Lucas said and then looked at Nicolette. "Why didn't you tell me about all this when we met in town after lunch?"

She pointedly glanced down at the boy who, despite all the excitement, had the droopy eyelids of exhaustion. "I didn't think it was the time or the place."

Dillon frowned. "Lloyd is definitely a hothead, but I can't imagine him taking any grudge to this kind of a level. Still, I'll check him out, see what he has been up to tonight." He gazed at Nicolette and then back at Cassie. "Anyone else giving you any problems?"

"No, like you said before, we've scarcely been in town long enough to meet anyone." She looked at Adam. "And I don't think we've made anyone angry here at the ranch."

"It wasn't one of our men," Adam replied firmly. "Nobody here would want to bring harm to Cassie or Nicolette or Sammy. We're all trying to rebuild things since Cass's death, not destroy them."

"I just want to know that my son is safe," Nicolette said softly. In the past few minutes Sammy had drifted off to sleep, and she gently stroked his dark hair from his forehead.

Lucas found himself wondering what her touch would feel like across his forehead, what it would be like if she were his woman, if Sammy was his child. He focused back on Dillon, knowing his thoughts were about to take him into dangerous territory and there had already been enough of that on this night.

"I'll have my men check the window upstairs," Dillon said. "And if it's any consolation, I wouldn't assume that whoever was at the window intended harm for your boy. It's more likely it was just a matter of chance that that particular window was used."

"I hope you're right about that," Nicolette replied.

"I'm going upstairs to check out the window, and I know your men and mine are combing the area, but I think the excitement is probably over for the rest of the night."

As Dillon went upstairs, Nicolette shifted the sleeping boy in her arms and Lucas sat on the sofa next to her. Adam stood at the side of the chair where Cassie sat clad in a blue lightweight robe, her eyes still filled with fear.

"You don't have to worry," Adam said to her. "I'll have a man patrol the perimeters of the house for the rest of the night."

"And you also won't have to worry because I intend to move in," Lucas added. "I can bunk in with Sammy during the nights until Dillon gets this figured out, and that way nobody will be able to get past me to hurt anyone."

Nicolette stared at him in obvious surprise, but he also saw a hint of relief in the green depths of her eyes.

"You don't need to do that," she said, but it was only half a protest.

"Maybe I don't need to, but I want to," he replied. He looked to Cassie, who he knew would have the final say in the matter.

"You could at least stay in the extra bedroom in a queen bed rather than bunking in with Sammy on a twin," Cassie replied.

He looked at the kid, his handsome little face a picture of innocence in slumber. He'd been sleeping when his mother had screamed. He'd heard about a man at his window. He'd probably be afraid to sleep alone in that room ever again.

"I'd rather sleep in the small room with Sammy. He might need a roommate for a few nights after all the trauma," he replied.

He would have slept on a cow patty on a wintry night to receive the soft, grateful gaze that Nicolette gave him. What was wrong with him? He had never felt this protective surge for anyone except Cass, who had saved his life, his very soul by having him come to this ranch.

He would have died for Cass, and it shocked him that in the brief time he'd known Sammy and Nicolette he was starting to feel the same way about them. It didn't make sense, was completely irrational considering how little he knew about Nicolette, but it was there, nevertheless.

"While Adam and Dillon and his men are here, I'll just go get some things from my bunk," he said, suddenly feeling as if he needed some distance from the very scent of her, from the emotions she evoked in him.

As he stepped out the front door and headed around the house where the ladder still stood leading up to

Sammy's bedroom, a new fiercely burning knot formed in the pit of his stomach.

He dismissed his crazy thoughts about Nicolette and instead his mind filled with all kinds of questions. Had the incident in the café with Lloyd Green prompted some sort of crazy attempt at retribution?

Everyone knew Lloyd was a mean soul, but a little milk on his jeans didn't warrant this kind of reaction. Still, with Lloyd and his group of buddies there was no telling for sure. He might have just thought it would be fun to terrorize Sammy and Nicolette.

Lloyd worked for Raymond Humes on the ranch next to Cass's. Throughout the years there had been plenty of bad blood both between Raymond and Cass and the cowboys who worked for each of them.

Lucas's feelings toward Nicolette and Sammy were definitely confusing, but the ladder against the house felt ominous, and as he reached the bunkhouse, he smelled more than a hint of danger in the air.

Dillon and his men finally left. By the time they did Nicolette had laid Sammy on the sofa and she was pacing the floor, trying to wrap her mind around that unexpected and frightening face in the window.

Cassie and Adam were in the kitchen seated at the table and talking about rotating men outside the house each night for the next couple of nights or until Dillon came up with a guilty party and a reason for the ladder.

Nicolette heard only the murmur of their voices as she was mentally focused on the vision of that ski mask and those eyes that had appeared to hold such glittering malevolence.

Who could it have been and what had he wanted?

Was it just an accident that he'd been about to enter the room where her vulnerable son was soundly sleeping? Dillon had told her the window was still closed, but that didn't mean if Nicolette had been three minutes longer climbing up the stairs the man wouldn't have been through the window and into the bedroom.

And then what? She couldn't imagine, for everything she thought of was too terrifying to contemplate.

She stopped pacing as Lucas came in the front door, carrying an oversize duffle bag and a sense of security she welcomed. The only thing better than the sight of him would have been if he'd cradled her in his arms to steal away the cold wind that had blown through her since the instant she had seen the man at the window.

As if reading her mind, he dropped his duffle bag to the floor and stepped forward, his arms open to welcome her. She didn't hesitate. She ran into his embrace, a sob escaping her the instant he enfolded her tight.

His body was hard against hers, yet seemed to meld around her. He stroked her hair with one hand while his other slowly rose up and down her back in an obvious effort to comfort her.

"I was so scared," she whispered.

"There's no reason to be scared anymore," he replied.

She buried her face in his chest, breathing in the scent of night and the faint fragrance of a spicy cologne. She told herself it wouldn't matter whose arms she was in, as long as they were big and strong, but she knew that wasn't true. She needed *his* arms, Lucas's arms around her.

She'd known him for only three short days, but it didn't matter. Already he'd become safety and security for her and her son.

She didn't know how long they stood together, locked in an embrace, before she realized the cold that had been inside her was gone and she wasn't just warmed, but a new fire had begun to burn in the pit of her stomach. It was a fire that had nothing to do with comfort or a feeling of security, and when she recognized it for what it was, she finally stepped away from him.

"Sorry about that," she said, her gaze not meeting his. "Just chalk it up to a moment of weakness."

He stepped toward her and took her chin in his fingers, forcing her gaze to meet his. "It's going to be all right," he said. "Dillon is a good man. He'll figure it out, and in the meantime I'm here to make sure nobody gets inside this house." He dropped his hand back to his side, and at that moment Adam and Cassie came into the room.

"Sawyer is going to keep an eye on the house through the rest of the night," Adam said.

"That really isn't necessary since I'm going to be in the house," Lucas replied.

"We'll have him on duty tonight and then tomorrow figure things out." Adam raked a hand through his hair, his gaze lingering on Cassie. "I don't want you to worry. We aren't going to let anyone harm you. I'll talk to you in the morning." He looked at his watch. "It's already after midnight. Why don't we plan to meet here around ten."

"That's fine with me," Cassie replied. "And now that the excitement is over, I'm going to bed." She looked at Nicolette. "Are you coming up?"

Nicolette shook her head. "I'm too wired to sleep. I'll be up a little bit later."

Adam left, Cassie disappeared up the stairs and

Lucas looked at Nicolette. "Do you want me to carry Sammy upstairs?"

"Only if you're going up now."

"I'm a little wired myself," he replied. "Why don't we go into the living room, where we won't bother Sammy," he suggested.

She nodded and followed him from the great room into the smaller, more formal living room. She sat on one side of the sofa and he sat on the other.

"You should have told me what happened in the café when we were in town this afternoon," he said.

"I didn't want to make a big deal out of it in front of Sammy. He was so upset when it happened and the only thing that made his world okay again was a cookie and ice cream from Daisy and the cowboy boots from you."

"Still, I could have settled it with Lloyd right then and there." His jaw clenched tightly, making him even more handsome and slightly dangerous looking.

She smiled. "Then I probably would have had to figure out how to get the money to pay bail for you."

His jaw softened and he returned her smile. "You got that right. Lloyd and his fellow cowboys are nothing but a bunch of bullies and thieves. Cass couldn't abide Raymond Humes or any of the men who worked on his ranch. The bad blood goes both ways, which is unfortunate since his ranch is next to this one."

"Why the bad blood?" she asked curiously.

Lucas shrugged. "I don't know where it all began. Things were already bad when I first came here, and that was fifteen years ago."

"Fifteen years—you must have been a baby."

"I was just shy of seventeen years old and I hadn't been anybody's baby for a very long time." He paused and took off his holster and set it with his gun on the coffee table before them. "What's your story? How did you come to be here with Cassie?"

She leaned back against the sofa. "In order to tell you that I have to start at the beginning when I got married, and it's a long story."

"We've got all night," he replied easily.

"I can sleep in tomorrow, but you have chores to do."

"Tomorrow is my day off, so there's no problem," he replied.

Nicolette had a feeling his questions were less about wanting to really know about her past and more about wanting to take her mind off the horrible events of the night.

"I met Samuel when I was working as a salesperson in an upscale dress shop during the day and going to night school in the evenings. It was obvious to me that he probably didn't have to look at price tags and it was equally obvious that he was flirting with me. But, he told me he was looking for a dress for a woman about my size and wanted shoes to match."

She paused a moment, remembering the first time she'd seen her future husband. He'd had sandy brown hair, earnest brown eyes. He possessed boyish good looks and was exceedingly charming.

"Anyway, he bought a ridiculously expensive dress and shoes and after I rang up the purchases he told me to wear the clothes and meet him that night at a fancy French restaurant. Before I could protest, he left the store."

"And so you went to the restaurant to meet him?"

"I did, but I wasn't wearing the dress or shoes he'd bought. Before I left the store that day I put them back

on the rack and credited his account and then I met
him for dinner and told him he couldn't buy me with a
fancy dress and sparkly shoes. He was both surprised
and intrigued. I guess nobody had ever turned down a
gift from him before."

"That was the beginning of your relationship," Lucas
said.

"It was the beginning of a whirlwind romance. Samuel is a trust-fund baby who spent the first months of
our dating telling me about all the wonderful things
he intended to do, to be in his future. He talked about
charity work and altruistic causes and I believed him,
I believed in him. I thought that he had just been waiting for the right woman to be at his side, so when he
proposed I accepted and we got married in Las Vegas
and honeymooned there for a week in luxury."

"Then what went wrong?" Lucas asked and leaned
a bit closer to her.

"When I married him he spent most of his time
throwing away his money frivolously and partying until
he passed out. I kept waiting for him to grow up, to start
to be a productive member of society, to do something
worthwhile, and then I got pregnant with Sammy. I
thought that would be the catalyst for him to change. But
Samuel wasn't interested in being a father and he wasn't
interested in being a husband. By the time Sammy was
two, I knew that nothing was ever going to change. He
had his monthly money from his trust fund and didn't
have to do anything constructive, so I divorced him."

"I'm sorry he didn't turn out to be the man you
wanted him to be."

Nicolette shrugged. "I guess I should be grateful that
all Samuel ever cared about was money and partying.

When it came time for the divorce Samuel only wanted to hang on to his money and he didn't care about any custody of Sammy. So, I walked away with full custody of my son and a little bit of money that I'd had before I met Samuel."

"And Cassie?"

"She and I had met when I was going to college classes to become a teacher. We'd become best of friends and continued that friendship even during my marriage. When she heard about the divorce she insisted that Sammy and I move in with her temporarily until I got on my feet. Then I threw my money in on the store, and to be honest, I'm still waiting to get on my feet. But I'd rather live in a cardboard box with Sammy than live in luxury and have him endure a lifetime of his father's indifference."

"What about your parents? Couldn't they help you out?"

"My mother died a year after I married Samuel and my father passed away almost a year to the day after her. I think he just missed her so much he let go of life to be with her again."

She looked at him with a touch of humor. "Have I put you to sleep yet?"

He smiled, that crazy beautiful smile that always lit up a place deep inside her. "Not at all. I wanted to get to know you better, and part of the way to understand people is to learn where they've been."

"And where have you been?" she asked.

"Now, that is a story for another night," he said. She noticed how his eyes darkened slightly. He stood and buckled his holster back around his waist. "It's late. I think maybe it's time we both call it a night."

She also stood, slightly disappointed that she'd just shared so much with him about herself and he obviously wasn't in a state of mind to share anything with her. *He owes you nothing*, she reminded herself.

They walked back into the great room, where Sammy still slept soundly on the sofa. "I'll carry him upstairs," Lucas said. He picked up Sammy, who immediately wrapped his legs around Lucas's waist and nestled his face into the crook of Lucas's neck.

The sight of her son wrapped like a baby monkey around the strong, handsome cowboy pierced Nicolette's heart. How many times had she wished that Samuel would hug Sammy, give the little boy any kind of attention and love?

"I'll carry your bag," she replied. She picked up the duffle, turned off the lights downstairs and then followed Lucas up the stairs, trying not to notice how his worn jeans fit so nicely across his backside.

She dropped the duffle bag just inside the room that held the two twin beds and watched as Lucas placed Sammy in the bed he'd been pulled from by her scream.

Lucas tucked the sheet around the boy and then walked back to Nicolette just outside the doorway. "You can sleep peacefully knowing that he's safe with me," he said.

"You have no idea how much I appreciate what you're doing for us."

He took another step closer to her, so close she could feel his body heat, and her head once again filled with his heady scent. Her mouth was unaccountably dry as she saw a flash of desire light the depths of his eyes.

She knew he intended to kiss her. She also knew she should step back from him, but her feet refused to move her to safety. Cassie's advice about not getting close to anyone here was forgotten as she fell into the midnight blue yearning in Lucas's eyes.

She didn't see him move but found herself once again in his embrace, her breasts tight against his hard chest as his soft, warm lips claimed hers.

The kiss was like nothing she'd ever experienced before. Initially his lips were soft as butterfly wings against hers, and then the pressure increased and she couldn't help but open her mouth to him, allowing him to deepen the kiss.

Shivers raced up her spine along with his slow caresses up and down her back. His tongue swirled with hers, dizzying her senses, and she leaned closer into him.

He kissed her with mastery, stealing away her will for anything else but to acquiesce to whatever he desired from her.

She felt as if she were on fire when his mouth left hers and trailed a blaze of nips and kisses down her jaw and in the hollow of her throat.

More. She wanted more, and the idea snapped her back into reality. And the reality was that she had no business kissing Lucas Taylor. She had no business allowing him to kiss her until her knees were weak and she wanted more from him, of him.

She stumbled backward and raised a hand to her lips. She stared at him with both a sense of wonder and a bit of fear…the fear of her own desire for him.

"Sorry," he said as he took a step back from her. "I shouldn't have done that."

"*We* shouldn't have done that," she replied, dropping her hand to her side. His eyes still held a fire that tempted her closer, and it took every ounce of her will-power to stand her ground.

"But I have to be honest. If given the chance again, I'd take it." He turned and went into the room where Sammy was asleep, leaving Nicolette standing stunned in the hall.

Chapter 5

Nicolette awakened to the delicious scents of fried bacon and fresh coffee. She rolled over in the bed and sat straight up when she realized by looking at the alarm clock that it was after nine.

Sammy was usually an early riser and it had been his habit to wake her when he got up. Her heart beat fast for a moment and then she remembered that it was Lucas's day off and he was in the house.

That would explain Sammy's lack of interest in waking her. With Cowboy Lucas at his side, his mom was now just spare change.

She slumped back against the pillow and tried not to think about the kiss she and Lucas had shared the night before, but that seemed to be all she could think about. Never, even in all her years of marriage, had she been kissed so thoroughly. Never had her response to a kiss been so immediate and visceral.

Still, even the memory of his amazing kiss couldn't completely erase from her mind the fact that somebody had put a ladder against the side of the house with the obvious intent of getting inside.

Who? And why?

These thoughts pulled her out of bed. She grabbed clean clothes for the day and then scurried down the hall to the bathroom.

As she stood beneath a warm spray of water, she hoped that Chief Bowie stopped by later today to let her know if Lloyd had been behind the potential break-in or not. She almost hoped it was Lloyd. Otherwise it had been some unknown person, and she had no clue as to what the motive might be.

Maybe Chief Bowie was right. Maybe it had just been some creep who had known the house was occupied by two city ladies and a small child and saw the perfect opportunity for a robbery.

If that was the case, she still didn't understand why the intended point of entry had been an upstairs bedroom instead of the front or back door or even a window at ground level.

Or maybe it had been bored kids out for a night of fun, planning a party in a house they assumed was empty. But even as she thought of this, she didn't believe it. Kids wouldn't plan a party with twelve protective, armed cowboys on the property.

She dismissed all thoughts from her head as she finished her shower and then dressed for the day. No matter how much she ruminated on it, she wouldn't find an answer by herself.

As far as Lucas was concerned, her best course of action was to attempt to gain some distance from him.

She knew Cassie's plan to sell the ranch, although she'd promised Cassie she wouldn't tell any of the cowboys.

It was still bad enough that Sammy had instantly bonded to "Cowboy Lucas." If she wasn't careful, Sammy's heart wasn't the only one that would be broken when they left Oklahoma.

The bottom rung of the stairs creaked loudly as she stepped on it, and Sammy appeared as if by magic at the foot of the stairs. "Finally," he exclaimed with a dramatic roll of his eyes. "We've been waiting forever and ever for you to get out of bed. Cowboy Lucas and I are fixing you breakfast this morning."

He grabbed her by the hand and when he dragged her into the kitchen, she felt an uncomfortable shyness upon seeing Lucas seated at the table with a cup of coffee before him.

"Good morning," he said, and there was a simmering whisper of a secret in his eyes that made her believe he was thinking about the kiss they had shared the night before.

"Good morning," she replied, meeting his gaze for only a moment and then walking over to the counter that held the coffeepot.

Sammy stopped her before she could grab her cup. "You just sit, Mom. I'm going to take care of you this morning."

"Far be it for me to argue," she replied with a laugh. She sat across from Lucas and watched Sammy carefully pour the coffee into a mug and then carry it to her without spilling a drop.

"Thank you, sir," she replied.

"Lucas fried the bacon, but he showed me how to make pancakes. All I have to do is pour the batter on the griddle and then flip them at the right time." Sammy smiled at her proudly. "So, a short stack or a tall stack?"

"A short stack for me," she replied. "Although Lucas might want a tall stack."

"Sammy and I already ate," Lucas said. "He's been champing at the bit waiting for you to get out of bed so he could show you that he makes the best pancakes in the entire state of Oklahoma."

Sammy beamed and moved to the counter where a griddle and a large cup of batter awaited him. Nicolette tensed…hot griddle…little boy, her motherly instincts fired up.

"He can do it," Lucas said softly, as if he could read her thoughts and saw her concerns. "We've been practicing for the last half an hour and he doesn't have a burn mark to show for it."

She smiled at him gratefully and curled her fingers around the warmth of her coffee mug. "I'm assuming Adam and Cassie have already left for her tour of the ranch."

"They left about an hour ago. I don't expect them back for quite some time. It's a big spread with lots of outbuildings."

"Mom, watch, I'm going to flip the pancakes now," Sammy said. He flipped the two that were on the griddle perfectly.

"That's great, Sammy. I'm so proud of you," she replied. He was growing up so fast, faster it seemed here at the ranch than in the city. He was experiencing so many new things and appeared to be thriving.

It took only minutes for Sammy to deliver to the table a plate with two pancakes and two pieces of perfectly cooked crispy bacon. The butter and syrup were already on the table, and she helped herself to both.

"I feel bad eating in front of you two," she said.

Lucas got up from his chair. "No reason to feel bad. While you're enjoying your breakfast I'm going to supervise Sammy's cleanup."

As she ate her breakfast, she gazed out the window and listened to Lucas's soft voice explaining to Sammy how to clean the griddle and load a dishwasher.

Outside the window the sound of chain saws at work indicated that some of the men were busy taking care of the tree damage the spring storm had left behind. It sounded like the beginning of the end because once the storm damage was repaired, Cassie would be ready to put the sale of the ranch in the hands of a local real estate agent and they'd all return to New York.

By the time she'd finished eating, Lucas and Sammy had made plans with her permission to go out to the stables, where Lucas was going to teach Sammy how to brush down the horses.

Finding herself alone in the house, she remained seated at the table, sipping coffee and trying to stay out of her own head.

She felt out of control, bound by what Cassie decided and attracted to a man who hadn't given her any signs that he was a forever kind of man. For goodness' sake, he'd only kissed her once and he certainly hadn't been particularly forthcoming about his background when they'd talked the night before. She really had no idea who Lucas Taylor was except that he was kind and patient with her son and his kiss had tasted of pure sin.

With time on her hands and nothing else to do, she went upstairs and got her sketch pad and colored pencils, even though she wasn't particularly in the mood to work on fashion drawing for a clothing line that had been only busywork for the woman who had been Samuel's wife.

It had been an acceptable little hobby that he'd talked about financing when the time was right, a hobby that Cassie had then encouraged with the idea of both of them becoming creative entrepreneurs.

While Cassie had real talent, as Nicolette thumbed through her pages of designs, she knew in her heart of hearts that she was mediocre at best. She had allowed Cassie to fool her into thinking she could make it in the fashion world because after she'd left Samuel, Nicolette didn't know where she fit into any world.

She continued to gaze at her designs, and she made the decision that when they got back to New York City, she'd somehow figure how to get back into school and complete her teaching degree.

She had only a year to go to get her degree. It would be tough, working and going to school and being a single parent, but somehow she'd make it work. Many women had made it work before her.

Something about being away from the city had made her rediscover what her dream for herself had once been, and that was to teach second- or third-graders. That had been her life goal when she'd first met Samuel, and somehow she'd allowed herself to get thrown off course.

Nicolette needed to have a talk with Cassie. She needed to tell her friend that once she sold this ranch, she wanted Cassie to buy Nicolette out of the store.

Nicolette had lived Samuel's life, and for the past couple of years she'd been living Cassie's life. It was time she began to figure out how to live her own, whatever that life might be.

She looked down and realized that while she'd been thinking, she'd been drawing, and she hadn't sketched cute little skirts or romantic blouses. Instead she had drawn a picture of a man with attractive crinkles at the corners of his eyes, dark, slightly shaggy hair and lips curled up in simmering sensuality.

She dropped the black chalk pencil and slammed the book closed. A faint irritation rode her shoulders as she took her sketchbook back up the stairs and stuffed it away in the pocket on the side of her suitcase. She sat on the edge of the bed, wishing Cassie was back from her tour of the ranch.

The problem was that she had far too much time on her hands, too much time to think, too much time to fantasize about a man she had no business fantasizing about.

She had just about decided to go outside and check on her son when a knock sounded at the front door. She hurried down the stairs and looked outside to see Chief of Police Dillon Bowie standing on the front porch.

She opened the door and stepped outside into the late-morning sun. "Chief Bowie," she said in greeting.

"Nicolette, right?" he asked.

"That's right."

"Is Cassie around?"

Nicolette shook her head. "Cassie is with Adam someplace on the property. I'm the only one here right now. Are you here about what happened last night?" She looked at him eagerly, hoping he had an answer that would make some kind of sense.

"I just came by to tell you all that I talked to Lloyd

Green last night and according to him he was no place near here."

"Of course he would say that," she scoffed. "He wouldn't just come out and confess to being here last night."

Dillon looked at her sympathetically. "Unfortunately he had a couple of his buddies who provided an alibi for him. According to them they were all at Greg Alberton's apartment in town drinking beer and telling tales most of the night."

"And you believe this?" she asked.

He frowned, his dove-gray eyes deepening in hue to a steely gray. "It doesn't matter whether I believe it or not," he replied. "Unless one of his buddies tells me differently, or I get more information, I have to assume he was where they all said he was."

"Then, who could have possibly tried to get into the house last night?" Nicolette asked.

"I still think it's possible that somebody from town knew there were two city women here and that it was probably an attempted robbery. I want to assure you that this isn't a closed case by any means. I intend to continue to ask questions and investigate until we know who was on that ladder outside the window."

"I appreciate it," Nicolette replied, although she'd been hoping that creepy Lloyd Green was guilty and his reason would have been to scare the "spoiled city brat" and his tea-throwing mother.

"Just as I suspected, we didn't get any prints off the ladder and it's a common make and model that's sold both at the feed store and the hardware store. Most ranches in the area have more than a couple."

"Then you probably won't learn where it came from," Nicolette replied with disappointment.

"Probably not," he replied.

"I appreciate your candor, although I wish you had some answers for me."

"I'll get the answers, Nicolette. Trust me, that's my goal," he replied.

Minutes after Dillon left with a promise to stay in touch, Nicolette headed out the back door toward the stable area. The sound of chain saws still rode a faint breeze, and she enjoyed the scent of fresh wood chips mingling with the sweet spring air.

She had just reached the large building when Sammy and Lucas stepped outside. Lucas had his hand on Sammy's shoulder and the two of them were laughing. Her heart squeezed at the sight of her son's utter happiness.

"Well, don't you two make a fine pair," she said.

Lucas clapped Sammy on the shoulder. "Your son is a natural around the horses."

"It was so cool, Mom. I got to brush Lucky and Lady and Jasper, but only Forest gets to brush Demon. He's a half-wild horse that belongs to Forest and only Forest takes care of him."

"Forest?" Nicolette shook her head as she tried to place the man. "I guess it's going to take me several more days before I can put names to all the faces around here."

"Lucas wants to take us to lunch today at the café." Sammy's smile faltered a bit. "He said he wants to make a good experience where we had a little bit of a bad one."

A wave of distaste swept through her. She really had no desire to return to the café, although she knew she was being silly. The café hadn't been the problem. Only one of the men who had been a customer had been an issue.

"That sounds like a good idea," she agreed. The last thing she wanted was for Sammy to think his spilled milk and the over-the-top result had been a big deal.

"Good. Why don't we all meet in the great room in about an hour? That will give Sammy and me time to clean up," Lucas replied.

"Sounds like a plan," she agreed.

They headed toward the house and Sammy dominated the conversation, telling her each and every detail about brushing and grooming horses.

She listened absently and tried to still the dread that chased through her at the thought of potentially running into Lloyd Green and his band of buddies once again.

Cassie tried to focus on everything that Adam pointed out to her as they rode in a small golf cart–like vehicle around the property. But her mind kept racing with thoughts of New York City and how much she wanted to be back where she belonged.

How much merchandise would the store have moved in the days they had been gone? Would she have sold a painting or two? She longed for the customers drifting in and out of the shop, the conversations about happenings in Central Park and the madness of whatever else might be happening on the city streets.

This ranch had been her aunt's dream, never hers. She didn't want to learn everything there was to know about the ranch because she didn't intend to keep it.

Still, Adam was a handsome man and she didn't mind his company at all, although he was taking his teaching of her a bit too seriously. But he was the last person she wanted to know that she intended to sell the place, so she tried her best to stay focused on his desire to educate her.

"Tomorrow you might want to be in the lower pasture. We're going to be tagging cattle all day," he said, pulling her from her inward vision of the hustle and bustle of Times Square at noon.

"Tagging cattle?" She turned and looked at Adam and couldn't help but notice the very strength that rode his lean features, the solidness of his broad shoulders.

"For years we didn't brand the cattle in any way at all. Your aunt believed it was an out-of-date, rather barbaric tradition. Then we found too many of our cattle missing. We always suspected Raymond Humes of encouraging his men to rustle our cattle whenever possible, and eventually your aunt decided to microchip them instead. So, tomorrow right after sunup, Dr. Dan—Dan Richards, the local vet—is coming out to put the chips in the ears of all the cattle."

"How long will it take?" She couldn't imagine getting up at dawn to watch the whole process of tagging hundreds of cattle.

"He'll probably finish up sometime just after noon or so."

"Then I'll try to make it out before then."

She pointed to the shed in the distance. The storm damage was instantly visible, as half the building had collapsed to the ground. "What was that used for before the storm?"

"Hay storage and equipment for the winter months," he replied.

"Can it be repaired?"

"Doubtful. Part of the wooden floor collapsed when the building fell. There's just too much damage to try to repair. It's probably going to have to be pulled down and another one built."

"Once the trees are all cut up, I think that should probably be the next project. There's enough money to build a new one, and we'll need the shed space come winter." And by then the last of the storm damage would be taken care of and Cassie and Nicolette could get back to the city, where they belonged.

It was a coincidence that Daisy led the three of them to the same booth where they had eaten lunch before. Instead of curious gazes from the other diners, Lucas was greeted by most of the people, friendly smiles moving from him to embrace Nicolette and Sammy, as well.

"I guess the friendliness of the crowd depends on the company you keep," she observed once they were seated with Sammy next to Lucas across from her. "It's obvious you're well liked around here."

She was surprised to see Lucas's cheeks grow dusty with faint color. "It's not so much because of me personally. It's more the fact that I was one of Cass's cowboys. Other than Raymond Humes and his gang of thugs, most people had high regards for Cass Holiday." His eyes darkened with obvious grief.

He sat up straighter and plucked Sammy's hat off his head and handed it and his own hat across the table for Nicolette to put on the seat next to her.

"A real cowboy never sits at a table and eats with his hat on," he explained to Sammy.

"What else does a real cowboy do?" Sammy asked.

Lucas frowned thoughtfully. "A real cowboy protects the innocent and the helpless. He never tells a lie because his word is his honor. He's trustworthy and always helps people in trouble. He's a good friend and takes pride in his work." Lucas paused with a grin. "And I think that's enough for you to take in for one day."

At that moment Daisy appeared at their table to take their orders. While they waited for their meals to arrive, Lucas explained the tagging that would take place the next day with the cattle.

"Kind of like what people do with their dogs," Sammy said. "That way if their dogs get lost they can find them." He shot a longing look at Nicolette. "I wish I had a dog."

"You know we can't have pets in the apartment," she replied.

"But if you all are planning to stick around here, I know a good breeder…" Lucas let his voice trail off as Nicolette narrowed her eyes at him. "Anyway, nice day, isn't it?"

Sammy frowned at Nicolette, as if he knew she'd halted the talk of any dog. Thankfully Daisy returned with their meals and the conversation turned to favorite foods.

"Give me a good steak any night," Lucas said and then took a bite of his oversize burger.

"Pizza," Sammy replied. "Give me a good pizza any night."

It amused Nicolette that Sammy had used the exact same wording as Lucas. There was definitely more than a little bit of hero worshipping happening between her son and Lucas.

"Cookie makes great pizza," Lucas replied. "When

I know he's going to make pizza, you can come down to the bunkhouse for dinner."

Lucas looked at her, his eyes holding a faint simmer that made her think he might be entertaining thoughts of the kiss they had shared. "What about you? What do you like?"

Your lips against mine. She forced the inappropriate answer out of her head. "Steak is good. Pizza is good, but my all-time favorite is a BLT, heavy on the B. In fact, you could put bacon on pretty much anything and I'd eat it."

Sammy and Lucas continued to talk about food and cowboy things and Nicolette simply ate her salad and enjoyed the happiness that shone on her son's face, the happiness that she felt at this very moment.

She shouldn't be feeling so happy just seeing her son and Lucas interact. She shouldn't feel so happy just remembering the sinful slide of Lucas's lips against her own.

When was the last time she'd felt truly happy? She couldn't remember. Maybe in those early days with Samuel when she'd really believed he was going to set up charity foundations and build a company and do worthwhile things. Had she been truly happy then? She honestly couldn't remember.

Certainly the day that Sammy had been born she'd known true happiness, but there had been too many days since then filled with disappointments, heartaches and worries. Right now she'd found her happy and she simply enjoyed the moment.

She held on to that happiness until Lloyd entered the café with three scruffy-looking men just behind him and they all took seats at the counter. Thankfully

Sammy and Lucas had their backs to the counter so Sammy didn't see the man who had terrified him as they finished their meals.

It was only as they got up to leave that Lucas saw Lloyd. Lloyd turned around on his stool, as if anticipating a problem. Nicolette put her arm around Sammy's shoulder and grabbed Lucas's arm with her other hand. She didn't want any trouble, but apparently Lloyd had other ideas.

"Have you been demoted to babysitting patrol, Lucas?" Lloyd smirked from his stool.

Lucas cast his gaze to the men with Lloyd. "Looks like you're the one doing the babysitting, or maybe you're the one who needs babysitting."

Lloyd's eyes narrowed. "Now that Cass is gone, maybe some of the people around here will remember that all of her cowboys were nothing but street scum before coming here to Bitterroot."

Lucas stepped closer to Lloyd, and Nicolette's hand slipped off his arm and her heart beat a little faster with a dreadful anticipation.

"Just a word of advice, Lloyd," Lucas said, his voice soft and deceptively pleasant. "You ever verbally abuse or touch the boy or his mother again, and you'll be sipping beer without teeth for the rest of your life."

It was at that moment Nicolette realized she was just a little bit in love with Lucas Taylor.

Chapter 6

Night had fallen once again, finding Nicolette sitting alone in the great room. The television played softly, but she scarcely paid it any attention.

Cassie had gone to bed, as had Lucas at the same time as Sammy. Despite the fact that she was tired, Nicolette hadn't been ready to call it a night and go to bed.

She found herself playing and replaying the scene in the café, working through the hateful words that Lloyd had thrown at Lucas…something about everyone now remembering that the men who worked here had been nothing but street scum before Cass had taken them on.

Her curiosity about Lucas's past had definitely been piqued, but as the afternoon had progressed she hadn't had an opportunity to ask him about it, nor did she believe it was any of her business.

The afternoon had flown by quickly. Cassie returned

from her tour and Lucas had taken Sammy to his bunk-house to show the boy where he had lived for the past fifteen years. Her son had come back to the house more determined than ever to not only become a cowboy, but to work on this ranch and earn a room in the cowboy motel.

Nicolette wanted to remind him that they weren't staying, that this would never be their home, but after giving it some thought decided not to say anything.

She'd promised Cassie that she wouldn't tell any of the ranch hands Cassie's plan to sell out, and with the close relationship between Sammy and Lucas she feared that Sammy would spill the beans—or had already.

The less said in front of Sammy, the safer Cassie's secret would be. Nicolette already feared she'd said too much to her son about their future plans.

She'd just about decided to go upstairs to bed when she heard the faint creak of the lower rung on the stair-case. She looked to see Lucas come into the room. She sat up straighter on the sofa. "Couldn't sleep?" she asked.

"No, and it's been my experience that it's a waste of time to toss and turn and chase after sleep that isn't ready to come." He sat on the opposite side of the sofa and set his gun on the coffee table in front of them. "Did you know your son snores?"

"Is that what's keeping you awake?"

"Nah, he snores real soft. I've slept beside cowboys who rattle windows and sound like bullfrogs." He raked a hand through his shaggy hair, looking ridiculously sexy. "I just couldn't sleep and saw the light on down here and figured you were still awake."

"Cassie has apparently embraced the old saying of

early to bed and early to rise. She has so much on her mind. This all has been such a huge shock to her," Nicolette replied.

"You don't just step into ranching without experience or a good teacher. Adam will help her, and eventually it won't be so overwhelming for her." He was so handsome in a plain white T-shirt that stretched across his broad shoulders and his jeans.

Although the gun on the table in front of them was a reminder that he was on bodyguard duty, he appeared completely relaxed and she decided it was the right time to ask him about what Lloyd had said that afternoon in the café.

"At the café today when you spoke to Lloyd, he said something about now that Cass was gone maybe everyone would remember where you all came from. What did he mean by that?"

He stared at her for a long moment, his eyes holding a mix of emotions she couldn't begin to sort out. "Remember I told you it was a long story?"

"We have all night," she replied lightly, returning to him what he had told her on the night when she'd bared her past to him.

He sat forward, his gaze growing distant, as if he was accessing memories not often thought about. "I never knew my father. I was raised by my mother, and I use the term 'raised by' loosely. Like your ex-husband, she was a partier. She loved her drugs, her alcohol, and when she remembered I like to think she loved me."

Although he spoke the words starkly and without any emotion, Nicolette slid a bit closer to him, sensing the pain that he held back.

"We always had a roof over our head, mostly cheap

apartments that were government subsidized in Oklahoma City. There was also usually a little food in the house unless she sold all of our food stamps to somebody for cash to buy drugs. I learned to be fairly self-sufficient early on because when I woke up in the mornings I never knew for sure if she'd be home or not."

He paused to draw a deep sigh and once again leaned back against the chocolate-brown sofa. "In any case, we managed to survive, at least until I was fifteen."

"And what happened when you were fifteen?" She scooted closer, wanting…needing to touch him, but was afraid in this moment he wouldn't welcome her touch. He looked like an island, his features taut with tension as his gaze radiated out an inner pain.

"When I was fifteen years old I came home from school as usual and was stopped by Mr. Blackworth, our landlord at the time. It wasn't unusual for him to stop me occasionally to tell me to remind my mother that the rent was overdue. But that day, he handed me a hundred dollars and a duffle bag and told me early that morning my mother had moved out and left no forwarding address."

He laughed, a harsh, bitter sound. "No forwarding address, can you believe that? She just disappeared and I never saw her again."

Nicolette could help herself no longer. She placed a hand on his muscled arm in an effort to comfort the young boy he'd been. "What did you do?" she asked softly.

Some of the tension left his features and he shrugged. "One thing I knew for sure was that if anyone found out that I was homeless and motherless, Social Services would step in and I'd be placed somewhere. That was the last thing I wanted. For the next month or two I managed to go to school every day and spend the night at friends' homes. But after I'd stayed at any one place for more than two or three nights, parents got suspicious and so I finally quit school and took to the streets."

Nicolette tried to imagine Sammy at fifteen, on the streets and all alone. She couldn't bear the thought of it, and she couldn't bear the thought of Lucas in that position either.

"Oh, Lucas. How did you survive?" She tightened her grip on his arm, as if she could pull him out of the dangers he'd faced so long ago.

"Day by day," he replied. "I met up with other groups of kids who were homeless or runaways. We slept under bridges and in parks. We sweated through the summer and froze in the winter. The money my mother had left me didn't last long. Lots of the kids were into drugs, but I never touched them. But I did steal food to eat, I rummaged in garbage cans behind restaurants, did whatever I needed to do to survive."

He frowned and drew in a deep breath. "I think the worst part of it all was that no matter what kind of person my mother had been, I loved her and she just left me behind."

He shook his head, as if unable to believe the life he'd led. He gazed at her and covered her hand with his. "And then I was saved."

"Saved how?" she asked.

"By a social worker named Francine Rogers and a force of nature named Cass Holiday. Francine often visited the lost boys, as we called ourselves. She'd come in the evenings after her day job and try to talk the runaways into going back home, the addicted to get into treatment and the boys like me to get into the system."

"She was friends with Cass?"

"Good friends. This was all around the time that Cass had lost her husband and most of her employees had abandoned her and her ranch. None of them believed a fifty-two-year-old widow had the chops to keep the ranch running. They vastly underestimated Cass Holiday."

"So Cass decided to restaff her ranch with boys Francine brought here?" Nicolette asked. She moved close, closer to him still, until their thighs touched.

"The ranch was already in bad shape. Cass's husband had been sick for some time before he passed. Cass didn't just decide to restaff the place. She decided she was going to start again with cowboys she built from the ground up. I had just turned seventeen when Francine brought me here."

"You must have been scared."

He smiled at her and the shadows that had filled his eyes were gone. "I was terrified," he admitted. "I didn't know anything about ranching or being a cowboy, but I also knew that if I stayed where I was on the streets, then there were really only two outcomes… death or arrest."

"Tell me about Cass." Nicolette realized that at some point in the conversation she'd leaned against him, her body snuggled against his.

"I don't even know where to begin." His voice filled with a mixture of love and respect. "She was the strongest woman I've ever known, and when I first met her she scared the hell out of me. Adam was already here working for her and if he hadn't helped me along those first weeks and months, I might have not stayed."

He took her hand in his, and it felt incredibly normal to have his big hand wrapped around hers. "Cass was tough, determined to make us from little boys into the kind of cowboys she wanted. She gave us rules and consequences for breaking those rules, but she also gave us love and respect and self-esteem. This was a kind of last-chance ranch for most of us. If we hadn't made it here, who knew where we'd all be."

"She made you into the wonderful man you are now," Nicolette said.

He looked at her and smiled, a slow teasing grin that made her conscious of every single place their bodies touched. "You think I'm a wonderful man?" His face was suddenly intimately close to hers.

Despite the temptation to lean closer into him, she sat back. "I think Cass must have been a wonderful person." She couldn't allow another kiss to happen because she knew one would never be enough. "Did she get all of you men the same way?"

He released a sigh, as if sorry that she'd put a little physical distance between them. "Yeah, we were all brought here by Francine. There were others, but they either ran away or were taken away by Francine. They were the drug addicts who pretended to be clean, young guys who refused to abide by the rules or just plain didn't cut it."

"It seems like you are all a good bunch now," she replied.

"We're like brothers and Cass was the mother we'd never had. All of us who are here now would have died for her. You know she died between here and the bunkhouse. We think she was running to warn us about the tornado when she got hit in the head by a tree branch. She died trying to save us."

Emotion choked in his throat and he stood abruptly. "I think that's enough for tonight." He smiled tightly as he grabbed his gun from the table. "I guess talking so much about myself has tuckered me out. Good night, Nicolette."

"Good night, Lucas," she replied and watched as he left the room and went up the stairs.

She almost wished he hadn't told her about his tragic past because knowing his struggles and seeing the kind of man he'd become only made her admire him more.

She didn't know who had tried to get into the house using a ladder. She didn't know how long it would take before Cassie put the ranch up for sale and headed back east.

All she knew for certain was that Lucas Taylor was getting way too deep into her heart.

Despite the fact that Lucas had told Nicolette he was ready for bed, when he climbed into the twin bed sleep was the last thing on his mind.

He'd just needed to escape from her, from the feminine curves that had fit so neatly by his side, from the warmth of her so close against him. He'd had to get away from the scent of her and most important the compassion and then the admiration that had filled her eyes as he'd told her his story.

Now his head was not only filled with Nicolette but also old memories that he hadn't entertained for years. He tried never to think about that day he'd returned home from school to find his mother gone…vanished.

He'd run down the hallway to the apartment that had been home and had used his key to open the door, stunned to find everything gone. Even though he and his mother had gone through many bad times, he couldn't believe that she'd just abandoned him like an old piece of furniture she didn't want to move to a new place.

He'd thought he was over that pain of abandonment, but his discussion tonight had made him realize there were some things you never really got over, you just moved on.

As he listened to the faint snore of the six-year-old in the bed next to his, his heart expanded with affection. Sammy would never know abandonment from his mother. Nicolette's love for her son was evident every minute of every day.

He lusted for her, but he also admired her maternal instincts. He wanted her in his bed, but he also didn't want to break her heart, and he had a feeling she was the kind of woman who wouldn't give herself to a man easily. One kiss with her hadn't been enough. As he drifted off to sleep, he dreamed he was kissing her once again.

He awoke just before dawn and silently left the room. He showered and dressed, and then crept down the stairs. No lights were on downstairs, letting him know that he was the first one up in the house.

He made a pot of coffee and then stood at the kitchen window sipping it as dawn began to streak across the sky. He hoped to talk Cassie and Nicolette into heading to town for breakfast this morning.

Since it was cow chipping day, they would need all hands on deck in the lower pasture and he didn't want to worry about the women and Sammy being all alone in the house while all the cowhands were occupied so far away in the pasture.

He'd just started on his second cup of coffee when Cassie walked into the kitchen, clad in a blue bathrobe and with her blond hair making messy curls around her head.

"Thank goodness you made coffee," she murmured as she beelined toward the counter where the hot brew awaited her.

"I have a favor to ask you," he said once she'd poured her coffee and was seated at the table across from him.

"What's that?" She blew across the top of her cup and then took a drink.

"I think maybe it would be a good idea if you three went into town for a leisurely breakfast this morning. It's going to take all of us ranch hands to round up the cattle and herd them where they need to be for the chipping."

"But Adam thought it was important I see this chipping operation," she replied.

"If you head into town for a couple of hours, then you'd probably be back in plenty of time to see how it all works. If you do come down to the pasture, I'd like Nicolette and Sammy to be with you."

She took another sip of her coffee and studied him thoughtfully over the rim of her cup. "Do you think it's dangerous for the three of us to be here in the house all alone?"

"Probably not, at least not in the daytime," he said thoughtfully. "I can't imagine anyone bringing danger during the day when they would know we're all up and around, but today all the men will be down in the pasture. I still think it would be safer if you were having breakfast at the café and then return and come to where we'll all be."

"So, you don't think the danger to us is over," she said, her eyes slightly widened.

"It might be over, but I won't feel completely comfortable until I know who was climbing up that ladder and why," he replied. "I don't particular like unsolved mysteries."

"Okay, we'll get out of here and head into town and when we get back we'll go to the pasture," she agreed.

"Since none of you ride, you can take one of the cars to drive you down there."

"Cars I do, horses not so much." She finished her cup of coffee and stood. "I'll go wake up Nicolette so that you can get out of here. It shouldn't take us long to get ready."

True to her word, within half an hour, all three came down the stairs, dressed and ready for a trip into town. "Is the café even open this early?" Sammy asked as he scrubbed a fist in one still-sleepy eye.

Lucas smiled at him. "The café is open before the sun first peeks over the horizon. Lots of hungry cowboys eat there before they start their day at work."

"Okay, then let's go!" Sammy exclaimed.

Lucas laughed and his gaze connected with Nicolette, who looked stunning despite the early hour. Her hair was loose and fell to the shoulders of a bright red blouse that made her eyes appear even greener than usual. The tight black jeans showcased the long slender length of her legs, and he couldn't help the knot of desire that formed in the pit of his stomach.

He was grateful when minutes later they pulled away from the house in the car that had belonged to Cass. He locked up the place and headed for the stables, knowing he was already late to get to work.

Lucky and three others were the only horses left in the stable, indicating that all the other men had already gone to the lower pasture for the day's work. He saddled his horse and tried not to think about the woman who haunted his dreams and the little boy who had wormed a path dangerously close to his heart.

Maybe it would be better if he got somebody else to bunk in with Sammy. The minute the idea formed in his mind he rejected it as a streak of unexpected jealousy swept through him.

There was no way he wanted another man to see Nicolette first thing in the morning, with her hair still bed-tussled and her green eyes sleepy and sexy. There was no way he wanted another pair of male eyes to feast on her wrapped in her silky robe as she drank her first cup of coffee.

He mounted Lucky and gave the horse a light rein. As he rode, he breathed in the clean morning air and noticed how much work the others had accomplished the day before in their tree and brush cleanup.

He passed the nearly destroyed long shed that stood as a constant reminder of the storm that had ripped through the area and had taken Cass's life. He'd be glad when they got it torn down and rebuilt it, and then maybe it wouldn't be a constant reminder of loss.

Loss. He'd had enough, and even though Cassie hadn't told the men, Sammy had mentioned to Lucas that she intended to sell the place and head back to New York City.

A vision of the young boy filled his head. Sammy. He'd never seen a kid so eager to learn and so eager to please. He'd never known a kid so open to love, so hungry for the love of a strong male.

Lucas would put his heart on the line for the kid, but he wasn't willing to do the same for Nicolette. Besides, although she hadn't told him Cassie's plan, she had to know what her friend intended.

Nicolette was probably just wasting time with a rugged cowboy who had been judged as unworthy by his own mother. He and Nicolette came from completely different worlds.

He liked to believe that when it came time to say goodbye to Sammy, he'd have the knowledge that he'd been a part of teaching the kid about hard work and discipline, about affection and praise. He'd know that he'd been a father fill-in temporarily.

But he knew in his heart that he couldn't be a temporary lover to Nicolette. He had sworn he'd never allow any woman into his heart again. He'd sworn that he would never give another woman the power to hurt him.

He had a feeling she could hurt him, that if he allowed it she could crawl under the shield he'd erected around his heart that day that his mother had left him.

He was grateful to see the herd of cows in the distance and his fellow workers, some on horseback and some standing by the chute where the cattle were herded in five or six at a time so that Dr. Dan could chip them.

A hard day's work in the warm sunshine with his fellow cowboys and a big herd of cattle was just the ticket to drive thoughts of a beautiful, desirable woman right out of his mind.

Chapter 7

Breakfast at the café was a treat. Cassie chattered with Sammy about the ranch while Nicolette sipped her coffee and tried not to think about what Lucas had shared with her the night before.

She watched Sammy dig into his thick French toast and did her best not to consider how many mornings Lucas had gone hungry in his life.

Fifteen wasn't grown and ready to face the world all alone. How could a mother just walk away from her child and leave him to the mean streets of the city? She couldn't imagine the horror of being all alone, of being afraid and having nobody to turn to for comfort.

As breakfast progressed she found herself sharing some of the story with Cassie. "According to Lucas that's how all the men came to be here. It took less than a year for her to get all her young cowboys at the ranch. Your aunt must have been an amazing woman."

Cassie released a sigh. "I wish I would have known her better. Adam talks about her like she was a little bit saint and a little bit mama bear. He told me she had a temper and could crack a bullwhip within an inch of a man's face. In fact during the local fairs and such she'd put on a show with her bullwhip."

"Maybe Lucas could teach me how to crack a bull-whip," Sammy said, and then licked a glob of syrup off his lower lip.

"Not a chance, buddy," Nicolette replied and handed him an extra napkin. "You could put your eye out with one of those things. Maybe it would be better if you asked Lucas to teach you to ride a horse."

"Really? That would be awesome." Happy with his mother's reply, he continued digging into his breakfast.

"Maybe you could follow in your aunt's footsteps and learn to handle a whip," Nicolette said to Cassie.

"Ha, the only whip I'm interested in is the whip of my gorgeous locks on a windy day," Cassie replied airily.

"You're so shallow," Nicolette said teasingly.

"I know. That and oil and acrylic painting are the only real talents I have."

"Have you managed to get any painting done in between meetings with Adam?"

Cassie frowned. "Not much, but we've only been here a couple of days. I'm hoping now that Adam has given me the crash course in ranch management I'll have a little extra time to spend on my painting." She took a sip of her coffee and then continued, "To be honest, I'm already homesick."

Sammy looked up from his plate, obviously stricken by her words. "But we aren't leaving yet, are we?"

"Not yet, little buckaroo," Cassie replied. "We've still got plenty of work to do to get the place in tip-top shape."

"I hope it takes forever and ever to get the work done," Sammy exclaimed. "I don't want to leave here for a long, long time."

Nicolette mentally added her own wish to her son's. She wasn't ready to leave the ranch and Oklahoma yet. She hadn't tired of the vastness of the starlit sky at night, the clean spring air that greeted her every morning. She wanted to explore the wildflowers that dotted the pasture, take in the scent of hay and leather.

In truth, even though she hated to admit it, she wasn't ready to leave Lucas yet. His story had stirred her on all kinds of levels. She'd wanted to mother the child he had been, she'd wanted to nurture the lost teenager and she'd wanted to make love to the man he had become.

It was a good thing he'd gone upstairs when he had last night because if he'd kissed her, if he'd caressed her in any way, he would have had her right there on the sofa if he'd wanted her.

Heaven help her, she'd known the man less than a week and she already wanted to take him to bed, learn every nuance of his heart and soul. It was crazy. She was crazy.

"Earth to Nicolette," Cassie said.

Nicolette looked at Cassie blankly, realizing she'd been lost in her head and had no idea what had just been said. "I've asked you three times if you're ready to go," Cassie said.

Nicolette looked down at her plate, surprised to realize that while she'd been thinking about Lucas she'd eaten all of her breakfast.

"Unless I intend to eat the silverware, I guess I'm ready to go," she replied and loved the sound of her son's responding giggle.

By the time they'd paid, it was still early enough that they stopped into the shop where Lucas had bought Sammy's cowboy boots. Nicolette had decided she needed a pair of her own.

"They'd be a great novelty item when we go back to New York," Cassie said while Nicolette perused the various styles and colors.

The minute she saw the muted red boots with the black embroidery of roses, she knew they were meant for her. She left the store with them on her feet, knowing that they were an extravagance she could ill afford and yet rationalizing to herself that she needed them to be out in the pastures and around the ranch with Sammy. They weren't a luxury, they were practical, she told herself firmly.

It was nearly eleven by the time they reached the house. Cassie parked the car and then brought around a golf-like cart so they could head to the area where the men were working.

"Look at all the cows," Sammy said as they rode up a small hill.

The valley on the other side was an impressive sight that nearly stole Nicolette's breath away. Lush green grass and a sparkling pond partially surrounded by trees looked like a beautiful rural painting.

The herd of cattle and the cowboys on horseback appeared like a scene from a Western. Reddish-brown dust stirred beneath the horse hooves and the cattle moos made a peculiar chorus that was a pleasant sound.

Nicolette instantly identified Lucas among the men

on horseback. He sat tall and proud in the saddle, as if confident he was exactly where he was supposed to be and doing what he loved.

She envied him that, the obvious sense of belonging he'd found here with Cass and his fellow cowboys. She couldn't imagine what he'd do when Cassie sold and if the new owner let him and the others go.

Where would he go? Where would he find a family like the one Cass had built here? She kept telling herself he wasn't her problem, but she couldn't help but worry about his future, about all of the cowboys who might be displaced.

Cassie parked the cart and she and Sammy got out and began the walk down toward where the action was happening. Nicolette chose to stay in the cart. She didn't want to get in the way of the work. Cassie needed to see what was happening, and she knew there was no way she could hold Sammy back from being a part of it all.

She was perfectly content to remain in the cart and feast her eyes on the cowboy who had already subtly marked her heart. It was strange. All of Cass's cowboys were good-looking men, as if the old woman had chosen to surround herself with eye candy. But no matter how handsome the others were, it was Lucas who caught and held Nicolette's attention.

The morning waned and finally the work was done with the cattle appearing no worse for the wear.

Cassie and Sammy returned to the cart, Sammy chattering excitedly that Lucas had agreed to give him horse-riding lessons later that afternoon.

"Did you see all the cows, Mom? They're so big up close," he continued as they rode back to the house.

"The bigger the better." Cassie spoke like the true

owner of the ranch who knew those black Angus were her cash cows.

Maybe there was some hope that Cassie would change her mind over the next few weeks and decide to make her life here, where her aunt had built a dream.

Although Cassie spoke of being homesick, she could put the ranch up for sale at any time, without further repairs being done, and still make enough money to probably never have to worry again. She could leave tomorrow with the ranch in the hands of a real estate agent and head back to the city she professed to love. But so far she didn't seem to be in a huge hurry to cut and run.

It wasn't long after lunch that Lucas returned to the house. He'd apparently showered and cleaned up at the bunkhouse, for his dark hair looked freshly shampooed and he smelled of minty-clean soap.

"I heard there was a little cowboy around here who wanted to learn to ride a horse," he said.

Sammy jumped up off the sofa, his hand in the air. "Me, you know that it's me." His entire body vibrated with excitement.

Lucas looked at Nicolette, his gaze drifting down to her new boots. "I like the new footwear. You wear them well."

It was ridiculous how much his compliment meant to her. "I figured they were more appropriate for around here than the sandals and heels I brought with me."

"I like a woman with good sense," he replied.

"And I'd like to get on a horse," Sammy exclaimed, obviously wanting action rather than any more conversation. He ran toward the kitchen door and Nicolette and Lucas followed.

"I hope you don't intend to put him on one of the big

horses you all ride," Nicolette said, unable to halt the tinge of worry as she thought of her little boy on the back of a big beast.

"You know I'd never do anything to put Sammy at risk. Surely you trust me enough to believe that."

"Of course I trust you, Lucas. I think I've trusted you since the moment you knelt beside Sammy's bed and told him that real cowboys bathed every night."

For a brief moment she wanted to dive into the softness that filled his eyes. She wanted to forget that he could only be her temporary cowboy.

He broke the moment. "We'd better get outside before Sammy chokes on his own excitement."

She laughed, an excitement of her own building inside her as she thought of her son's happiness and the opportunity to spend more time watching the two most important men in her life interact together.

Sammy stood by the stables, waving to them to hurry. "Come on," he yelled. "I'm so ready."

"And I've got the perfect mount for you," he said to Sammy once they'd caught up to him. "Her name is Candy because she's so sweet-tempered. She used to be Cass's horse." He paused a moment, as if needing to tamp down the grief that he must feel whenever he thought of Cassie's aunt.

"Funny," he continued. "Cass was the strongest, most independent woman I've ever met, but she had a bit of a fear of horses. Wait here."

He disappeared into the stable and minutes later returned leading a brown-and-white-dappled horse that was smaller than the horses the men rode. He also had his own horse saddled and ready to ride. "You might want to introduce yourself to her," he instructed Sammy.

"She isn't one you met when you were in the stables before."

Sammy moved to the front of the horse. "Hello, Candy. My name is Sammy Kendall and it's nice to meet you."

Lucas burst out laughing. The deep rumble wrapped around Nicolette's heart despite the fact that she knew it was at her well-mannered city boy's expense.

"That's not quite what I had in mind." Lucas pulled a lump of sugar from his pocket and handed it to Sammy and then showed him how to offer it to Candy from the palm of his hand. "Now, scratch her nose and let her smell you. That's how you introduce yourself to a horse."

Sammy smiled blissfully as the horse nuzzled his hand and then sniffed his face. He stroked Candy down her nose and giggled as she nuzzled the hollow of his throat. "I think she likes me."

"She definitely likes you," Lucas replied. "Now, you two hold tight and I'll go grab Candy's saddle. Before you actually get to ride, you have to learn how to saddle a horse properly," Lucas said.

While Sammy continued to get acquainted with Candy, Nicolette watched Lucas walk away. The man had the rolling-hip swagger of a sexy gunslinger down pat. He made her fantasize about pulling him down in a stall full of fresh hay and stripping him naked.

Lucky was apparently well trained, as the big horse didn't move, although he turned his head in the direction of the stable as if impatient for Lucas to return.

Lucas had been gone only a couple of minutes when the sound of horse hooves filled the air, coming from around the side of the house where no horses were stabled. Nicolette turned just in time to see a rider on a huge black horse riding toward them.

His face was hidden by a ski mask, and by the time alarm bells went off in her head the rider swept past her, grabbed Sammy and threw him on his belly across the saddle in front of him and continued on.

The scream that had momentarily been trapped inside her by abject horror released, the high-pitch sound of sheer terror.

The scream shot adrenaline through Lucas as he raced out of the stable. He saw the rider heading out toward the main lane to leave the ranch, and he saw the absence of Sammy next to his mother.

His heart slammed into his ribs as he lost no time. He flew onto Lucky's back and nudged the horse's sides with his heels. Lucky responded, racing after the other horse as Lucas filled his hand with his gun.

The black horse was bigger, but Lucky was faster, and it didn't take long before Lucas was close enough to hear Sammy's screams of fear, his grunts of pain as his body slammed up and down on the saddle.

Rage seethed through Lucas. Who was on that horse and why had he taken Sammy? It had been a brazen act in the middle of the day with Nicolette standing right next to her son.

He urged Lucky faster, knowing that if he somehow managed to fall behind the black horse then Sammy would be gone and nobody would have a clue how to get him back or who had been responsible for taking him.

Sammy's cries stabbed Lucas in the heart. He had to be bounding around with each galloping step, possibly breaking ribs or being injured further.

"Stop!" he shouted when he was close enough to be heard. "Stop and let the boy go or I swear I'll shoot you in your back." To prove his point he pointed to a nearby stand of trees and fired.

The sound of the gunshot pierced the air and the black horse slowed just a bit. "The next shot will kill you, or at the very least make you wish you were dead," Lucas shouted.

He pointed his gun in the center of the man's back, no doubt in his mind that he would shoot if necessary. There was no way in hell he would allow this man to ride off to some unknown destination with Sammy in his possession.

They were at the black gates that formed the entrance to the ranch. He fired another shot just over the left shoulder of the rider. That was apparently enough for the man to know he meant business. Slowing his horse just a bit, he tossed Sammy to the ground, where the little boy rolled to the side of the lane and into the brush and remained unmoving.

Lucas's heart stopped beating. As the rider on the black horse once again began to gallop away, Lucas pulled up and dismounted, but before he could rush to Sammy's side the sound of pounding horse hooves came in the distance and he was passed by six of his fellow cowboys on the trail of the perpetrator.

Thank God. Hopefully they would catch up to the man, but right now Lucas's entire concern was for the unmoving child on the side of the road half-hidden by brush. When the horsemen passed, Lucas rushed to Sammy's side.

"Sammy?" he said and knelt down. Sammy's eyes were closed and once again Lucas's heart began to beat, but too fast, too frantically. Did the little boy have broken bones? Had he suffered internal injuries from the tumble?

"Sammy, you're safe now," he said, and holstered his gun so he could get to his cell phone to call for help. Before he could dial a number, Sammy's eyes opened and he slowly sat up.

Lucas nearly wept with relief. "Sammy, are you okay?"

"I think I'm okay." The young boy's voice quavered, but Lucas hoped it was more with fear than with the pain of serious injury.

"Can you stand up?" Lucas asked.

"I think so. Everything hurts, but nothing hurts really bad." With Lucas's help, Sammy got to his feet. He threw his arms around Lucas's waist, held tight and began to cry.

"Shh, it's okay. You're with me now and nothing bad is going to happen to you again," Lucas said as he patted Sammy's shoulder. He wanted to kill somebody as he heard Sammy's cries, felt the warmth from him as he clung to him. He was just a little boy, for crying out loud.

"Thank you for saving me," Sammy said and finally released his hold on Lucas. He swiped the tears from his eyes. "Why did that man take me?"

"I don't know, little partner, but we're going to find out. Now we'd better get you back to your mother before she has a complete heart attack. You can ride back in front of me on Lucky, but you'll sit tall in the saddle like a cowboy should."

Sammy eyed the horse warily. "I didn't like riding

that other horse so much." He rubbed his stomach. "It hurt me."

"This won't hurt," Lucas promised. He grabbed Sammy by the waist and put him in the saddle. "Now I'm going to sit right behind you." Lucas mounted Lucky but made sure Sammy had most of the saddle. He wrapped his arms around Sammy's sides, taking no chances with his precious passenger.

They rode silently until they reached the stables, where Nicolette was surrounded by Cassie, Nick and Dusty, who were obviously keeping her in place by bodily force. Cassie had her arms wrapped around Nicolette and Nick had a hand firmly on her shoulder. The two of them stepped back from her as Lucas rode in.

Her sobs filled the air when she saw them and Sammy called to her. "I'm okay, Mom. Lucas saved me."

Lucas didn't know if Nicolette would fall to the ground with relief. She looked so fragile, so broken, but she straightened her shoulders and rushed to where Lucas had halted Lucky.

"Thank God," she said as she reached up to help her son down. She dropped to her knees and hugged him tight, still weeping tears that Lucas knew were a mixture of both terror and relief.

"Mom," Sammy protested as he looked at the other cowboys and wiggled in her arms. "Mom, it's okay. You can let me go now. I'm safe and sound."

Lucas dismounted at the same time Sammy managed to escape his mother's hug. Nicolette got up from the ground and ran directly to Lucas and threw her arms around his neck.

"Thank you, thank you," she whispered over and

over again against the hollow of his throat. With her plastered against him, he was acutely aware of every curve in her body, of the scent of her that threatened to erupt desire in him.

He untangled her arms from around his neck and stepped back, feeling a little bit of Sammy's embarrassment at her effusive gratefulness.

"I called the police. Chief Bowie should be here anytime," Dusty said.

Lucas nodded. "Whoever took Sammy tossed him off the horse. It probably wouldn't hurt to get Doc Washington out here to give Sammy a thorough check."

Dr. Eric Washington practiced in Bitterroot, but still clung to the old-fashioned notice that he practiced wherever patients needed him, and so he often made house calls around the area.

"I'll put a call into Doc and see if we can get him out here as soon as possible," Nick replied. "He might want to check out Nicolette, too. She was like a rabid dog. It took all of us holding her back."

Nicolette's cheeks grew pink. "Sorry, I was just so frantic." She started to grab for Sammy again, but he danced away from her, obviously embarrassed by all the mommy love displayed in front of the other cowboys.

"Why don't you and Cassie take Sammy inside," Lucas suggested. "We'll wait out here for Chief Bowie to arrive."

Nicolette nodded, as if grateful to get her son into the house, where he would be safe from crazed horsemen or any other unexpected danger that might appear out of nowhere.

When the two women and Sammy had disappeared

into the house, Nick turned to Lucas. "Did you recognize the rider or the horse?" he asked.

"The rider had on a ski mask. I can't even tell you what color his hair was," Lucas replied in frustration. "I didn't recognize the horse, either. It was a big black beast that I've never seen before, but thankfully it was slower on its feet than my ride."

He stepped over to Lucky and stroked her nose. She nuzzled him in mutual affection. "I threatened to shoot him in the back and fired two shots to let him know I meant business, and that's when he slowed down and threw Sammy off the horse."

"I guess we can now jump to the conclusion that the ladder against the house at Sammy's bedroom window was there intentionally," Dusty replied.

Lucas's stomach knotted with tension. What in the hell was going on here? Who would want to kidnap Sammy and why? "I just can't believe that Lloyd would go to all this trouble over a glass of spilled milk. And I've never seen any of the men on the Humes ranch with that horse."

"We don't really know that much about Nicolette. Maybe the danger to her son is something she brought to town when she arrived here," Nick suggested.

"Maybe," Lucas replied dubiously. He thought he knew Nicolette. She'd shared her past with him. Had she left something out? Were there secrets in her past that endangered her son? Had she left New York City with her friend to escape somebody only to have the person follow her here?

He was grateful when Chief Dillon Bowie arrived with several of his men. Lucas quickly filled them in on what had happened and that several of the other cowboys had given chase but had yet to return to the ranch.

"We called in Doc Washington, who should be here anytime as well to check on Sammy," Lucas said. "He seems to be fine, but he took a hard spill from the horse and I figure a checkup by the doctor wouldn't hurt."

"I guess the next step is to go inside and see what Nicolette can tell us," Dillon said. "I have a hard time believing somebody from Bitterroot would try to kidnap a kid. She's got some difficult questions to answer."

Lucas followed Dillon into the house. He wanted to hear her answers, too. Somehow over the past couple of days he'd become emotionally invested in Nicolette and her son. He needed to find out if she had dark secrets that threatened her son...that might threaten everyone else on the ranch.

Chapter 8

Nicolette felt as if she would never be warm again. As she relived the sound of those pounding horse hooves, that horrifying moment when the rider had reached down, grabbed her son and ridden away, icy fear renewed itself over and over again inside her.

What was going on? Why was somebody after her son? And who would make such a bold attempt to take him right from her side? This all felt like a nightmare and she couldn't wake up. Sammy sat in the chair across from the sofa, his handheld video game in his hand.

She didn't want him out of her sight. Dear God, she'd been standing right next to him when he'd been carried away. If it hadn't been for Lucas's quick action, Sammy might have disappeared forever. And for what?

She rubbed two fingers across the center of her forehead, where a killer headache attempted to bloom. She wanted to wrap Sammy in Bubble Wrap packaging and send him to some isolated island where she was certain he would be safe for the rest of his life.

She wanted to wrap him in her arms and not let go until he was a full-grown man and could handle any danger that might find him.

What on earth was happening here? Was Lloyd Green so evil he would do something like this? Over a glass of spilled milk? It just didn't make any sense.

When Chief Bowie walked in followed by Lucas, she sat up straighter and tried to pull herself together for whatever questions might come, questions she knew she had no answers for.

"Rough day?" Chief Bowie asked, his gray eyes soft as he gazed at her.

"That's an understatement," she replied. "Sammy, why don't you take your game and go upstairs with Cassie so I can talk to Chief Bowie." Although it was difficult to send him out of her sight at the moment, she didn't want him to hear things that might frighten him even more.

"Come on, buckaroo," Cassie said. "Let's see if we can make a tent out of bedsheets in my bedroom."

"Cool," Sammy agreed and within moments the two had disappeared up the stairs.

"Can you tell me exactly what happened?" Dillon asked.

She recounted the events, and the cold inside her returned full force. She wrapped her arms around herself and then smiled gratefully as Lucas sat down next close to her, his body heat warming her.

"The man had on a ski mask so I can't identify him. He just appeared out of nowhere and scooped up my son. I can't imagine why anyone would want to take Sammy," she said.

"What about his father?" Lucas asked.

Nicolette looked at him in surprise. "If Samuel wanted to see Sammy, then he has my phone number. We'd make arrangements. He certainly wouldn't try to kidnap his own son. We haven't even heard from Samuel since my divorce from him over two years ago."

"What about old boyfriends?" Dillon asked.

"There are none," she replied. "I've been far too busy as a single mother and the owner of a business to even consider romance."

"Is there any business-related issue that might have followed you here? Does the business owe money to people who might want to grab Sammy for some sort of ransom?" Dillon's gaze had gone from soft to steel.

A hysterical burst of laughter escaped her lips. "Anyone who knows me knows that I wouldn't have money to pay a ransom. I'm broke and the store is barely functioning in the black."

She shook her head. "There's no way the answer to this is that somebody is seeking a ransom."

"But isn't your ex-husband wealthy?" Lucas asked.

She turned and looked at him thoughtfully. "Samuel has a healthy monthly trust fund amount that his mother set up for him before her death, but anyone who knows Samuel would know that he'd rather hang on to his money than pay a ransom for his son." The words came out a little more bitter than she'd intended, but truth was truth.

She glanced back at Dillon. "Honestly, I can't imagine that anyone from Samuel's life would be behind this. He lives a party lifestyle and I would guess that most of the people he now surrounds himself with don't have a clue that he was ever married or even has a son."

Although she felt Lucas's gaze on her, she couldn't look at him. She was ashamed by her choice, by her foolish belief that Samuel would be the man she'd thought he would be for her sake, for the sake of their son.

Samuel had been a spoiled brat when she'd married him and when she'd divorced him. She had no reason to believe that he had changed since then.

"You can't come up with a single name for me?" Dillon asked. "Not a name from your past or since you've been here?"

"Lloyd Green is the only man I've had any issues with here and I can't imagine him taking it to this kind of a level," she replied. "Sammy could have been killed being thrown from that horse."

"Maybe you should check Lloyd out again," Lucas said. "He and I exchanged some heated words at the café. He knows I'm quite fond of Sammy." He shrugged his shoulders.

"What kind of words were exchanged?" Dillon asked.

"I warned him not to mess with Sammy and Nicolette. I might have stirred the pot a little bit," Lucas admitted.

"I'll check him out, but I have to tell you, this just isn't Lloyd's style. He's an in-your-face kind of guy, not the type to sneak an attack on a defenseless kid."

At that moment a knock fell on the door and Lucas answered and introduced Nicolette to Dr. Eric Washington. He was a tall, white-haired man whose blue eyes looked both sharp and kindly.

"I understand there's a little patient I need to see," he said.

Nicolette started to rise. "He's upstairs."

Dr. Washington motioned her back on the sofa. "If I have your permission, I'll just head upstairs and give him a look."

Nicolette hesitated but when Lucas touched her shoulder and gave her a reassuring nod, she sat back down. "Just let me know if you have any concerns."

"Of course," the doctor agreed and then headed up the stairs.

When he'd disappeared from her sight, Nicolette turned her attention back to Dillon. "I don't know what else to tell you," she said in frustration. "I don't know how to help you. I wish I had a clue, I wish there was somebody from my past who could be responsible for what happened, but I don't know. I simply don't know."

Her voice cracked as emotion rose up to fill the back of her throat. Somebody had tried to get to her baby twice now and nobody had any answers for her.

Lucas placed his hand on her knee and she knew it was in an effort to comfort her, to somehow assure her that everything was going to be all right. But as far as she was concerned, nothing was going to be right again until they found the man responsible for what had happened to Sammy.

"Who went after the man?" Dillon asked, turning his attention to Lucas.

"I think it was at least Forest, Jerod, Sawyer and maybe Clay. They blew by me so fast I just got a glimpse of them," Lucas said. "I was more focused on getting to Sammy to make sure he was all right."

"I hope I don't have to arrest any of them for murder," Dillon said drily.

"I hope they do kill whoever it was," Nicolette blurted out and then was horrified by her own words. Tears misted her vision as she thought of those agonizing moments when she didn't know if Lucas would be able to catch the man and save her son or not. "I'm sorry, I shouldn't have said that," she said, feeling as if she were about to shatter apart.

Sammy was all she had. She was all he'd ever had, and the thought of him being gone from her was too horrifying to fully take in.

"I understand your feelings," Dillon replied, his gaze once again soft as he looked at her. "If I had a son and somebody had done this to him, I would want the perpetrator hung by dusk. Unfortunately even in a small ranching town we have to abide by the laws."

Dillon finally sat in the chair Sammy had vacated. "If you don't mind I'll just stick around here until those cowboys return."

Heavy footsteps coming down the stairs announced the return of Dr. Washington. He smiled at Nicolette in reassurance. "No broken bones, although he's a bit banged up and bruised. I have a feeling he won't feel so great tomorrow. He'll be achy and sore, but other than that he should be just fine."

Nicolette released a sigh of relief, although the doctor just confirmed what she had thought. Sammy had taken a hard tumble, but he'd be fine. Thank God for small favors, she thought.

Dr. Washington had been gone for only a few minutes when the sound of horses approaching thundered through the open window. Both Lucas and Dillon were on their feet immediately.

They headed out the kitchen back door with Nicolette at their heels. Nicolette gasped as she saw the four horsemen from the ranch, one of them leading a man with his hands tied to the saddle horn of a familiar big black horse.

The man had dirty blond hair and a scraggly mustache and beard. His pale blue eyes held both belligerence and a hint of fear. Nicolette had never seen him before in her life, but apparently everyone else knew who he was.

"Jeff Bodine, you bastard," Lucas said in obvious surprise. "What the hell, man?"

"I'll take it from here," Dillon said.

All the other men dismounted from their horses and Dillon stepped up to the horse where Bodine was tied. "Forest, untie him and get him down."

Forest lived up to his name in that he was as big as a giant oak with muscled arms and legs. He untied the man in the saddle and then bodily removed him from the horse.

Dillon whirled Bodine around and slapped handcuffs on him and then turned him back to face him. "You've got some explaining to do."

"I ain't saying nothing," Bodine replied defiantly.

Nicolette stepped closer to him, her heart beating frantically. "Who are you?"

"Allow me to make the introduction," Lucas said, scorn deepening his voice. "Jeff is our resident dopehead. He'd sell his own mother if he thought it would get him drug money. Isn't that right, Bodine?"

"Why did you take my son?" Nicolette stared at the man, willing him to make sense of things.

"Right now you're looking at charges of kidnapping, endangering the life of a child and whatever else I can tack on to make sure you spend plenty of time behind bars," Dillon said. "Talk to me, Jeff. Make me understand why in the hell you'd do something like this."

Jeff rocked back on his heels. "If I cooperate will you go easy on me?"

"You know that's not up to me, but I'll make sure the prosecutor knows that you were cooperative," Dillon replied.

"Money," Jeff said grudgingly. He looked at Nicolette. "I was offered two thousand dollars to get the kid and promised another two when I delivered him."

Nicolette stared at him in stunned surprise. Who would pay four thousand dollars for Sammy? This wasn't just a fight between two cowboys in a café. It wasn't about a glass of spilled milk and a thrown cup of tea. It was something far more insidious, far more evil, and a new chill of horror swept through her.

Minutes later they were all seated back in the living room. The only person standing was Jeff, who was still cuffed with his hands behind his back.

Lucas sat next to Nicolette on the sofa, but he wanted to smash Jeff's face in, he wanted to beat the man until he could barely stand. He thought about Sammy's fear, about the fall from the horse that could have been deadly, and his rage was barely contained.

Nicolette appeared shell-shocked, her face pale and her fingers curled tightly in her lap as Dillon continued to question Jeff.

"Now that we're all settled in, you need to tell me who offered you the money to grab the kid," Dillon said.

"I don't know who he is. I never met him. Yesterday I got a phone call and this man told me he needed to get the kid, that if I was in then my total payday would be four thousand dollars." Jeff licked his lips, as if on the verge of drooling. "I've never seen that much money in my whole life. At first I thought it was some kind of a joke, but the man insisted he was serious."

"Once you had Sammy in your custody what were you supposed to do with him?" Dillon asked.

"Call the man and take Sammy to a motel for the night and then tomorrow night I was supposed to meet the man in a restaurant to do the handoff. I was to be there at midnight and give the kid a pill so he'd be asleep."

Jeff shifted from one foot to the other. "Last night I found an envelope in my mailbox with two thousand dollars inside and a pill that I was to give to the kid. There was also a motel room key."

"What motel?" Lucas asked, still needing to punch something, preferably Jeff's face.

"The Cowboy Inn." Jeff didn't look at Lucas, as if he could feel the animus radiating from him and didn't want to do anything to cause an explosion that might wind up causing him bodily harm.

"That's a cheap motel almost halfway between here and Oklahoma City," Lucas said to Nicolette.

"And what restaurant were you supposed to meet him at?" Dillon asked.

"Darryl's Diner. Look, I had no intention of hurting the kid. The man told me he didn't want the kid harmed." Jeff looked at Nicolette and then back to the chief. "I thought maybe it was some sort of an ugly custody issue of some kind. You hear about this stuff on television all the time."

"There is no custody issue," Nicolette said, her voice strained with barely suppressed emotion.

"Where did you get that horse and how was it that you just happened to be at the side of the house at a time when Sammy was vulnerable?" Dillon asked.

"The horse belongs to Bill Janko over at the Breckenridge Ranch. Bill and I are friends and I asked him if I could borrow his horse for a little while this morning. I'd been hiding out around the side of the house for a couple of hours before I saw the kid standing next to his mother and nobody else around."

Jeff sighed. "I've told you everything I know. Can't we just chalk this up to one of my boneheaded mistakes and forget about it?" For the first time his voice held no belligerence, but rather a pleading.

"I know what I think we should do," Lucas said before Dillon could respond. "I think we should put Jeff behind bars until tomorrow night and then I think he should make the phone call and meet this guy at the restaurant."

"And we'll all be waiting," Dillon replied, his eyes lighting with the shine of a hunter smelling prey.

"Why stop with the bonehead when we can get the man behind the plot?" Lucas asked rhetorically.

"But Sammy wouldn't be there," Nicolette said. "I don't want him anywhere around any of this. He's been through enough already."

"Sammy stays here. Jeff can tell the man that he's asleep in the back of his car. If it gets that far we'll make sure we've got a lump of blankets there that appears to be a sleeping child." Dillon turned his attention back to Jeff. "How are you supposed to identify this man when you get to the diner?"

"He's going to be wearing a black-and-red shirt," Jeff replied. He bowed his head, as if a confession had been beaten out of him.

"At that time of night in that dive, I'd be surprised if there was anyone else in the place," Lucas said.

"You'd be surprised at how many drunks and low-lifes wind up there in the middle of the night," Dillon replied. He rose from his chair. "Why don't I get this creep out of here and we'll talk tomorrow about specific plans for tomorrow night."

Minutes later Nicolette and Lucas were alone. The only sound in the house was Sammy's giggles and Cassie's laughter drifting down the stairs.

"You know Sammy is probably the least traumatized of all of us about this," Lucas said softly.

"I know." She unclasped her hands and instead reached two fingers to the center of her forehead and lightly rubbed.

"Headache?" he asked. She looked achingly vulnerable, as if she might shatter to pieces if she moved wrong, if he said the wrong thing.

To his surprise she straightened her shoulders and gave him a small smile. "Life ache would be more like it."

He took one of her hands in his, marveling at how small, how delicate it was against his own and yet how much inner strength she possessed. "Hopefully by tomorrow night we'll have all the answers to satisfy us and the bad guy will be in custody."

She squeezed his hand. "I hope you're right. I just

want all of this to be over." She released his hand and stood. "It's late. I need to get Sammy into the bathtub and into bed."

"I'll make sure the house is locked up tight," Lucas said and got up from the sofa, as well.

What he wanted to do was wrap his arms around her and hold her tight against him, hold her until the simmer of fear no longer darkened the beauty of her eyes. He'd like to kiss her long and deep, until he banished every thought of what had happened, what might have happened, and instead filled her head with hot, sweet desire.

But he did neither of those things. He watched her walk up the stairs and then he went around the house, locking doors and checking windows.

His mind whirled with the events of the day. The fact that Jeff had been lured to commit such an act wasn't a huge surprise. The man was an addict who had no moral compass when it came to getting the funds to get his fixes. The real question was who was behind the kidnapping attempt. Who had paid Jeff to do the job?

He lingered at the kitchen door, reliving the moment he'd heard Nicolette's terrified scream. He never wanted to hear that kind of sound from her again.

Thank God for the resilience of children, he thought. Sammy was young enough not to fully process the real danger he'd been in, and from the giggles Lucas had heard from the upstairs bedroom throughout the interrogation of Jeff, Sammy had already put most of the trauma behind him.

It was the adults who would not be able to just make a tent of bed sheets and forget the whole thing. This would haunt Nicolette and him until they had all the answers they needed to stamp the case closed in their minds.

He was just about to leave the back door when a soft knock fell. He peered out to see Nick standing on the back porch. Lucas opened the door and Nick stepped just inside.

"I just wanted to let you know that a couple of the other guys and me are going to take turns guarding the outside of the house for the night."

"I appreciate it," Lucas replied. He knew that Nick had problems of his own. When the waitress Wendy Bailey had initially gone missing, Nick had been under scrutiny for her disappearance.

"I just wanted to let you know we're out here so if you see us you don't think we're the bad guys and decide to shoot us," Nick replied with a wry smile.

"I'll keep that in mind. I'd hate to shoot one of the good guys."

Nick left and once again Lucas locked up the back door. By the time he climbed the stairs, his bunk buddy was already bathed and in bed with Nicolette seated on the twin bed beside him.

She stood as he entered the room and Sammy gave him a sleepy smile. "I was just telling him to have sweet dreams," Nicolette said.

"Cowboys always have sweet dreams," Lucas replied.

"And I'm a real cowboy." The words slurred from Sammy and then it was obvious he was asleep.

Lucas walked with Nicolette out into the hallway. She looked up at him, her eyes shimmering in the faint light spilling from Cassie's bedroom.

"I don't think I really thanked you enough for saving

him," she said. Her lower lip trembled slightly. "He's my world, you know. I can't imagine what my life would be like without him."

Lucas couldn't stand it any longer. He had to touch her in some way, somehow. He raised a hand and stroked it softly down her cheek, and before he realized how it happened, she was in his embrace.

She wrapped her arms around his neck and he took her by the waist and held her tight, breathing in the scent of her hair and the soft floral and slightly fruity perfume that muddied his head.

He rubbed his hands up and down her back as he felt her shivering despite the fact that the hallway was warm. Fear was a terrible place to dwell. He knew that more than most people.

He remembered the fear of sleeping beneath a highway overpass or in the back of a dark alley, terrified that somebody would sneak up on him in the middle of the night and slit his throat and steal what meager items he'd managed to collect.

"It's going to be all right," he murmured against her ear. "We aren't going to let anything happen to Sammy."

She raised her head to gaze up at him and her beautiful eyes swam with so many emotions he couldn't begin to discern any one in particular.

All he knew was that she looked as if she needed to be kissed…badly. And he wanted to kiss her…badly. He recognized that they'd both been on an emotional roller coaster and the ride hadn't stopped.

Following instincts alone, he lowered his lips to hers, stunned when she tightened her grip around his neck and pressed closer against him.

She tasted of sweetness and heat. She opened her

mouth to allow him to deepen what he'd intended simply as a kiss of compassion, of support. The kiss became so much more complicated than that as their tongues swirled together and a fire in his veins flamed hot. The kiss stole his breath away and finally he broke it and instead slid his lips down her jaw and under her chin.

She dropped her head back and pressed her hips more firmly against his. *You've got to stop*, a little voice whispered inside his head.

It was as if she heard the little voice. She suddenly stepped back from him, her green eyes glowing and her breathing labored.

Before he could mutter an apology, she grabbed his hand, hers feeling hot and fevered. "Come to my room, Lucas. Come and make love to me."

It never entered his mind to deny her. After all, a real cowboy never turned down a lady's request.

Chapter 9

Nicolette knew she was all kinds of fool, but at the moment she didn't care. She'd deal with the morning-after issues when they'd shared their night before.

She could pretend to herself that she was out of her mind, that Sammy's near abduction was the reason for the bad decision she was about to make.

The truth of the matter was she wanted to make love with Lucas. She thought she'd wanted him since the moment she'd gotten out of the car and saw him standing so tall, so confident and sexy, by the front porch.

The minute she closed her bedroom door behind them, she was in his arms once again and his lips claimed hers in a kiss that torched fire through her from head to toe.

She didn't want to think anymore, and being in Lucas's arms brought not just a welcomed sense of security, but a desire that overrode anything else.

Sammy was safe and she wanted Lucas. It was as simple and as complicated as that. As their lips remained locked, he grabbed the bottom of her T-shirt and broke the kiss only long enough to pull it over her head and toss it aside.

The only light in the room was the soft glow from the bedside lamp on the nightstand that cast the room in hazy gold and shadows.

He pulled his own T-shirt off and then reached for her again. She loved the feel of his bare, muscled chest against her. She nestled her face into the hollow of his throat, breathing in the scent of sunshine and a fresh, clean cologne.

Their hips moved against each other, friction from their jeans creating a new well of heat inside her. She knew he wasn't her happily-ever-after, but he was her happy for tonight and that was enough.

She broke away from him and moved toward the queen-size bed. Shoes and socks disappeared and she unfastened her jeans and wiggled out of them. A glance at him showed that he was doing the same thing.

As he stood before her in only a pair of navy briefs, her breath caught in her chest at his physical perfection. Lean muscles rode his body in every place they belonged, and she couldn't wait to feel all those muscles against her. The faint illumination appeared to play and dance on his perfect physique.

She quickly unfastened her bra and allowed it to fall off her, unashamed as she once again stood to face him clad only in a wispy pair of white lace underpants.

"You are so beautiful," he said, his voice lower… deeper than she'd ever heard it before. He reached up and tangled his hands in her hair, as if wanting to touch each and every strand.

"I was just thinking the same thing about you," she replied. She stepped away from him and moved to the bed and pulled down the quilt that covered it, exposing pale blue sheets that beckoned them.

She slid beneath the sheets and he followed. He immediately placed his hands on each side of her face. "I've dreamed of this since the moment I first saw you when you got out of that rental car," he said softly.

"I've had the same dream," she confessed. His lips took hers in a soft, gentle kiss that stirred her on all levels. Gone momentarily was the stress, the horror of the day. She knew it all would eventually return, but for right now Lucas's kisses, his caresses, provided a temporary respite from her worries.

Their kisses grew deeper, longer, and at the same time his hands found her breasts, cupping them, his fingers sliding over her nipples and forcing a gasp of pleasure to escape her as they tautened to meet his touch.

Her hands played down the length of his back, loving the feel of moving muscles beneath his sleek, smooth skin. They were close enough that she could tell he was fully aroused, and that only drove her desire for him higher.

It wasn't long before their underwear was gone and their naked bodies slid against each other as if needing to make up for days of sensory deprivation.

She wanted to touch him everywhere, and at the same time he explored her intimately, touching…tasting her as if she was a delectable dessert he couldn't resist.

She was wet and ready for him as his fingers slid

into her and then out. He focused on the core nub to bring her to climax.

Her breath came in quick pants as his fingers worked faster, his gaze locked with hers as if he wanted to see the moment that utter, mindless passion swept her completely away.

And then she was there, rolling waves of pleasure drowning her. He moved between her thighs and entered her. The waves continued to overwhelm her.

She gasped his name and clutched his back, wanting him closer and deeper, wanting to keep him with her not just for this single night, but for forever.

He pulled back and then stroked into her once again. The waves of pleasure intensified their frenzied movements.

He had already taken her to a place she'd never been before, even in all the years of her marriage, and he was sweeping her away once again.

She clung to him as he took her over the edge yet again and cried out his name. He stiffened against her, finding his own release.

They remained locked together, his weight on top of her lightened by him holding himself up on his elbows. He gazed down at her, his eyes filled with a tenderness, a softness that almost pulled tears to her eyes.

"That was nothing short of amazing," he said.

"You'll get no argument from me," she replied.

He rolled to the side of her and propped himself up on one elbow, his eyes glowing in the illumination from the lamp on the nightstand. "So, should we have the morning-after talk now or tomorrow?"

"Do we need to have a morning-after talk?"

"I don't know. You tell me," he replied. "I figured

after you had a little bit of time to think about it you would have all kinds of regrets and get all weird on me."

She released a small laugh. "Get all weird on you? Is that normally how women react after you've been intimate with them?"

"I don't get intimate with anyone very often. I just don't want you to wake up tomorrow morning and have regrets about this…about us."

"No regrets, I promise," she replied, and meant it. No matter what happened between them, she would never regret this night with Lucas. Her body still hummed with pleasure she'd never known before.

"Cassie is going to sell the place, isn't she?" His gaze didn't leave hers.

She couldn't lie to him, not here with him so close to her and not now, with the memory of his body still burned into hers. Besides, he had to already suspect.

"That's her plan right now, but she didn't want any of you men to know."

"Why?"

She sat up and pulled the sheet up to hide her bare breasts. Despite what they'd just shared she felt more naked now than she had before as his gaze remained on her. This was not a conversation she wanted to have with him.

"She was afraid if you all knew then you'd leave and she'd have nobody to get the work done that needs to be done before she can get the place on the market." She frowned. "Do the others know that she plans to sell?"

"No, at least not that I know about. Adam certainly believes she plans to stay on. Otherwise he wouldn't be spending so much time trying to teach her about management of the ranch."

"Are you going to tell them?"

He was silent for a long moment. "No, I'll keep Cassie's secret, but eventually she's going to have to let everyone know her true intentions. We all have our own lives to think about."

He rolled out of the bed and grabbed his underwear from the floor and stepped into them. "I'd better get back to my little roommate." He put on his shirt and then pulled on his jeans.

"Lucas…" She called his name as he was about to step out into the hallway. It all felt suddenly awkward, as if he'd slammed a door between them. He turned back to look at her.

"Are we okay?" she asked, her heart beating an unsteady rhythm. She hadn't realized until this moment how much she'd come to depend on Lucas's strength and support. She hadn't realized until now how much she'd come to care about him.

"We're okay, Nicolette. You just reminded me that city girls like to play for a little while in the country, but the city always calls them back."

He didn't wait for her reply, but left the bedroom and disappeared down the hallway. Nicolette rolled onto her back and stared up at the ceiling.

What should have been a magnificent end to a dreadful day had taken a sour turn, and she didn't understand exactly what had happened.

Had he gotten angry because she'd merely confirmed Cassie's plan to sell, when he'd admitted that he'd already figured that out? But his coolness didn't make sense if he'd already known about Cassie's plans.

His last comment played and replayed in her head.

City girls like to play in the country for a while, but the city always calls them back.

Had that been some sort of indictment against Cassie, or had it been directed at her?

She got out of bed, grabbed a nightgown and crept out into the hallway and to the bathroom. Sammy's room was dark and her heart squeezed tight as she thought of Lucas sharing that room with her beloved son.

Had she merely reminded Lucas that not only was Cassie and her time here limited, but that his own time here might be limited, as well?

Country girl…city girl…she wasn't sure where she fit. She'd grown to love it here, but the idea of staying here, of turning her back on the life that she knew in New York City, was more than a little bit daunting.

She finished in the bathroom and, clad in her nightgown, went back to her bedroom. She got into bed and shut off the bedside light.

Her question about what kind of a lover Lucas would make had been answered. He'd been masterful yet tender, taking and giving with an intensity that had stolen her thoughts, her very breath away.

Now, although the sheets smelled of him and his body heat lingered in the bed, her thoughts turned to the trauma of the afternoon and the near abduction of her son.

She'd nearly lost him. If Lucas and his men hadn't rushed to the rescue, Sammy would have been gone. Why? Who? Who had paid Jeff Bodine to take her son away from her?

Making love with Nicolette had been a big mistake, a mistake that haunted Lucas's sleep and continued to haunt him throughout the next morning.

He wasn't working outside today and didn't intend to again until he knew for sure that Sammy was safe. Besides, he was eager to hear from Dillon about the plans for tonight to get to the man behind Jeff Bodine.

He'd tried to keep things as normal as possible between him and Nicolette during the morning hours, but the truth was he'd let her in too deep, allowed her access to places in his heart he'd never shared.

Tomorrow he would know her one week, but it felt as if he'd known her for months. Their living conditions, the circumstances of the danger to Sammy, had drawn them together in an intense way that had nothing to do with time.

Making love to her had been amazing, but their conversation afterward had simply served to remind him that she wasn't going to be around here forever. The last thing he wanted to do was fall in love with her. She and Cassie and Sammy might be here a month or two, but ultimately he believed Nicolette and her son would follow Cassie back to the life they'd had before Cass had died.

For the first time in years he wondered where his mother was, if she was even still alive. Her complete and total abandonment of him had created a shattering of his heart that he'd believed nobody could ever heal again.

And then he'd met Cass, who had been both employer and mother figure. She'd given him back his self-worth, built in him a self-respect that had been lacking when he'd first arrived here at the ranch.

She'd rebuilt his heart piece by piece with her love and support, with her expectations and assurance that he could be a man proud of who he was at his very core.

Her death had been like a second abandonment, and

he knew if he allowed himself to fall in love with Nicolette only to have her leave, his heart would shatter once again and there would be no more picking up the pieces.

He wouldn't let himself go through that kind of pain again. He'd be here for Nicolette and Sammy as long as they needed his protection, as long as they needed his support, but he refused to give them any more purchase into his heart.

He now stood at the kitchen window, watching in the distance as his fellow cowboys went about the daily chores. His shirt pocket that held his cell phone burned with the need for it to ring, for him to know how Dillon and his men intended to play out the continuing drama of Sammy's near kidnapping.

They'd managed to get through breakfast and had just finished lunch with only a slight tension between Nicolette and him, a tension that obviously wasn't noticed by Cassie or Sammy.

The other three had gone upstairs when lunch was finished, leaving Lucas alone with his thoughts. At the moment he was pretty sick of his own introspection. He needed something to happen, some answers, some sort of closure as to what had happened yesterday. He knew that Nicolette needed the same thing.

There was no question in his mind that the tension that radiated from her throughout the morning wasn't just a result of their night spent together, but also the need to know who was behind the scheme to take Sammy.

"No word yet from Dillon?" Nicolette's voice pulled his attention from the window.

He turned to face her and tried not to process how pretty she looked with her hair loose, and dressed in a pair of jeans and a forest-green blouse that accentuated the green of her eyes. Desire instantly leaped back into his veins, a desire he consciously ignored.

"No word," he replied. What the hell was wrong with him? Why whenever she was near did he fight the desire to touch her, to want her?

"Surely he intends to do what we talked about yesterday," she said and sat at the table.

He took the chair across from her and set his coffee cup in front of him. "I can't imagine that he wouldn't do some sort of a sting tonight to catch the man who is behind all of this."

"I want to be there," she said.

He looked at her in surprise and then narrowed his gaze. "I don't think that would be wise."

She lifted her chin just enough to show her steely determination. "I think it would be very wise," she countered. "Sammy will be fine here with Cassie, and you could get a couple of the other men to guard the house."

She leaned forward, bringing with her the scent of her fruity, floral perfume, a fragrance that had been in his head for what seemed like forever. "I *need* to be there, Lucas. I need to see the man behind the curtain. I might be the only one who can immediately identify him. In any case, nobody is going to stop me from being at that diner tonight at midnight."

She held his gaze, her eyes now narrowing slightly. "You can either stay here or you can come with me. It's your decision."

"That's not much of a choice," he replied drily. "I can't let you go off half-cocked into this kind of a potentially dangerous situation. In any case, it's really not our call. It's all up to what Dillon thinks is best for everyone."

She leaned back in her chair. "I don't care what he says. I have the name of the diner and a vehicle at my disposal and I intend to be there whether he thinks it's a good idea or not."

"This is a side of you I've never seen before," he said.

"What do you mean?"

He couldn't help the smile that twitched at his lips. "Bullheaded. I've never seen your stubborn side."

"Well, take a good look at me because I'm feeling totally bullheaded about this issue." She held his gaze and then continued, "I might be stubborn, but I'm not stupid. I don't plan on getting in the way of Chief Bowie and his men. I'll stay hidden someplace outside the diner until they get the man arrested. But I want my face to be one of the first he sees when he's led out of the diner. I want his face to be the first one I see."

He couldn't blame her. If he was in her position and it was his son who was at the center of a kidnapping scheme, he'd want to be there, too.

"Fine, when I talk to Dillon I'll tell him that you and I intend to be at the diner," he said.

Her gaze softened. "Thank you, Lucas."

"Don't thank me yet. I'm still not sure this is a good idea." He broke eye contact with her, the soft green of her eyes threatening to pull him into places he didn't want to go. He took a sip of his coffee and stared out the window.

"Lucas?"

Reluctantly he looked at her again. "About last night…" she began.

"I thought we weren't going to have a morning-after talk."

"I've changed my mind," she replied. "I just want you to know that it was strictly a physical-attraction thing and I certainly don't expect anything else from you except maybe your support while we get through this thing with Sammy."

Her words should have caused a river of relief inside him, but he was stunned that they didn't. Somehow they made what had happened between them last night even worse.

He gave her a curt nod. "I ride alone, Nicolette. Don't expect anything else from me. I care about you and Sammy. I care about your welfare, but I'm glad you recognize last night for what it was…an explosion of desire between us that won't happen again."

At that moment his cell phone rang. He got up from the table and left the room when he saw that it was Dillon's cell phone number on his caller ID.

He stepped out the back door to talk to the lawman, not wanting to speak in front of Nicolette. He had no idea what Dillon had planned, and if it wasn't what Nicolette wanted then he didn't want her to hear it firsthand. He'd have to figure out a way to make her accept that Dillon knew best how to handle the situation.

He listened as Dillon outlined the plan for the night, and after a ten-minute discussion things were finally settled. He returned to the kitchen to find Nicolette seated where he'd left her at the table.

"It's all set," he said as he resumed his seat.

Nicolette sat up straight, a thrum of energy radiating from her. "Tell me the plan."

"It's pretty basic. Dillon is going to have a man inside the diner around eleven. Dillon's men will surround the diner and stay out of sight. He's planning on riding with Jeff to the diner and once Jeff arrives he'll sneak out of the car while Jeff goes inside."

"How do we know that Jeff won't somehow warn the man to run?" she asked, her worry creasing a fine line across her forehead.

"By that point it won't matter. The place will be surrounded and anyone running out of the diner will be put under arrest. Apparently last night Dillon spent the night at the motel with Jeff and was there when he made the call telling the man he had the kid and will make the rendezvous tonight."

"Did you tell Dillon that you and I are going to be there?"

"I did, and I have to say he wasn't exactly overly thrilled by the idea, but I assured him we'd park and stay in the car until the whole thing goes down. He just doesn't want anything to spook the guy or screw up the operation."

Her eyes shimmered in the afternoon light. "So tonight, just after midnight I should know the identity of the man who's trying to kidnap my son."

Chapter 10

Darryl's Diner was definitely a dive, Nicolette thought as Lucas pulled his vehicle around the front of the building and then to the side to park.

It had taken twenty minutes to get to the place, which lit up the lonely dark highway with flashing neon signs more appropriate on a Las Vegas casino.

It was just after eleven and Nicolette had never felt so wide-awake in her entire life. Nerves jumped in the pit of her stomach and danced electric tingles throughout her veins.

There had been only one car parked in front of the building, and she assumed it was whomever Dillon had assigned to be there. It would be somebody Dillon knew wouldn't be recognized by the staff of the diner, somebody who would be unkempt and appear half-drunk to blend in with the usual local clientele at this time of night.

Her heart beat rapidly as she thought of what was going to go down in the next hour or so. She prayed it would work, that by the time she placed her head on her pillow tonight the danger to Sammy would be permanently vanished and she'd have all the answers she needed to finally be at peace.

"You okay?" Lucas asked softly.

"I feel like my nerves are trying to jump right out of my skin, but I'm also hopeful," she replied.

"You sure it isn't your ex-husband who is behind this?" Lucas asked. He unfastened his seat belt and turned to face her.

"I can't imagine why he would do something like this. Kidnap his own son." She shook her head. "If Samuel called me tomorrow and wanted to spend time with Sammy, I would encourage it. I told Samuel at the time I left him that I would never stand in the way of his relationship with his son. Samuel has just never been interested in having any relationship with Sammy."

"And therefore it doesn't make sense that he would be behind all this," Lucas replied.

"Exactly." She unfastened her seat belt as well, wanting to be able to get out of the car as quickly as possible when the right time came.

They both fell silent. Nicolette checked her watch, wishing that the minutes would pass faster, that she'd have some sort of answer that made sense right now, right this very minute.

She released a deep sigh. It was still forty minutes until midnight. For the first time in her life time felt like an enemy, an emotionless entity keeping her from what she needed most…answers that would ensure her son's safety.

By the time another five minutes had passed, she became aware of shadowy shapes moving in the semi-darkness around the building. "That will be Dillon's men getting into position," Lucas said.

A new tension filled her. The ladder at the window at the house, Jeff's unexpected crazy horseback kidnapping attempt to steal away Sammy. They were crazy events without an apparent motive. Hopefully every question she had would be answered in the next half an hour.

She hated that they were parked on the side of the building, where they couldn't see anything but car lights pulling into the parking spaces in front of the building.

She wanted to see Jeff arrive in his car with the fake sleeping boy in his backseat. She wanted to see the man he was meeting pull up and park, get a glimpse of the car he drove, anything that would give her a hint about whom would be arrested tonight. And she hoped and prayed there would be an arrest.

She stiffened as she saw headlights that indicated a car had pulled up at the diner. It was still twenty minutes until midnight.

"Maybe that's him or Jeff and Dillon," she said and broke the silence.

"Or maybe it's some drunk wanting hotcakes and eggs to try to sober up," Lucas replied. "There's no way to keep out the usual customers without blowing the whole thing."

She released another sigh and rolled down her window partway. The air that drifted in smelled of fried onions and spoiling garbage, causing a faint nausea to roll in her stomach.

"If you don't calm down you're going to have a heart attack before midnight ever arrives," Lucas said, his voice a soft whisper in the interior of the car.

"I'm trying to stay calm, but my heart is beating so hard I'm surprised you can't hear it."

"I think I can." He reached across to her and covered one of her hands with his. She welcomed his touch and curled her fingers around his, drawing strength and comfort from the simple connection.

He had been so distant for most of the day, as if he wished he could take back their lovemaking, as if he wished he was back in the pastures instead of embroiled in the complications of her life.

"I'm sorry I got you involved in all this," she said and tightened her fingers with his. "I never meant for you to get entangled in this mess."

"You didn't get me involved. I got myself involved." He smiled at her, his features barely visible in the illumination from the corner of the building where a neon sign hung advertising homemade biscuits and gravy. "I'm not just doing this for you. I'm doing it for a little boy who dreams about being a cowboy just like me."

Nicolette's heart swelled when she heard the obvious love in his voice. He might not want a forever-after with her or any other woman, but Sammy had definitely crawled under his defenses.

If she decided to return to New York City when Cassie sold the ranch, then she'd have a little broken-hearted cowboy to deal with, for she knew that Sammy loved Lucas, too.

Lucas pulled his cell phone from his pocket and held it to his ear. He must have had it set on vibrate because there had been no ringtone, but it was obvious some-body had called him.

He listened for a moment and then replied "Okay" and hung up. "That was Dillon. Jeff is in place inside and now we just wait for the man of the hour to arrive." He slipped his phone back into his pocket.

"Maybe he won't show up. Maybe Jeff somehow managed to warn him off with his phone call. Maybe he'll change his mind and set up a different meeting or call Jeff again to change the date and time."

Suddenly Nicolette was filled with doubts and fears. *What if it all goes very wrong tonight and we don't get the answers I want so badly? What if the man who paid Jeff manages to somehow escape?*

"Or it all can go as smoothly as Dillon has planned," Lucas countered. He gave her hand a final squeeze and then released it. "We'll know if things are screwed up in the next ten minutes or so."

Ten achingly agonizing minutes. She definitely felt as if she would have a heart attack before that time. Her chest tightened with tension and she wondered how long her heart could sustain its frantic beat.

She needed answers. She needed to know that after tonight Sammy would be safe and they all could spend the rest of their time at the ranch in peace and happi-ness.

She had no idea what the future held for her. She was conflicted between her loyalty to Cassie and her building desire to form some kind of a life in Bitterroot.

There was no thought about whether or not Lucas would have a place with her if she decided to stay. She'd like to believe he would, but she couldn't forget that he'd told her he rode alone—and he hadn't just meant during his chores.

However, she didn't need Lucas for any future plans she might make. She was falling in love with him and would like him to be a part of that future, but she and Sammy would be fine without him as long as this night passed with questions answered and danger vanished.

Just when she thought she couldn't stand it another minute, another set of headlights bounced in the darkness as a vehicle turned into the diner parking lot.

She heard the sound of the engine shutting down and then a car door slamming shut. She wanted to fly out of the vehicle. As if sensing her need, Lucas reached over and grabbed her arm.

"Not yet," he said.

She trembled with both fear and anticipation. It was midnight. Everyone was in place. She just wanted this all to be over.

Seconds ticked by in loud clicks in her mind, a form of torture that might have driven her insane. Lucas kept his hand on her arm, preventing her emotions from getting the best of her and ruining the plans.

What was happening? Who was in there? Would she recognize him? Her brain tried to access anyone from her past who might now be in the diner, but she couldn't think of anyone.

Lucas once again reached into his pocket and grabbed his phone. He listened for a moment and then returned the phone to his pocket. "It's over. We can go inside."

Nicolette stared at him, frozen now that the time she'd been waiting for had arrived. They'd heard no gunshots, so apparently Dillon and his men had handled the situation exactly the way they'd hoped.

The frozen inertia passed and she scrambled for the door handle to get out. When she reached the front of the vehicle, Lucas was there. He took her arm and together they walked around the side of the building to the front door.

They entered and it was like a scene from a crime movie. Both Jeff and another man in a black-and-red dress shirt stood in the middle of the diner, hands cuffed behind their backs and surrounded on all sides by Dillon's men with their weapons drawn and centered on the two.

Nicolette looked at the man Jeff had met and a trembling began inside her. His dark hair was slicked back with an excess of gel and his eyes were the dark, flat color of a shark's. He was tall and muscular, and she'd never seen him before in her life.

"I don't know you." Her voice sounded unnaturally loud in the otherwise silent diner. "I don't know who you are." This time a light edge of hysteria crept into her voice.

She took a step toward him. Lucas tightened his arm on hers, but she pulled away from him, lost in a sea of incomprehension, of rage. Nobody moved as she approached the suspect.

She stopped just in front of him, her heartbeat smashing against her ribcage and echoing inside her head. "Who are you and why do you want my son?"

"I don't have to say anything to anyone," he said with a sneer.

Before Nicolette knew her intention, she slapped

him. The slap was hard enough to sting her hand and redden his cheek. She sobbed and began to pummel him in the stomach until Lucas pulled her away and Dillon stepped between her and the man.

"I was wondering if you were going to let that bitch throw any more punches while I'm cuffed and defenseless," he said to Dillon.

Lucas pushed Nicolette behind him and stalked toward the man. Dillon and several of his men grabbed Lucas. "I can't let this go any further," Dillon said to Lucas. "We all need to calm down here."

Nicolette could feel Lucas's energy, his angry tension snapping in the air. She knew that anger had been driven by the fact that the man had called her a bitch. But he finally stepped back and instead placed an arm protectively around her shoulder.

"According to his identification his name is Del Hawkins and he lives in Oklahoma City." Dillon looked at Nicolette as if maybe the man's name would somehow ring a bell of recognition in her head.

She leaned into Lucas. "I don't know him. I've never seen or heard of him before in my life."

"I just stopped in for the biscuits and gravy," Del said. "I don't know what's going on or why I'm under arrest. You all are making a big mistake here."

"Shut up," Dillon said to him. "Let's get these two in a squad car and get them out of here and to the station."

As several of the other officers took charge of the prisoners and led them outside, Nicolette remained weak and boneless against Lucas's side.

Dillon approached where they stood. "Hopefully with a little time in jail he'll be more willing to talk. In the meantime we'll be checking out whatever we can about him, and by sometime tomorrow I should have some information for you that will resolve everything."

"Thanks, Dillon," Lucas said. "We'll be anxious to hear from you tomorrow." Nicolette couldn't speak as tears chased down her cheeks and sobs welled up inside her.

She'd hoped it would all be over. She'd hoped that tonight would be the end, but they were leaving here with more questions than they'd come with and absolutely no answer as to who was after Sammy.

Despite the late night, Lucas awoke before dawn, the sound of Sammy's deep, rhythmic breathing oddly comforting. For now he was safe, and Lucas would do everything in his power to keep him that way.

He was just a kid, for crying out loud. Who would want to take him from the mother who loved him so deeply? He rolled over on his back in the small twin bed and stared unseeing at the still-dark ceiling.

Nicolette had been a basket case on the way home from the diner. She'd cried the entire drive back to the ranch. The sound of her weeping had cut him to the core. He had no words of comfort to give her, could think of nothing to say that might ease any of her pain. He hadn't felt this impotent since he'd been a kid trying to survive on the streets.

He could only hope that today would bring her answers, that somehow Dillon could ferret out what and who had put Sammy at the center of a kidnapping scheme.

Unable to stay in bed any longer, he grabbed clean

clothes from the closet and then crept down the hallway to the bathroom. He tried to keep his mind completely blank as he showered and then dressed for the day.

By the time he was finished and headed downstairs, the house was still silent around him. He made coffee and when it was finished he carried a cup to the table and sat down. It was only then that the blessed blankness of his mind filled with myriad thoughts.

Last night had been a nightmare, and he hoped that Nicolette had found comfort in sleep without dreams. His dreams had been on the unpleasant side.

They had begun happy enough with a dream of him and Nicolette in bed making love, but it hadn't taken long for that scene to melt away and instead he and Nicolette were wandering the ranch, screaming out Sammy's name.

Finally that scene had disappeared and Lucas was once again a young teenager, homeless and hungry and knowing that danger could come for him at any moment. He wanted his mother and then he transformed into Sammy, crying out for his own mother.

A tense, terrible night followed by nightmares that had chased him through sleep. Still, despite the lack of peaceful sleep, he felt wide-awake and alert.

His fingers now tightened around his coffee cup. He never wanted Sammy to be in a position where he was alone and afraid and crying for his mother. Lucas knew the scars that lingered and he never wanted Sammy to possess those kinds of scars.

He looked up as he heard the back door unlock and open, and Adam came inside. "Morning," Adam said and headed directly for the coffee. "How'd it go last night?" He joined Lucas at the table.

Adam frowned and sipped his coffee as Lucas filled him in on the night's events. "Hopefully Dillon can get some answers from Del Hawkins and this danger to Sammy will be over once and for all," Lucas finished.

"Speaking of Sammy, Cookie told me to tell you that tonight is pizza night so if you want to bring the boy for dinner he'll set an extra plate."

"If you talk to him, then tell him to set that plate. Sammy would love dinner with the other cowboys." Lucas smiled as he thought of Sammy's excitement. He was certain that there would be no issue with Nicolette letting Sammy go with him to dinner. Nicolette had to know by now that nobody would get to Sammy as long as Lucas was around, and he intended to be near them at all times now.

"You've gotten close to them," Adam said. "Not just to Sammy, but also to Nicolette."

Lucas wanted to protest Adam's assessment, but instead he took a sip of his coffee and then formulated his reply. "Yeah, I've gotten close to them," he agreed. "It's impossible not to get close to a kid like Sammy. He's open and curious and wants to be a cowboy just like me. If I had a son, Sammy would be like what I'd want."

"And Nicolette?"

Lucas leaned back in his chair and frowned. "I'll admit she's gotten under my skin more than a little bit. But, you know I have no desire to have anything permanent with any woman. None of us have ever sought any real relationships in all the years we've worked here. The twelve of us, we're all damaged goods."

Adam sighed and raked a hand through his dark hair. "Cass would kick your butt for saying that. She had always hoped that she'd rehabilitate us to the point where we could all live normal lives. She fantasized that we'd all eventually fall in love, get married and have families of our own. She wanted to rock our children, be a beloved grandma."

"But, she's dead now," Lucas said flatly. "And I know we're all still grieving her."

Adam gave a curt nod, his dark eyes filled with pain. Lucas knew Adam had been the first young teenager that Cass had taken on. He'd been especially close to Cass and his grief still clung to him. "We just need to move ahead as if she were here."

"And you really think we can do that with Cassie in charge?" Lucas didn't want to betray Nicolette's confidence that Cassie had no intention of sticking around for the long term.

"I don't know…maybe. She seems like she's trying to learn the ins and outs of the ranch business." Adam shrugged. "She's no Cass. She's much more fragile, but she might toughen up. Time will tell. She's supposed to meet me in just a few minutes. I'm driving her out to the Garmand Ranch to look at a bull."

"Are my ears ringing?" Cassie walked into the kitchen, dressed in jeans and a long-sleeved blue blouse. "If somebody would have told me a couple of months ago that I'd be getting up at the crack of dawn to drive to a ranch to look at a bull, I would have told them they were full of bull."

Adam smiled at her and in his smile Lucas saw genuine affection. It seemed the foreman might have a little crush on the new boss, and for some reason that depressed Lucas. He hoped Adam didn't get any romantic ideas about the new owner, because he was fairly sure she was here only temporarily and, like all the others on the ranch, Adam had already had more than his share of heartache.

Cassie and Adam had been gone for only about fifteen minutes when Nicolette made her first appearance of the day. Clad in an emerald green robe, with eyes red and still swollen from the tears she'd wept the night before, the sight of her moved him on all kinds of levels.

He had to fight his need to pull her into his arms and onto his lap and cradle her in his comforting arms. She'd obviously had a rough night of sleep.

"Nightmares?" he asked and watched as she shuffled her way barefoot to the coffeemaker.

She poured her coffee and then turned to face him, her back leaning against the counter. "That was only when I finally managed to fall asleep. I had trouble turning off my brain for a long time."

"Did your brain come up with anything new that might be helpful?" he asked.

She joined him at the table and curled her fingers around her cup. "Nothing specific." She took a drink of her coffee and then continued, "Four thousand dollars is a lot of money to pay for the kidnapping of a child, and that was only what Jeff was being paid. Surely somebody was paying Del, as well. No matter how I twist it around in my head, I just can't make sense of it. I mean, is there some kind of child trafficking ring working here in town?"

"Not that I'm aware of," Lucas replied. "I haven't heard of any other kids in town being in danger or kidnapped. Hopefully Dillon will have some answers for you later today," he replied. "On a different subject,

Cookie is serving pizza tonight for dinner and I'd like Sammy to eat with us at the bunkhouse. Would that be all right?"

Her smile lit up his heart. "That would be more than all right," she replied. "He'll be absolutely thrilled." Her smile lasted only a moment and then defaulted into a frown. "I just wish I knew who was behind these attacks on Sammy."

"You need to let Dillon do his job."

"I know. I just want all of the answers now." She took another drink of her coffee and the frown disappeared from her forehead. "Now you're seeing yet another side of me that you probably didn't know about."

"And what's that?"

"Impatience."

He offered her a small smile. "Maybe in this case, but I don't think impatience is a normal emotion for you. I've seen your patience with Sammy too often to believe that."

"Speaking of Sammy, I think maybe I'll just keep him inside today. He can play his video games and watch movies and just have a quiet day. I need a quiet day. I'll keep him inside until it's time for him to go with you for dinner."

He recognized that what she really wanted was her son nearby, close enough that she wouldn't have to worry about his safety, and he couldn't blame her.

"I think that sounds like a good idea. Maybe I can teach him how to tie a rope and we can practice some lassoing skills in the great room."

"Just as long as you don't rope anything valuable," she replied. "Maybe I could act like a cow and run around the room and you could teach Sammy to lasso me."

And that's exactly the way they spent the morning after breakfast. It was a couple of hours of welcomed laughter as Nicolette ran back and forth in the room with her fingers at her forehead like horns and Sammy tried to lasso her.

She even made mooing noises, causing Sammy to fall to the floor in a fit of giggles more than once. He got close several times but never managed to get the rope over his mother.

Lucas finally took the rope from him and easily roped Nicolette over her head and pulled the rope tight, trapping her arms against her sides. He slowly reeled her toward him and Sammy laughed and clapped his hands.

Nicolette was laughing as Lucas pulled her close to him. He saw the laughter in her eyes, heard the giggles as Sammy danced around them, and he wanted to reel her all the way into his arms. He wanted to pull her close enough to feel her body intimately against his. This all felt like home. It felt like family.

He dropped the rope and stepped back from her, needing to stop the fantasy, halt the thoughts that suddenly raced through his mind. "And that's how you rope a lady cow," he said to Sammy.

"Hey, who are you calling a cow?" she asked, but her laughter faltered just a bit. She unwound herself and stepped out of the rope. "I think that's enough lassoing for the day. How about we eat some lunch?"

After a lunch of sandwiches, Nicolette and Sammy disappeared upstairs and Lucas paced the lower level, willing his cell phone to ring and for Dillon to call them with some answers.

He wanted this whole thing solved so that he could

gain some distance from Nicolette. He had to get out of this house and back on Lucky.

He needed the fresh pasture-scented air to sweep Nicolette's sweet fragrance out of his head. He needed to be in the barn oiling saddles with the soft neighs of the horses. He needed to be back at the bunkhouse, sharing evenings with his fellow cowboys and not fantasizing about a family he'd never have.

It was just after three when he finally got a call from Dillon. "What have you found out?" he asked.

"Absolutely nothing," Dillon replied, his frustration obvious in his voice. "Del Hawkins lawyered up faster than we could blink our eyes, and it's not some local-yokel ambulance-chaser lawyer. It's Raymond Russell from Oklahoma City."

Lucas whistled beneath his breath. Raymond Russell was part good old boy and part barracuda. The defense lawyer had made a name for himself two years before on a national level when he'd defended a prominent doctor who'd been accused of killing his wife. Against nearly insurmountable odds, he'd gotten the doctor off and had made a reputation for himself.

"Does Del Hawkins have the money to pay for that kind of a defense?" Lucas asked.

"Not according to what little we've managed to learn about him. He's single, a car salesman and in fact has a gambling problem that has his finances on the brink of disaster. Somebody else is paying for his defense and all we know is that it's an anonymous donor."

Lucas frowned, wondering how on earth he was going to tell Nicolette this new twist. He knew that she'd hoped that Del Hawkins would talk and the mystery would finally be solved. But, this was simply more bad news. It was obvious Del Hawkins was just another link in a chain of evil.

Chapter 11

Lucas had managed to escape the house with Sammy for dinner without telling Nicolette that he'd spoken to Dillon earlier in the day. He felt bad about holding on to the information of Del's representation by a shark lawyer, but with Sammy in Lucas's custody for the evening meal, she and Cassie had decided to drive into Bitterroot and eat at Tammy's Tea House, a quaint little eatery in town that catered more to the womenfolk in Bitterroot.

He hadn't wanted to ruin her evening, and thankfully she hadn't asked if he'd heard anything from Dillon, so he hadn't lied outright except by omission.

He and Sammy watched the two women drive off and then he clapped a hand on Sammy's shoulder and together they began the walk to the bunkhouse.

"I'd even eat liver and onions to have dinner with you and the rest of the cowboys and I totally hate liver," Sammy said. "But pizza is a lot better."

"I agree," Lucas replied. "Liver isn't one of my fa-vorite foods, but pizza is terrific."

Lucas's heart squeezed tight as Sammy slipped his small hand into his. "I think this is the very best time of my life," Sammy said.

Lucas's heart squeezed a little bit tighter. "I'm glad you're having a good time now, but I hope your future has lots of good times."

If he had a future, Lucas thought, and tightened his hand around Sammy's. They'd been lucky twice in saving Sammy, but Lucas couldn't help but wonder how long that luck would hold and when danger might threaten again.

"I just wish my mom and I could stay here forever. I could grow up and be one of Cassie's cowboys and ride horses and do cowboy work."

Cassie's cowboys. In their hearts they were still Cass's cowboys, and it would take a long time of hard work on Cassie's part to earn their respect and their hearts.

Sammy stumbled on a dirt clot, but Lucas's fast grip steadied him and they walked on. "I'm trying to talk Cassie into staying here," he continued. "Then Mom and I could stay here forever."

"Are you making any progress?" Lucas asked.

Sammy smiled up at him. "Maybe a little bit. Cassie told me she was going to start doing some paintings of the ranch. Maybe if there was someplace in town where she could sell her paintings, then she'd get rid of the shop in New York and stay here forever."

By that time they had reached the bunkhouse dining room, where the scent of tangy sauce, yeasty crust and cooked beef and vegetables filled the room.

Dusty was the first one to greet them. He thumped Sammy on his hat and offered him a grin that displayed Dusty's dimples. "Glad you're here, Sammy. That makes you the youngest cowboy in the building instead of me."

"I'm glad I'm here, too," Sammy replied. He looked up at Lucas. "Lucas is my best partner, but I like all of you." Sammy leaned a little closer to Dusty. "Except Cookie…he scares me a little bit."

Dusty laughed. "Don't worry, Cookie scares all of us a little bit."

Lucas and Sammy hung their hats on hooks inside the door and then found seats at one of the picnic tables. While they waited for the others to arrive, Lucas thought about the man who had been the ranch hand cook since he'd first arrived here.

None of the men knew much about Cookie other than he had worked at the ranch for Cass when her husband had still been alive. Cookie didn't share downtime with the other men and he definitely didn't talk about where he'd come from or where he'd been before being here.

He had a small one-bedroom bungalow on the property and, as far as they all knew, spent his off time there alone. None of them even knew how old he was, although the guesses ranged from forty-five to sixty-five. He had the kind of unlined face and a strong physique that made it impossible to gauge his real age.

Thoughts of Cookie flew out of his mind as the rest of the men began to arrive, each of them greeting Sammy with high fives and knuckle knocks. Sammy beamed with happiness and Lucas was reminded of just how much he trusted these men, how much they had become his family.

Even though Cass was gone, her cowboy "children" lived on, caring about each other, supporting one another as she would have wanted them to do.

He didn't want to think about what would happen if Cassie decided to sell. He would have to face that particular pain if and when it happened.

Tonight he just wanted to focus on Sammy and pizza. And that was what he did. The rest of the men came in and the dining room filled with laughter as they gobbled up Cookie's delicious variety of pizzas and teased Sammy and each other.

Sammy took the ribbing well, especially seeing how the others reacted good-naturedly to jabs and taunts from each other. Lucas knew the kid probably felt as if he was part of a special club.

It *was* a special club…a pack of society rejects who had found safe haven and love in the heart of a special woman, and no matter what happened in his future, these men were forever in his heart as brothers.

Sammy ate two big pieces of pizza and drank a large glass of milk and then pronounced himself full to the brim. Lucas ate three pieces of pie and then they lingered a little while just enjoying the fellowship.

It was after six thirty when Lucas and Sammy started the walk back to the house. Once again Sammy grabbed his hand. They walked in silence for a few moments and then it was finally Sammy who spoke.

"Can I tell you a secret?" he asked.

"You can tell me anything," Lucas replied.

"I love you and I wish you were my dad." Sammy didn't look at him as he spoke the words.

The wistful tone in his voice pierced through all of

Lucas's defenses. His tongue seemed to twist in his mouth as he thought carefully before speaking.

"I love you, too, Sammy, but you know I can't ever be your dad."

The boy finally looked up at Lucas and gave him a sad little smile. "I know, I just wanted you to know what I felt inside." He gazed toward the house. "It looks like Mom and Cassie are home."

"Hopefully they had a nice time at their girlie dinner," Lucas replied, grateful when Sammy giggled. The conversation had gotten too real for Lucas and the last thing he wanted was for Sammy to be a casualty of Lucas's unwillingness to have anything permanent in his life.

Thankfully, by the time they reached the house, Sammy ran inside and began to share with his mom the total awesomeness of pizza dinner in the bunkhouse dining room with all the other men.

Nicolette looked gorgeous in a deep purple blouse that highlighted her green eyes and long tailored black slacks that made her legs appear to go on forever.

"How was the lady meal?" he asked when Sammy finally paused to take a breath.

"Wonderful," Cassie replied. "We had cucumber sandwiches cut in little squares and a spring salad with all kinds of goodies and blueberry scones with honey butter."

"Cucumber sandwiches?" Sammy pretended to retch.

Nicolette laughed and Lucas hated that before the night was over he'd have to steal that laughter away. He couldn't go to bed tonight without sharing with her what he'd learned from Dillon that afternoon.

But now wasn't the time or the place. He would find

the time later in the evening when the two of them were alone. He knew she'd be upset and he didn't want Sammy to witness any of that.

The evening hours passed with Sammy showing Lucas how to play his favorite game on his player while Nicolette and Cassie small-talked with each other.

Finally Nicolette and Sammy disappeared upstairs for bath and tuck-in time. Soon after Cassie followed, murmuring a good-night to Lucas.

Once he was alone, he went into the kitchen and made a short pot of coffee, deciding to have a cup while he told Nicolette the latest news.

She would not be happy that Del hadn't talked. In fact, she'd be devastated when she learned he was lawyered up with one of the best defense lawyers in the Midwest.

He had a cup of coffee before him and was seated at the table when she came into the kitchen. "I think I'll join you," she said as she went to the counter and fixed herself a cup of coffee and then sat across from him at the table.

"Did Sammy behave for you tonight?"

He couldn't help the smile that curved his lips. "Sammy always behaves with me. That kid has a heart as big as the sky. Did you have a good time out with Cassie?"

The twinkling in her eyes told him his answer. "Cassie and I always have a good time together. We know each other so well and we become like teenagers when we're alone together. I think Adam might have a crush on her."

"Is it reciprocated?" he asked.

"Cassie thinks he's hot, but I don't think she'll let

things get out of control. She appreciates everything he's doing for her, but I think that's about the extent of her feelings for him right now."

She looked so relaxed, so at ease as she sipped her coffee and leaned back in the chair, and he knew he was about to destroy any well-being she felt.

"Cucumber sandwiches, huh? Doesn't sound too filling to me," he said, aware that he was putting off the inevitable.

She laughed. "Actually, the entire meal was quite filling. It was lovely and feminine, and everything we ate was also beautiful to look at. Cassie particularly enjoyed it. I've never really been into fancy-schmancy food."

"A lot of the women in Bitterroot love the place," he replied. "I suppose they figure it's a little piece of civilization in a no-count town."

"Bitterroot doesn't strike me as a no-count town. It's a lovely little town plunked down in one of the prettiest places I've ever seen," she replied.

He took a sip of his coffee and then set the cup back down. He drew a deep breath and released it slowly. It was time to come clean. "I heard from Dillon late this afternoon."

She sat forward, the glitter of her eyes now a single beam of focus. "Did Del talk? Did he say why he wanted to take Sammy?"

"Unfortunately no. In fact, Del immediately lawyered up and is now represented by a high-dollar, high-power defense attorney. He was arraigned this morning and charged with conspiracy to kidnap a child. His lawyer pled him not guilty. The only good news in all of this is he was in front of a hard-nosed judge who ordered no bail."

She stared at his mouth as he spoke, as if needing to see the words as they fell from his lips besides hearing them.

When he'd finished, all her features appeared to droop downward. A frown crossed her forehead and her eyes lost their twinkle. Her beautiful lips bowed down, and with a trembling hand she carefully placed her cup back on the table.

"Who hired the lawyer?" she finally asked.

"An anonymous source."

"I suppose I should at least be satisfied that both Jeff and Del are in jail, but that's little comfort when now we can assume Del was just another link in the food chain and I don't know who the man behind the curtain might be." She narrowed her eyes. "You said Dillon called earlier. Why didn't you tell me all of this immediately?"

"I didn't want to ruin your dinner out with Cassie."

"I should be angry with you, but actually I appreciate that." She released a weary sigh. "I've been on pins and needles all day wondering what Dillon had found out from Del, and now I know he found out nothing and that means Sammy is still in danger and we have no idea when somebody will strike at him again."

He needed to touch her, to somehow find a way to comfort her. He wanted to banish the fear that once again simmered in the depths of her eyes.

He reached across the table with his hand, grateful when she leaned forward to grasp it. "A real cowboy doesn't make promises easily, but I promise you now that I'm not going to let anything bad happen to Sammy. I'd kill for that kid. I'd die for him."

He was surprised to realize it was true. He'd give his life to save Sammy's. As her fingers squeezed his more tightly and tears glistened in her eyes, he realized he was more than a little bit in love with Nicolette, as well as her son.

He would die for Sammy. Lucas's words played and replayed in Nicolette's head long after she'd gone to bed. He would give his own life to keep her son safe.

She'd believed him without question. His affection... no, his love for Sammy was evident anytime the two of them were together. It shone from Lucas's eyes, was evident in the way he touched Sammy's shoulder or patted his back with encouragement.

Lucas had come from a place where he'd not known his own father, but that absence hadn't stripped him of his ability to love a child, to be the kind of man who would make a wonderful father.

I ride alone.

His words of warning were the last thing she thought of before she finally fell asleep. She awakened to the sun peeking over the horizon and the scent of coffee wafting up the stairs from the kitchen.

Lucas was probably up and around. It was still too early for Cassie to stumble out of bed. In fact, before she'd gone to her bedroom the night before she'd told Nicolette that she had no early morning meeting with Adam or anyone else this morning and intended to sleep in.

It was Saturday morning and she couldn't believe everything that had happened in a mere week. There had been two attempts to kidnap Sammy and she'd made love with a special cowboy. It felt as if she'd been here a month rather than a mere week.

She closed her eyes and wished she could sleep in a

little longer, but her mind was already awake and over-working as she thought of the information Lucas had told her last night.

She knew Jeff Bodine had been hired by Del Hawkins to kidnap her son. Was Del the man in charge? Why would he want Sammy?

Was it possible that Del ran some sort of child-trafficking scheme and had somehow seen Sammy? Had Del developed some kind of sick obsession for Sammy?

There was no question her son was a handsome little boy, with innocence oozing from him. The idea of any-one stealing him away and destroying that innocence nearly shattered her.

The thoughts that flooded her mind chased her out of bed and into the shower. There, as warm water pum-meled her body, her brain continued to work overtime.

An anonymous donor? Who would step forward to pay for Del Hawkins's defense? Somebody was throw-ing around money as if it was candy. Who could it pos-sibly be?

Maybe it was time she call her ex-husband and see if he had any information about what was happening here. This idea didn't spur her immediately out of the shower. The best time to contact Samuel would be sometime later in the afternoon. If he'd stayed true to form, and she had no reason to believe he'd changed, he would have partied most of the night away and wouldn't awaken until mid- to late afternoon.

He always shut off his cell phone when he went to bed and ordered the servants not to disturb him unless he was in some sort of danger.

She still couldn't imagine Samuel having anything

to do with what was happening, but maybe he had some nefarious associates he could name for Dillon to investigate.

She had to do something in an effort to figure this all out, and Samuel was the only person she could think of who might have come into contact with somebody who might see Sammy as a treasured hostage.

There was little comfort in the fact that Jeff had said he'd been instructed not to hurt Sammy. Del had apparently wanted Sammy alive and well, but accidents happened and little boys were so achingly vulnerable.

She finally got out of the shower and dressed in a pair of jeans and a purple T-shirt. She decided once again to keep Sammy in the house for the day, although she knew he wouldn't be happy with the arrangement.

He'd much rather be outside where the breeze smelled so clean you could wash in it, where the cowboys worked in the pastures and he could pretend that he was old enough to be one of them.

Once dressed, she made her way downstairs and found Lucas standing at the window and staring outside. Guilt ripped through her. He should be outside, doing his chores and joking with the other cowboys. He should be sleeping in his own bed instead of in a little twin bed in her son's room.

"Good morning," he said without turning away from the window.

"Good morning to you," she replied. She remained standing in place, her gaze lingering on the broadness of his shoulders, the muscles she knew that were now hidden beneath his black T-shirt.

Heaven help her but she wanted him again. She remembered the feel of those muscles naked against her, the mindless pleasure she'd found while they'd made love, and the desire to do it all over again blossomed inside her.

She wanted his mouth on hers, his hands sliding over her naked skin. She wanted to experience the wonder of being with him again and again.

He turned from the window and for just a moment she saw the same kind of desire she felt shining unabashed from his eyes. It was there only a minute and then it was as if curtains crashed down to hide his emotion. His eyes darkened and became unreadable.

She broke the gaze and walked to the counter to pour herself a cup of coffee. "I've decided I'm going to give Samuel a call later this afternoon and see if he can shed some light on what's been happening here."

Lucas moved away from the window and leaned with one hip against the counter near the table. "I thought you believed he had nothing to do with this."

"I do, but he tends to surround himself with losers and lowlifes. Maybe he angered somebody and that somebody is seeking some sort of crazy revenge."

She shrugged. "I have to do something, try to somehow come up with anything that might help find answers. Samuel is pretty much the only link I can think of that hasn't been pursued at all. I just need to make sure we've covered all the bases."

"When you make that call, I want to be there with you and I want it on speakerphone."

She looked at him in surprise. "Why?"

"I don't know him. Maybe I'll hear something in his voice that you won't notice because you know him so well."

"I used to know him so well, but okay," she agreed.

"In the meantime I intend to keep Sammy inside the house again today."

He raised a dark brow. "You're going to have to get pretty creative in keeping him occupied."

"We could always do the roping thing again," she said, and then felt her cheeks warm as she remembered Lucas roping her and reeling her toward him.

He'd pulled her so close to him that she'd seen the flare in the pupils of his eyes, felt his warm breath on her face, and once again desire for him had danced in her veins. But he'd quickly dropped the rope and stepped back from her as if she was a special kind of poison.

"I think maybe I'll grab some of Cassie's paints and a canvas and let him work on an art project. That will keep him busy for an hour or two."

Lucas nodded and then stepped back in front of the window. She wondered if he was remembering that moment when he'd wrangled her so close to him, their mouths mere inches apart before he'd released her.

"I know you'd rather be out there on your horse with your partners," she said, her voice laden with the guilt that weighed down her heart.

"I'm where I need to be." His tone was flat. "I'm where I want to be," he added, this time his voice filled with a hint of emotion.

Once again he turned to face her. "I'm here until I know with certainty that Sammy is safe from any harm. I made you a promise last night and I intend to keep it."

"I don't know how we got so lucky to find you," she replied softly. Her heart filled with love, a love that she wanted to declare to him, but wouldn't. She wouldn't burden him with her love.

I ride alone.

His statement had been a warning to her that he had no intention of falling in love, of becoming a part of a family, and she would do well to remember that. She couldn't help the way she felt about him, but she'd be a fool to fantasize that there was any kind of a future between them.

He was here with her and Sammy now, but once the danger passed, he would be back out the window and in the pasture, riding the range alone.

Cassie remained in bed even though she was wide-awake. This had been her aunt's room and it was decorated in a style completely opposite to Cassie's personal taste. The furniture was big and heavy, the bedspread a brown floral. Cassie preferred bright colors and modern furnishings, but there was no point in redecorating a room she wasn't going to live in that long.

When the sun drifted into the window, she looked at the wall that held a dozen photographs, each one of her aunt Cass and the cowboys who worked here. They were twelve men who had obviously loved and respected her aunt very much.

Cassie didn't know what it was like to be respected like that by anyone in her life. Even her own parents had claimed her to be weak and silly with her artistic leanings and emotional nature.

She turned over on her side so that she could no longer see the pictures. Outside the window she could hear the faint sound of chain saws and knew that some of the cowboys were still working to clear felled trees.

Guilt had become a constant companion as she thought of selling the place, perhaps displacing the men who had been such an integral part of the ranch's success.

But she'd never wanted a ranch. She wanted her store and New York City. She wanted artists and the special thrum of energy that the city contained.

Her head filled with a vision of Adam. He was so sincere, so patient as he continued to teach her everything about ranching and running this place specifically. He wanted her to succeed here.

She was attracted to him and there were times she believed he was attracted to her, too. But she didn't want to hitch her star to a cowboy. She didn't want to muck around stalls and worry about hay storage or feed bins.

There was no question that he'd loved her aunt, and sometimes she wondered if he was trying to make her into Cass. That wasn't going to happen.

She didn't have the fortitude that her aunt had possessed. She couldn't imagine owning the strength that Cass had displayed when her husband had died and she'd decided to build cowboys from street kids and create a successful ranching operation.

Cassie was a city girl and she couldn't imagine anything or anyone ever changing that. Her decision to get the ranch in order and sell it hadn't wavered, even though she felt like a Judas in betraying all the people who worked for the ranch.

The scent of coffee drifted to her nose, along with Sammy's giggle. That meant that Lucas, Sammy and Nicolette were already up and around.

Sammy. Who on earth was behind the attacks on him? He was like a beloved nephew to her and she couldn't imagine the horror of anything bad happening to him.

Thank God for Lucas, who had managed to chase down Jeff and rescue Sammy. She frowned thoughtfully. She was a little bit concerned about the relationship Nicolette and Lucas seemed to be building.

When she left here to return to New York she wanted her best friend and partner at her side. She couldn't imagine Nicolette really wanting to build a life here. Whether Nicolette knew it or not, she was a city girl, too.

Cassie knew she should get up, but instead she burrowed deeper beneath the sheets and closed her eyes once again, not yet ready to face a day where she was deceiving the men who worked for her and hoping her best friend didn't find love with a cowboy.

Chapter 12

It was just after three in the afternoon when Nicolette sent Sammy upstairs with Cassie to work on his new painting project so that she could make the call to her ex-husband.

Lucas sat next to Nicolette on the sofa in the great room. She stared down at her cell phone in her trembling hand and her face paled.

Was she afraid to call the man she'd once been married to? "Was he abusive to you?" Lucas asked, his chest suddenly tight with tension at the idea of her suffering any kind of abuse at the hands of her ex-husband.

She looked up at him in surprise. "No, never. The only thing Samuel was guilty of as a husband was being neglectful and selfish."

"Then why do you look scared to death to make the call to him?" Lucas asked.

"Because if he doesn't have any suggestions as to

what might be happening to Sammy, then I don't have any place else to go for answers. I'm scared because he's my very last hope for figuring things out and I desperately want him to tell me something that would make sense of everything."

"I hope we learn something," he said. He needed this to be over. He was spending far too much time fantasizing about making love to her once again. He spent far too much time thinking about what it might be like to live with Nicolette and Sammy permanently, and he knew those were a fool's thoughts.

Even if he acknowledged to himself that he was in love with Nicolette and her son, even if she professed herself to be in love with him, he had no intentions of doing anything about it.

He wouldn't believe her if she told him she was in love with him. She was so far out of her element, with danger surrounding her son, and he was simply the rock she clung to under what could be described only as a stressful situation.

Besides, if he gave her his heart, he knew the ultimate result would just be another abandonment of him. She might be a country girl now, but the city would eventually call her back home.

He couldn't believe he was even entertaining these thoughts after knowing her only a week. He needed to stay focused on what was important, and that was the threat to Sammy.

"Call him," he said as she moved the phone from hand to hand. "Call him and get it over with."

She gave a curt nod and punched a series of numbers into her phone, at the same time hitting the speaker button that would allow him to hear the conversation.

The phone rang three times before a male voice answered. "Nicolette? Wow, talk about a blast from the past. How ya doing?" There was the sound of a female voice in the background, a muffled noise of rustling sheets, and Lucas could only assume that Samuel was sending somebody out of his bed.

"Not so well," Nicolette replied, her voice neutral of any emotions.

"Don't tell me after all this time you're calling me for money," Samuel replied.

"That would be the very last thing I'd call you for," Nicolette replied evenly. Fewer than four sentences out of Samuel's mouth and Lucas already didn't like the guy. "Somebody tried to kidnap Sammy."

"What? How…when?" Samuel sounded genuinely shocked.

Nicolette told Samuel as succinctly as possible about the two potential threats to Sammy's life.

"A guy snatched him and rode off with him on horseback? In the middle of New York City?" Samuel's voice was incredulous.

"I'm not in New York right now. I'm in Oklahoma."

"Oklahoma?"

She proceeded to explain to him about Cassie's aunt's death and their trip out to the ranch.

"So, why are you calling me? What do you expect me to do about it? I'm over a thousand miles away. Are the cops involved? Is there an investigation going on?" Samuel asked.

"Yes, there's an investigation." Again she filled him in on Jeff Bodine's and Del Hawkins's arrests, but explained that at the moment the two of them led to dead ends. "What I need to know from you is if you've made anyone angry enough that they might seek revenge on you by trying to take Sammy. Or do you maybe owe somebody money?"

"You know I don't make people angry. I make people happy. As a matter of fact, last night we had a Hawaiian luau on the yacht. We had hula dancers and roasted pig and plenty of rum punch. As far as the money thing, I don't owe anyone anything. My pockets are deep enough to stay out of other people's pockets."

Nicolette closed her eyes, her fingers gripping the phone. "So, you can't think of anyone who might be behind the kidnapping attempts on Sammy?"

"Not off the top of my head, but if I think of somebody I'll let you know," Samuel replied. "I can reach you at the number you called from, right?"

"Yes, it's my cell phone." Nicolette opened her eyes once again and gave a slight shake of her head. "Think hard, Samuel. There has to be somebody."

The call ended but she remained seated with the phone still in her tight grasp. "He didn't even ask how Sammy was doing. If he was scared or needed his father." Her voice was dull, lifeless. "I'm embarrassed to think that I was ever married to him." She finally raised her gaze to Lucas. "What did you think? Did you hear anything 'off' in his voice?"

"Not really. He just sounded like a jerk to me."

A quick burst of laughter escaped Nicolette. "And that about sums him up." She set the phone on the table in front of them and raked a hand through her long dark hair. Lucas remembered too well the feel of those silky strands in his fingers.

"Maybe he'll call you back and have a name of somebody," he offered in an effort to somehow chase away some of the darkness in her eyes.

"Maybe," she said without any real enthusiasm.

"Nicolette, Dillon is going to continue to investigate the case. Just because Del Hawkins isn't talking doesn't mean that Dillon won't be doing everything in his power to find out everything he can about Del. He might be a small-town chief of police, but he's smart and his investigators are equally as smart. He'll reach out to everyone and anyone he needs to in an effort to get answers."

"Thank you," she said, her eyes swimming with gratefulness.

"Thank you for what?"

"For reminding me that we aren't in this all alone. You're right. I need to give Dillon a chance to do his job, to hopefully find the clues that will lead to an end to this."

"You definitely aren't alone," Lucas replied. "You don't just have the entire law enforcement of Bitterroot taking care of business but you also have me and eleven other men whom you can count on to help keep Sammy safe."

"I feel better already," she said. "And now, I think I'll head upstairs and see how the art lessons are going."

Lucas watched her leave and then walked back into the kitchen and pulled his cell phone from his pocket. It took him only seconds to connect with Dillon.

"Anything new?" he asked.

"We've been digging into Del Hawkins's background, but haven't found much of interest other than the fact that he's underwater financially. I've requested his phone records, both cell and home phone, and hopefully we'll find a number that will lead to somebody else involved. It's possible Del was the end of the line and thought he could get a ransom for Sammy."

"Somebody paid for his high-priced lawyer," Lucas reminded Dillon. "Nicolette doesn't believe the motive was ransom money."

Dillon gave a dry laugh. "We've got two men without two nickels to rub together. Maybe Jeff and Del figured if Nicolette didn't have any money, then your team of cowboys and Cassie would all pool together enough money to make them happy."

"But that doesn't answer the question of who gave Jeff Bodine two thousand dollars with the promise of two more. As you just said, Del didn't have that kind of money."

Dillon was silent for a long moment and then released an audible sigh. "That's why we're just at the beginning of investigating."

"I'd like you to see what you can find out about Samuel Kendall."

"Nicolette's ex? She was pretty adamant that he wouldn't have anything to do with this, that he has plenty of money and no desire to have his kid."

"She called him a little while ago and he seemed genuinely surprised about the kidnapping attempts, but no stone left unturned, right?"

"Right. He's in New York City?"

"Nicolette told me he spends a lot of his time on a yacht in the Hamptons. He also has a beach house there and an apartment in Manhattan."

"I'll make contact with some local authorities there and see what they can dig up. The only real news I have is that Del's lawyer is going around and telling everyone within hearing distance that his client was just an innocent diner who got arrested because a drugged-up dopehead told the police a lie."

"Let's hope the prosecutor has a better story," Lucas replied. The last thing he wanted was for Del Hawkins to walk away from all this unscathed. There was no question in Lucas's mind that he was part of a scheme to take Sammy somewhere and to someone. Jeff hadn't just invented a man in the diner in a black-and-red shirt.

The two men talked for a few more minutes and then ended the call. Lucas wandered around the lower level of the house, trying to escape the scent of Nicolette that seemed to linger in every room.

She would haunt him long after she'd left here. He would hear the echo of her laughter as he rode the fence line, remember the silkiness of her skin, the heat of her kisses as he polished leather or stacked hay bales.

His hand would occasionally burn with the memory of Sammy's smaller hand in his. The secret that Sammy had told him of wanting Lucas to be his dad would forever burn inside his soul.

They had managed to find parts of his heart that weren't scarred, that had been defenseless, and he hated that. But he knew that Nicolette's cute dusty-rose cowboy boots didn't make her a cowgirl.

She could pull on jeans and muck out stalls, but he'd never believe that when push came to shove she'd make a decision to remain here in Bitterroot.

Besides, how many times could a man put his heart on the line and get it kicked and battered beyond repair? His mother's abandonment of him had forever changed him, forced him to be guarded...to be afraid of personal connections.

He'd let Cass in but only after years of working with her. He simply refused to let anyone else into his heart, into his very soul.

Eventually life would go back to some sort of normal. Hopefully when Cassie sold the ranch, the new owner would see that he had a group of men already in place who could take care of business and he'd keep them all on.

When this was all over the best he could wish for was that Sammy would no longer be in danger, he and his partners would still have their jobs here and he could say goodbye to Nicolette without his heart involved in any way.

The afternoon seemed agonizingly long. Lucas paced the floor like a caged tiger and Sammy bounced off the walls with boredom. Cassie had left once again with Adam to head into town, where he could show her the places they ordered their supplies from, and they planned on eating dinner out.

Nicolette, unable to stand the growing tension, escaped to the kitchen to think about dinner preparations. She decided to throw together a quick sauce and make spaghetti. She opened cans of tomato sauce and grabbed a handful of spices, and while she worked she tried to keep her mind empty.

She knew if she allowed it, her brain would fill with chaos…the danger to Sammy, her desire for Lucas and the uncertainly of the future.

She chopped up cloves of garlic and tried not to be discouraged by the fact that Dillon had so far uncovered nothing that might move his investigation forward.

Time. She just needed to give the officials time and

surely they would come up with an answer. Time. She'd heard Cassie talking to Adam before they left and they had set a day next week to start work on the damaged shed. And that would be the beginning of the end of time here if she stuck with Cassie and her life before now.

Could she build a life here in Bitterroot without Cassie and without Lucas? It would be difficult to start all over again, to build a new support system, a different kind of lifestyle from those she'd ever led before.

She threw the garlic into the sauce and then added parsley, sweet basil and onion. When it was simmering, she gave it a stir and then sank down at the table and rubbed the center of her forehead. She felt as if she'd had half a headache since the night she'd seen the masked man at Sammy's bedroom window.

The sauce hadn't been cooking long when Lucas and Sammy came into the kitchen. "We thought maybe we could help with dinner preparations," Lucas said.

Nicolette got up from the table. "It's going to take the sauce a little while to cook, but I guess Sammy can set the table and you could make a salad."

"Salad duty it is," Lucas replied at the same time Sammy headed for the cabinet with the plates.

Nicolette stirred the sauce and got out a pot of water to use to boil the spaghetti noodles. She tried not to focus on Lucas's nearness as he brushed against her with a handful of lettuce and veggies.

He grabbed a chopping board and set up his workstation right next to where she stood in front of the stove. Despite the tangy scent of the sauce she could smell his scent, that slightly wild, slightly spicy fragrance that evoked such a longing inside her.

"Forks on the left, Sammy," she reminded her son as he began to lay out the silverware.

"Right," he replied.

"No, left," she said teasingly, a desperate attempt to break the underlying tension with laughter.

Sammy's giggles were her reward. "You're being silly, Mom."

"Somebody needs to get a little silly," she replied. "We've all been far too serious all day."

"Maybe we could have a spaghetti-slurping contest," Lucas said and sliced through a green pepper. "Whoever manages to slurp the longest piece gets a prize."

"What kind of a prize?" Sammy asked with excitement.

Lucas frowned thoughtfully. "The winner gets his or her boots polished by the other two." He looked at Sammy and then at Nicolette, the gleam of challenge in his eyes. He then glanced down at his boots. "And mine could sure use a good shine."

Sammy looked down at his own boots. "Mine are worse than yours," he said to Lucas and then grinned. "And I'm a good slurper. Just ask Mom. Sometimes I slurp when I'm not supposed to."

Those simple words spoken from a six-year-old effectively changed the mood of the day. Challenges flew fast and furious among all three of them as they finished preparing the meal and then sat down to eat.

They were quite civilized as they ate their salads. It was only when their plates were filled with spaghetti that civilization went right out the window and the contest began.

Lucas picked up a long piece of pasta and with a

quick inhale, it was gone. "Beat that," he said to Sammy with a grin.

Sammy's attack on the pasta was less delicate and by the time he'd tried to get a piece longer than Lucas's, his mouth was smeared with sauce and Nicolette thought she even saw a bit of it in his hair.

"Your turn, Mom," Sammy said.

Nicolette shook her head. "I'll admit defeat."

"Chicken," Lucas replied, his eyes glittering with suppressed laughter.

"I'm no chicken," she protested. "I just know when I've been bested. I guess I'll be polishing up two pairs of boots and hosing you both down after dinner."

"I'll show you how to polish them after we clear off the table," Lucas replied with the twinkle in his eyes that she could ride to the moon.

As they worked together to clean up the kitchen, her heart swelled with a happiness she knew she shouldn't feel, but this was all she'd ever really wanted…a complete family.

She'd hoped that Samuel would be a man to walk beside her, to laugh and have fun with their son and take pleasure in simple things like a starlit night or a spaghetti-eating contest. Samuel had fooled her for a while, made her believe that he would grow into that kind of man.

Lucas was that man, but he would never belong to her. He belonged to his scars, to his past and this land and maybe to the dead woman who had saved his soul.

"I'm going to play some video games," Sammy said after the kitchen had been cleaned up. He kicked off his boots and set them on the kitchen floor.

"Ah, just another rat jumping off a sinking ship," Nicolette said, her words making Sammy laugh as he ran out of the kitchen to get his game player.

"Are you running out on me, too?" she asked Lucas.

"No way." He sat at the table and pulled off first one boot and then the other. "I don't trust these babies to just anyone. I definitely have to supervise this process."

He got up and padded to the cabinet beneath the sink. "I think Cass used to keep her boot polish under here." He rummaged around and then with a grunt of satisfaction straightened with a can of polish and a couple of soft cloths.

He pulled his chair close against hers and showed her how to apply the polish and then shine the leather. His shoulder was against hers, warming her from the point of contact straight through to her heart.

His big hands worked the cloth meticulously and the memory of how he'd touched her, how he'd made her feel so precious, so treasured, swelled in her chest.

"I want you again." The words shocked her as they whispered from her own lips.

His head shot up and he looked at her in surprise and then with a raw hunger that blasted a shiver of sweet, fiery anticipation up her spine. "I want you again, too." His gaze remained locked with hers, stealing her breath away as neither of them moved.

He broke the gaze, looking back down at the boot he held in his hand. "But, we both know that going there again would be a big mistake. I can't give you what you need, Nicolette. I can't be the man that you want."

He glanced up at her again and the desire, the passion that had burned in his eyes only moments before, was gone, replaced by a dull darkness that gave nothing away. "It's best if we just keep things the way they are between us and don't go there again."

Her cheeks flamed with embarrassment. "Of course you're right. I just…the stress…" She allowed her voice to trail off.

"If you want to polish your boots, then the next time we go to town we'll need to buy some red polish," he said, looking down once again.

"Maybe I'll plan a trip into town later this week," she replied. It was a slightly awkward transition from desire to boot polish, but she was grateful to move on before she made a total fool of herself.

She was grateful when the boot polishing was finished and even more grateful when Lucas engaged Sammy in one of his games and she sank down on the sofa and withdrew into her thoughts.

She was almost glad Lucas had the sense to stop anything more between them before it could begin. She couldn't even believe she'd spoken of her desire for him out loud. It was as if she had momentarily lost her mind, lost herself in him.

He wanted her, too. At least that knowledge made her feel less foolish. He obviously felt the same kind of magnetic draw to her as she did to him. Still, there was no way that another bout of lovemaking would solve all the issues that faced her. He was right in that getting more intimate with each other would only make things worse.

She watched her son with Lucas and found herself thinking about the two kidnapping attempts on him. She realized there was one other person she should call to see if he had any idea about what was happening and why.

"If you two will excuse me for a few minutes, I'm going up to my bedroom to make a few phone calls," she said.

Lucas looked at her curiously, but Sammy merely waved his hand, his attention focused on the game they were playing.

She went upstairs and entered her bedroom, closing the door behind her. She grabbed her cell phone from her purse and held it in her hand.

During her years of marriage to Samuel, she'd always had a good relationship with his father, Joseph. Joseph Kendall was a hardworking multimillionaire who had encouraged Nicolette to leave his son long before she'd actually made the final move.

Joseph had been disgusted by his son's lack of drive, the absence of any ambition and his party lifestyle. Joseph had often said that the worst thing that had ever happened to Samuel was being the beneficiary of his mother's trust fund.

Was it possible Joseph held any answers? She'd thought of the old man often in the years since she'd left Samuel, but they'd agreed at the time of the divorce that it was best for her and Sammy to make a clean break from the Kendall family.

Before she could change her mind, she punched in the number for Joseph's residence, vaguely surprised that she'd retained it in her head after all this time.

The phone rang twice and then a female voice answered. "Kendall residence."

Nicolette recognized the female voice. Maddie Winston had been the housekeeper for Joseph for years. "Maddie, it's Nicolette. May I speak to Joseph?"

"Oh, Mrs. Nicolette, you can't."

"Is he not home right now?"

"He passed away, Mrs. Nicolette. Mr. Joseph died two weeks ago." A sob filled the line. "It was his heart. It just gave out and he left us."

Nicolette clutched the phone tighter against her chest, grief piercing her as she thought of the man who had helped her through some of the tougher times of her marriage. "I'm so sorry, Maddie. He was such a good man," she finally managed to say.

"Mr. Joseph's lawyer has been trying to reach you," Maddie said. "He's left messages both at the store and at your home phone number."

"I've been out of the state," Nicolette replied, wondering why on earth Joseph's lawyer would need to speak with her. Was it possible Joseph might have left a little money to Sammy in his will?

"The lawyer's name is Vincent Veringo. Wait just a minute and I have his card here."

While Nicolette waited for Maddie, she quickly grabbed a small pad and a pen from her purse. Maddie returned to the phone and gave Nicolette the number to Veringo Law Offices.

When the two women hung up, Nicolette stared at the phone number. With the time difference it was too late to call tonight, and she knew more than anyone that the odds of anyone working late on a Saturday night were doubtful. Whatever Vincent Veringo wanted to discuss with her would have to wait until Monday morning.

She tucked the notebook and pen back in her purse and then headed back downstairs. Lucas and Sammy still sat on the sofa, but she motioned for Lucas to follow her into the kitchen.

She led him toward the back door, wanting to make

sure Sammy didn't hear their conversation. "I decided to call my ex-father-in-law, Joseph," she said in a hushed tone. "I thought maybe he'd know something about what's going on."

"And did he?" Lucas took a step closer to her.

"He died two weeks ago." She swallowed hard.

"I'm sorry, Nicolette. Were the two of you close?"

"He was very supportive of me when I finally decided to leave his son. We both shared the same disappointments in Samuel. Anyway, Joseph's housekeeper gave me the number of Joseph's lawyer, who apparently has been trying to reach me. Unfortunately, I'm sure I won't be able to get hold of him until Monday morning."

"What do you think he wants?"

Nicolette frowned thoughtfully. "I think maybe he left some money or something for Sammy. Sammy is his only grandchild."

She looked up at Lucas and her stomach felt more than just a little bit ill. "I think the real question to ask is why didn't Samuel tell me about his father's death when I spoke to him?"

"So you think all of this has something to do with your father-in-law's death?"

"I can't imagine how, but yes." She wrapped her arms around herself as a cold wind blew through her. Although it seemed impossible that an old man's death had somehow put into motion some kind of danger to her son.

Chapter 13

Nicolette was quiet and distant as Sunday slowly crept by. Twice Lucas saw her with the lawyer's number in hand and she'd tried to call it only to hang up without getting an answer.

It was obvious that she wouldn't have a hope of getting in touch with the lawyer until the next day when the law offices or whatever would be open for business.

Sammy seemed to have taken a note from his mother's mood. He spent most of the morning quietly playing his video games in the great room and then after a quiet lunch he got out a baggie of little cars and played with them on the floor.

Right after lunch Cassie had gone with Adam for another tour of the place to check out all the damaged trees that had been cleared and the patching work that had been accomplished on some of the outbuildings.

It was now just after two and Lucas sat on the sofa

watching Sammy while Nicolette walked the length of the room back and forth.

The first thing she'd wanted to do that morning was call Samuel and confront him about why he hadn't said anything about his father's death, but Lucas had talked her out of it. If Samuel was involved in any way in the threat to Sammy, then Lucas didn't want Nicolette giving him a heads-up.

The plan at the moment was for them to do nothing until she spoke to Joseph's lawyer. Depending on what she learned with that phone call, Lucas hoped they would have a better idea as to what was going on.

He definitely didn't want Nicolette to do anything that would place herself in a dangerous position. When they had some kind of information, they'd take it to Dillon and let him work it. The only goal he and Nicolette had was to continue to ensure Sammy's safety.

"Why don't we all plan on eating tonight down at the bunkhouse?" Lucas suggested, breaking the silence that had been the rule for most of the day.

"Yeah!" Sammy said. "Sounds like a good plan to me."

"Surely the men wouldn't be comfortable if Cassie and I came to dinner," Nicolette replied.

"Cass used to pop in for dinner on a regular basis. The men won't mind if you two show up. Besides, we need a break from this house. We've all been cooped up in here for too long."

She stared at him and he could almost see her brain churning with all kinds of thoughts. "I'll make sure two of the men escort us there and back here," he said, guessing that one of her concerns might be safety issues.

It was a long walk to the bunkhouse and she was

probably wondering if another horseman would ride up out of nowhere to try to steal her son away.

"Come on, Mom. Let's go," Sammy said.

"It would be nice to take a break and get out of here for a little while," she finally agreed.

A swift relief flooded through Lucas. He needed some time and distance from Nicolette and Sammy. At least in the bunkhouse dining room there would be plenty of others around who would provide some relief from his nearness to Nicolette.

"Then it's settled," he said. "We'll eat at the bunkhouse tonight and maybe after dinner we can talk Mac into playing some tunes on his guitar. That man makes great music."

The darkness in Nicolette's eyes that had lingered all day lightened just a bit. "That sounds like fun." Her eyes once again darkened. "I think I'll make some coffee."

She disappeared into the kitchen and Lucas wished he could steal that darkness out of her eyes forever. But he knew that wouldn't happen until she knew what and who had put her son in danger.

No matter how he worked it in his mind, he couldn't figure out why Samuel might want to kidnap his own son. Even if Joseph had left a little money to Sammy, Nicolette had full custody of the boy and there had been nothing to indicate that Samuel wanted to change that fact.

Besides, he was tired of thinking about the whole mess, tired of trying to solve a mystery puzzle without all the pieces in hand.

He was also tired of the visions that haunted him, not just during odd hours of the days, but also his sleep. They were visions of Sammy and Nicolette being his family, of the three of them sharing a life together that others would envy.

Last night had been the worst. He'd dreamed of him and Sammy riding horses side by side, of snuggling beneath a layer of blankets next to Nicolette as a cold wintry wind blew outside. There had been no nightmares of abandonment and loneliness; his dreams had held only love and a contentment he'd never experienced in real life.

Heck, the odds of them even being here in the winter were slim to none. Still, he'd awakened with a yearning he'd never felt before, with a desire to make his dreams a reality.

It had scared the hell out of him.

When the scent of freshly brewed coffee filled the air, Lucas went into the kitchen and found Nicolette seated at the table and staring out the window, her fingers wrapped around a cup.

Lucas poured himself a cup of coffee and then joined her at the table. He mentally asked himself why when he craved distance from her and then consciously put himself in a position to be close to her.

"You've been distant all day," he observed.

She didn't argue with him but instead nodded as she turned to look at him. "I've been trapped in my own head all day. I keep trying to find a way to make Samuel guilty, but I don't know if it's because he really might be or if I just want a final answer."

"Even if Joseph left Sammy some inheritance, you'd be the custodial representative until he comes of age, wouldn't you?"

"I would assume so."

"So how could Samuel kidnapping Sammy change that?"

"I don't know," she admitted and took a drink of her coffee. The line of worry appeared on her forehead, a faint line that he wanted to rub away with his thumb.

"Even though Joseph didn't approve of Samuel's life-style, I can't believe that Samuel would be named as a huge beneficiary. Whatever little money that has been left to Sammy wouldn't be worth Samuel's time. And like you said, that doesn't answer the question of what Samuel would have to gain by kidnapping his son."

"Tonight when we go to eat at the bunkhouse dining room I want you to put all of this out of your head. There's nothing that can be done until we have more information. No amount of stirring it all around in your head is going to give you an answer. You need to do that for me, but more you need to do it for Sammy."

She looked stricken, as if just realizing that Sammy's quiet mood of the morning might be a reflection of her own. "The last thing I want is for him to worry or be afraid. He's managed to put the horseback ride with Jeff behind him. I want him to stay worry-free."

"That means he needs his mother to be herself, not withdrawn and tense," Lucas replied.

She surprised him by reaching across the table and grabbing his hand in hers. "Thank you for always having Sammy's best interest at heart and for kicking my butt to remind me that he takes his cues from me."

She tightened her fingers with his and he hated the contact because it only made him want more. "You love him, don't you?"

"I know he loves me," Lucas replied. "He told me so the night I took him to eat pizza at the bunkhouse.

He told me that he loved me and that he wished I could be his dad."

Tears filled her eyes. "I wish you could be his dad. You would make a wonderful father."

He pulled his hand from hers and turned to stare at the window, unable to stand the yearning in her eyes. "Since I didn't have a father in my life, I wouldn't know the first thing about it." He spoke around a lump that had formed in the back of his throat.

"But that's not true," she protested. "You've already proved in a hundred different ways that you're wonderful father material. You care about Sammy. You want only the best for him. His thoughts and feelings are important to you, and I think if you looked deep inside your heart, you'd realize that you love him."

He looked back at her as he felt the defensive walls building inside his chest. "Don't mistake my protectiveness for a young boy in danger as love. I don't have the capacity to love anymore, Nicolette. I've told you, I care about your and Sammy's welfare, but never mistake it for love."

He got up from the table, leaving his coffee, and left the room, unable to stand being near her a minute longer.

He hated the mother who had abandoned him, and he hated Cass for dying on him, but more than anything he hated himself for the sadness he'd seen in Nicolette's eyes just before he'd left her sitting alone at the table.

Nicolette was determined to have a good time tonight. Despite the fact that she still didn't know who was after Sammy and why, in spite of the fact that Lucas had once again reminded her that he was unavailable emotionally to any kind of love, she needed to let herself go so that Sammy could fully enjoy the evening.

She dressed for dinner in a clean pair of jeans, a red-and-black sleeveless blouse and her boots. She pulled her hair up in a high ponytail and found a red kerchief to tie around it, giving her a cowgirl flair.

She'd just finished putting on a little mascara and spritzing herself with her perfume when Cassie appeared in the bathroom doorway.

Although Cassie also wore jeans, she topped them with a silky coral blouse and gold jewelry. "You look more like you're going to a fancy restaurant than to a cowboy's dining room," Nicolette said.

"All my T-shirts were dirty and I didn't feel like washing clothes. Did Lucas tell you what Cookie planned for the meal?"

"He didn't say. Whatever it is I'm sure it will be good." Together the two women went downstairs, where Sammy and Lucas awaited them.

"Our escorts should be here anytime," Lucas said. Nicolette couldn't help but notice that he wore his holster and gun. With him and two more armed cowboys, her son's safety would be ensured as they walked the distance between the house and the cowboys' quarters.

"I can't wait to eat Cookie's food and listen to Mac play his guitar. It's gonna be a great night," Sammy exclaimed with excitement.

"Yes, it's going to be a great night," Nicolette replied. She was determined to make it so.

Sammy looked out the window. "Here they come. It's Clay and Brody."

"I don't know if I'll ever figure out who is who among them all," Nicolette said ruefully.

"Clay has blond hair and Brody has brown hair," Sammy explained. "Clay is a womanizer and Brody is a hard-ass." Sammy clapped his hand over his mouth and stared at his mother as Lucas released a deep rumble of laughter.

"Who told you that?" he asked.

"That's what Dusty told me when I had pizza with everyone," Sammy replied. "Sorry I said the A word, Mom. It just slipped out."

"Well, let's go meet Mr. Womanizer and Mr. Hard-Ass and head to dinner," Cassie said.

The four of them stepped out on the back porch as Clay and Brody arrived. "Don't you ladies look positively lovely tonight," Clay said.

Cassie and Nicolette exchanged glances and instantly the two of them got a case of the giggles. Lucas frowned, Brody glared, Clay was clueless and Sammy looked at Cassie and his mom as if they'd both gone crazy.

The two females quickly got themselves under control and they all set off to the building in the distance. Both Clay and Brody wore holsters with guns, and the sight of them sobered Nicolette as she thought of the reason for their armed escort.

She mentally shook herself, refusing to go down that path, not now, not tonight. Hopefully, when she spoke to Vincent Veringo the next day she'd finally be able to make sense of everything that had happened since they'd been at the ranch.

Sammy walked between Lucas and Clay while Brody followed behind the women. The lights of the bunkhouse beamed out in the semidarkness of evening as if welcoming them.

They circled around to the back of the building to the dining room. The savory scent of cooking meat filled the air.

"Roast and potatoes with Cookie's gravy," Clay said. "You all are in for a culinary treat tonight."

They entered the door to find several of the cowboys already lounging behind the picnic tables on the sofas. All of them stood at the sight of Cassie and Nicolette.

"Down, boys," Cassie said. "Tonight I'm just here for a meal and a little music." She turned to look at one of the tall handsome cowboys. "Mac, I understand you're going to entertain us with your guitar after dinner."

Mac nodded and eased back down on the sofa. "That's the plan. I want to see if Sammy can kick up his boots and dance to the music." His eyes twinkled as he gazed at Sammy.

Sammy looked up at Lucas. "Can you dance to the music?" he asked.

"I've been known to handle myself on the dance floor if I have the right partner," Lucas said, and his gaze slid to Nicolette.

"Then, you can dance with Mom and I'll dance with Cassie," Sammy replied.

"Your mom and Cassie will have plenty of partners tonight if they feel like dancing," Clay said.

They all turned as several more cowboys entered the dining room, and it got noisier with each arrival. Finally they were all present and Cookie announced that the meal was ready.

The food was served buffet style in large warmers set on a solid table close to the kitchen. The men insisted Nicolette, Cassie and Sammy fill their plates first.

There was pot roast with tender potatoes and carrots,

a tub of thick brown gravy, green beans and an apple cobbler that made Nicolette's mouth water. At the end of the table sat plenty of hot coffee and several pitchers of iced tea.

Nicolette suspected that on most nights beer was also on the menu, but there was no sign of alcohol tonight. The three of them sat at a nearby picnic table and were joined there by Lucas, Clay, Brody, Mac, Forest and Adam.

Cassie had a good handle on who was whom and greeted Flint, Jerod, Sawyer, Tony, Nick and Dusty, who sat at the table next to theirs. Nicolette was vaguely impressed with her friend for being able to greet all twelve men by name. Maybe she was becoming more involved here than she realized.

The mood was light and the men teased and tormented each other and occasionally ribbed Sammy, who radiated happiness with their attention. If Sammy wanted Lucas to be his father, then he'd want these men to be his big brothers, and they treated him as if he were a beloved little brother.

Conversations swirled around Nicolette as she ate the delicious meal. There was love in this room. Remembering what Lucas had told her about where the men had all come from, how they had all happened to be here, was it any wonder that they'd formed a family based on love and respect of each other?

The possibility that Cassie might sell the ranch and destroy all of this broke Nicolette's heart. These were men who gained strength from each other, who had forged friendships based on the common traumas of their pasts. It just didn't seem right to tear down what had been built over the years here.

"You're very quiet," Lucas said, leaning close to her.

"Just taking it all in," she replied.

"There's a lot of testosterone in the room," he replied.

She laughed. "That's okay. It's obvious you all care about each other."

His eyes darkened for just a moment. "This is my family." She knew he must be concerned about what the consequences would be to each of them if and when Cassie decided to sell.

"Tell me about them," she said.

His eyes lightened as he began to tell her about his fellow cowboys. He didn't talk to her about their pasts, but rather focused on the kind of men they were now.

He told her that Clay's reputation as a womanizer was highly exaggerated and that Dusty had a crush on a waitress in town. He said that Forest was a gentle giant, and that Sawyer usually had to be carried home from the Watering Hole in town because he was the biggest drinker of the group.

As he spoke, she began to see them not just as a bunch of cowboys but as individuals with good characteristics and some flaws. She was just grateful these men were on her side, that they had shown her in a million ways that they took care of their own and, at least at the moment, they considered Sammy and Cassie and herself as part of their family.

After dinner, Mac broke out his guitar and the men shoved the picnic tables to one side, baring an area that could be used as a dance floor.

Initially, Mac played soft songs that Nicolette had never heard before and they all lounged around him on the sofas and chairs. Sammy leaned against Nicolette, a smile never leaving his face while he watched Mac strum the strings to create beauty.

After playing several slow songs, Mac began to tap his foot and burst into a rousing rendition of a popular country song with a dancing beat.

Adam pulled Cassie up from the sofa. "Come on, boss, let's see if you can dance better than you do book-keeping."

At the same time Clay grabbed Nicolette by the hand. "Let's dance," he said as he pulled her up from the sofa.

Before long Sammy was dancing with Dusty and then Cassie danced with Brody and Sawyer took the place of Clay. Nicolette danced song after song, partners changing frequently and laughter abounding.

She couldn't help but notice that Lucas didn't dance with her, although he took a turn with Cassie, proving to be adept on his feet and with plenty of rhythm.

Just when she thought Mac was winding down, she was spun around and into Lucas's arms. "I think I gave everyone else a chance. Now it's my turn," he said, tightening his arm around her waist.

"Are you having fun?" he asked as they moved seamlessly together with the music.

"It's been a wonderful night, just what we all needed," she replied. She was half-breathless by his nearness and overwhelmed by the familiar scent of him. "I have a feeling this is a night Sammy will never forget. I know I'll never forget it."

"I'm glad you had a good time," he replied, his breath warm on the side of her face.

"Did you all used to do this with Cass? Have a night of dancing?"

"Once in a while." He smiled in amusement. "Cass

wasn't as light on her feet as you and Cassie. Dancing with her was more like dancing with a hardheaded bull who insisted on leading."

She laughed and then sobered. "I don't think I've ever told you that I'm sorry for your loss, for everyone's loss. She must have been such a strong, special woman."

"She was the glue that kept us all together, that kept us grounded."

The music ended and he stepped back from her. "It's probably time we get back to the house. It's after nine."

"After nine?" She was shocked by how time had flown. She looked around for Sammy and found him seated next to Dusty on the sofa. He looked happy, but tired.

It didn't take long to round up a couple of escorts to walk them all back to the house. Dusty and Lucas walked on the outside of the three of them and Forest brought up the rear.

It was a quiet walk with the stars twinkling overhead and the scent of the pasture grass and the evening dew creating a sweet fragrance.

Once again Nicolette found herself never wanting to leave this beautiful piece of the country. She could envision herself in a small house with a back porch where she could sit in the evenings and smell the country air and watch Sammy run around the yard catching fireflies. She thought of small-town socials and homemade ice cream, of barn dances and going back to her original desire to become a teacher.

What she didn't think of was a life here in Bitterroot with Lucas. He'd made it clear in a dozen ways that he didn't intend to be a part of anyone's future.

Could she stay here and build a life for herself and

Sammy, knowing that she would probably run into Lucas in the café or at a store? Could she do that and not have her heart break each and every time they accidentally ran into each other?

They reached the house and Cassie pulled the house key from her pocket. Cassie, Sammy and Nicolette stood with Lucas on the back porch while Dusty and Forest went inside to make sure that nobody had broken in while they'd been gone.

While she waited for the all clear, Nicolette stared up at the stars, wishing she had all the answers they needed to solve the danger surrounding Sammy, wishing that she knew what was best for her future and Sammy's.

She looked up at the man who stood next to her. She knew he loved her son. If only he loved her, too.

I ride alone.

His words thundered in her head, reminding her that not all wishes made on stars came true.

Chapter 14

As usual Lucas was up before dawn and seated at the kitchen table. He was on the verge of a foul mood prompted by the dreams he'd suffered all night long.

Once again they hadn't been nightmares from his traumatic past, but rather dreams of what could be if only he allowed himself to let go of all control where Nicolette and Sammy were concerned.

Watching her last night dancing with the other cowboys had shot a shocking swell of possessiveness through him even as her laughter had warmed his soul.

He'd never wanted another woman in his life. He'd been comfortable occasionally seeking company from several women in town who had no interest in anything but a sexual relationship.

Sex with Nicolette was better than with anyone else he'd ever been with, but his emotions toward her were so much more complicated than just lust and physical desire.

Her happiness was important to him. He wanted to know what her future held, what her deepest dreams for herself and her son were and if she'd find the man who could be her everything, be Sammy's everything.

And that irritated him.

He sipped his coffee and stared out the window blankly, his mind racing with thoughts he shouldn't possess, thoughts that shouldn't even be entertained.

Surely once they figured out and neutralized the danger to Sammy, then he could get back to the bunkhouse, back to his real work, and these crazy feelings for Nicolette and Sammy would eventually vanish.

He wondered what the lawyer would have to tell her today. Did he hold the key to who was behind the kidnapping attempts on Sammy?

Lucas hoped so. He needed to get out of this space, away from Nicolette's daily presence, and go back to being a cowboy with nothing more on his mind than work and an occasional Saturday night spent at the local bar and dance hall, the Watering Hole.

He told himself the smartest thing to do was to get another cowboy to bunk in here for a few days so that he could gain the distance he desperately needed, but he'd promised Nicolette he'd see this through, and in his heart he knew that Sammy would be upset if it was anyone else but him in the spare bunk in his room.

He was on his second cup of coffee when he heard the patter of little feet and Sammy appeared in the kitchen doorway, his eyes huge and his lower lip trembling ominously. "I had a bad dream," he said.

The kid definitely looked little and fragile and in

need of a hug. Lucas scooted back from the table and patted his lap. "Why don't you crawl up here and tell me about it."

Sammy didn't wait for a second invitation. He scurried to Lucas and into his lap. He leaned against Lucas's chest and released a trembling sigh.

"I'm not sure I want to talk about it. I'm too scared," Sammy said. He looked up at Lucas, his eyes filled with innocence and fear. "Do real cowboys get scared?"

Lucas nodded. "Real cowboys sometimes get scared."

"What do they do about it?" Sammy asked as he snuggled his warm little body closer against Lucas.

"They face their fears."

"Then I guess I should tell you about my dream. That way I'm facing my fear like a real cowboy. I dreamed that Mom was missing and you and all your cowboys couldn't find her anywhere."

As he continued to describe the night terrors that had plagued him, Lucas marveled at how good it felt to hold the little cowboy on his lap, to feel the complete and utter trust and love that flowed from Sammy.

This was what it was like to have a child, to care deeply about something…someone outside of yourself. Lucas didn't remember ever being held and comforted by his mother and if he was to guess, Sammy had no memories of being cuddled against his father.

Sammy finally wound down but remained on Lucas's lap for several long minutes. "I faced my fear and now I feel better," he finally said. "Maybe we should make breakfast for the women this morning." He climbed off Lucas's lap.

"How about you set the table and I'll start frying up

some sausage," Lucas replied. "We'll make some biscuits and gravy for breakfast."

While they worked, Sammy chattered about the bunkhouse fun the night before. "Tony told me his mom was Italian and his dad was a real Indian."

"He's Choctaw Indian. His last name is Nakni, and that means *warrior*," Lucas explained. He added a couple of strips of bacon to the awaiting skillet.

"Cool," Sammy replied. "Are they all nice to me because of you?"

Lucas looked at him in surprise. "No, I think they're all nice to you because they like you."

Sammy nodded in satisfaction and continued to set the table.

"Do you have a lot of friends back in New York?" Lucas asked.

Sammy set the last spoon in place and then sat at the table. "Not really. I mean, I had some school friends, but usually after school I had to spend most of my time at the store with Mom and Cassie." Sammy smiled at him. "But, now I've got you and the other cowboys as my friends."

Until they left here and Sammy had to return to his life in the city, Lucas thought. And then the odds were good he'd go on to be a latchkey kid, lonely and easy pickings for the wrong crowd of friends.

Not your problem, Lucas reminded himself firmly.

By the time the sausage was fried, Cassie was up and dressed for the day. "Good morning," she greeted them cheerfully as she walked toward the coffeemaker.

"You sound chipper this morning," Lucas replied.

"I've still got Mac's guitar strumming playing in my

head." She carried her cup and sat at the table next to Sammy. "It was such fun last night."

She took a sip of her coffee and then continued, "And Adam and I agreed last night that one week from today we're taking down the shed. He's going to arrange for a bulldozer or whatever equipment we need to take it all the way out and then we'll lay new flooring and re-build."

Then you'll sell out and take Nicolette and Sammy back to the city with you. The thought depressed him more than it should. Aside from the fact that her move would place the lives of twelve cowboys in limbo, he would miss these early morning minutes with his little cowboy. He would miss sitting outside on the porch under the starlit skies with Nicolette. He would miss their laughter, their energy that filled the space around them.

He focused his attention back on Cassie, who was talking about the plans Adam had made for the shed takedown. "He's renting a couple of big Dumpster containers from Gus and we'll have the flooring ripped out in no time and then he assures me that all of you know how to build a new structure."

Lucas nodded. "We're all as quick with a hammer as we are with our guns. We helped build the barn on the Swanson Ranch and got it up and functional within two days."

"Men of all talents. I like that," Cassie replied. "I appreciate the way you have all worked for me since we arrived. I was afraid you'd all up and leave without Cass here anymore."

"We're doing it for you because of our love for Cass," he replied. "We're still at heart Cass's cowboys."

"I thought you all were Cassie's cowboys now," Sammy said.

Lucas looked at the woman who was the temporary boss. "It depends on Cassie whether we all eventually consider ourselves her cowboys. It will take time before she proves herself worthy of our total loyalty." And he didn't figure she'd be around long enough for that to happen.

"Speaking of time," he continued, "I say it's time we get the rest of breakfast fixed. I imagine it won't be long now before Nicolette makes an appearance."

By the time the biscuits were browned and the gravy was bubbly, Nicolette had joined them in the kitchen, and they ate together, the topic of conversation the fun they'd all had the night before.

Lucas noticed that throughout the meal, Nicolette checked her cell phone several times. He assumed she was keeping an eye on the time, wanting to make the call to the lawyer the minute the law offices opened in New York.

Although she appeared upbeat and chatty, she only picked at her breakfast, and he was surprised to realize he'd come to know her well enough to not be fooled by her cool-and-calm behavior.

Inside she had to be screaming in dreadful anticipation…hoping…praying that her phone call this morning would end the mystery surrounding her son.

It was exactly eight o'clock when she excused herself from the table and went into the great room to make her call. Lucas insisted that he and Sammy would clean up the breakfast dishes, and after a small protest, Cassie gave in and went upstairs.

"Did Cookie teach you how to make that gravy?"

Sammy asked as he helped Lucas carry plates and silverware to the sink.

"Actually, my mom showed me how to make it," Lucas replied. The memory tied a small knot of tension in his chest. "I was about twelve when she taught me. Biscuits and gravy are a cheap, easy meal."

"Where's your mom now?" Sammy asked. He set a glass into the sink and then turned to look at Lucas. "Does she live around here?"

"I don't know where she is. She ran away when I was fifteen."

Sammy's eyes widened. "She ran away? Moms can do that?"

"I didn't have a very good mom and good moms don't do that." The last thing he wanted to put into Sammy's head was any possible thought that Nicolette might just up and decide one day to run away from him.

Sammy walked over to him and grabbed his hand. "I'm sorry you had a bad mom. I have a good one. She'd never run away from me. I wish you'd had her as a mom."

The last thing Lucas felt toward Nicolette was any kind of maternal feelings, but Sammy's sweet words of support chipped away another piece of Lucas's defenses. Damn, but it was going to be hard to have to say goodbye to this miniature cowboy.

They had just finished placing the last of the dishes in the dishwasher when Nicolette returned to the room. Her face was pale, her eyes huge as she stared at Lucas and then looked at her son.

"Sammy, why don't you run upstairs and make your bed and get dressed."

"Okay, I'll be right back," he replied as he flew out of the kitchen.

Nicolette stumbled to the table and sat down hard, as if her legs couldn't hold her up a minute longer. Lucas sat across from her, waiting to find out what had her looking as if she'd just suffered a severe shock.

"I spoke to Vincent," she said. She placed her cell phone on the table next to her and stared at it. "Apparently he's been trying to reach me for the past week or so but only had the phone number to our apartment and the store. Anyway, apparently Joseph named me as a beneficiary in his will."

She looked up at him, her beautiful eyes holding more than a little bit of disbelief. "It's enough money that I shouldn't ever have to worry again."

"But that's wonderful," Lucas replied, happy that she'd be able to have the financial means to pursue whatever dreams she might want for herself and for Sammy.

"That's not the big news," she replied. "The really big news is that Joseph left the rest of his estate to Sammy. My son is now a multimillionaire."

Lucas's stomach knotted. "And that makes him a perfect target for kidnapping and ransom. We need to let Dillon know about this new information. We now know the probable motive, and all Dillon has to do is find out who has this knowledge and who would go to the lengths to attempt such a crime."

"There's only one person who would know what was in the will besides the lawyer and me, and that's Samuel." Her voice was flat as she held Lucas's gaze.

"Then Dillon will coordinate with the New York authorities and we'll get the bastard who obviously sees his son only as a dollar sign," Lucas replied firmly.

"And in the meantime?"

"In the meantime we keep doing what we're doing— we live our lives and we protect Sammy."

She reached across the table to grab his hand. Hers was cold, as if all of her fear pooled in her fingertips. She didn't say anything. She didn't need to. He felt her emotions without her needing to speak words.

For the first time in his life Lucas wondered if fate had somehow placed him here at the ranch specifically for the day that a wonderful woman and a little boy would need him.

And for the first time in a very long time, he felt as if he were exactly where he was supposed to be.

Nicolette sat on the back porch alone, breathing in the sweet-scented night air and listening to the chirps and clicks of insects that filled the silence like a miniature chorus.

A half-moon hung in the starlit sky and the faint breeze was comfortably warm.

It had been a little over a week since she'd found out about Joseph's will, nine days since Dillon had all the details and was investigating with the aid of a couple of New York detectives.

Samuel was under close scrutiny, but they could find no ties between him and either Jeff Bodine or Del Hawkins. He'd insisted to the officials that he hadn't been surprised by his father's will, that he'd never expected his father to leave him anything.

If not Samuel, then who? The question had haunted her all week, and that wasn't all that had haunted her.

Along with her concerns for her son's safety was the realization that she was completely and totally in love with Lucas Taylor.

There was no way she was going to leave this ranch unscathed by heartbreak. What a loser she was when it came to love. The first time around she'd fallen in love with a man who had loved his money and himself far more than he'd ever loved her.

Her second love was with a man who had proclaimed from the very beginning that he had no interest in a long-term relationship, that he was a man unable to emotionally invest in anyone.

All week she'd watched Lucas interact with Sammy. All week she could have sworn there had been times when he'd felt a deep yearning inside him, not just for her son, but for her. Yet, for the past nine days he'd managed to keep an emotional distance between them that had made her want to scream.

As if conjured up by her very thoughts, she heard the faint squeak of the screen door and instantly smelled his scent. He eased down on the stoop next to her.

"Long week," he said.

"One of the longest of my life."

"You know law enforcement is doing everything they can."

"I know," she replied. "I just want this over and done with. I want Sammy to be able to go outside and play without bodyguards around him and I want the person responsible for all this to be behind bars."

"Even if it is Samuel?"

"Especially if it's Samuel," she replied. "And all clues point to him."

"But I still don't understand what good he thought it

would do to take Sammy. You're still his legal guardian and therefore in charge of his inheritance."

She looked up into the night sky, which had become like a welcome friend for so many nights while she'd been here. "I can't begin to think like Samuel might think. Maybe he figured if he kidnapped Sammy, then I'd tap into the trust fund to pay a huge ransom to get him back. I don't want to believe it's the man I was married to, the man who fathered Sammy, but the fact that I'm even considering him as a potential suspect speaks to the fact that I don't believe he has any integrity, any morals at all."

"If he's behind this, then sooner or later he'll be caught."

She gazed at him, noting how the moonlight turned his eyes a silvery blue. "It's the *later* in that sentence that has me frustrated. It's been three weeks and both you and I know this situation can't go on forever. You need to get back to your real work, and to be honest, I need to get away from you."

She looked back up at the sky and released a deep sigh, deciding to speak exactly what was in her heart. "I've fallen in love with you, Lucas. I know we haven't known each other that long, but my heart doesn't know the space of time. I see you with Sammy and I want you to be a constant in his life. I look into your eyes and I yearn for things I know I can never have from you."

He stiffened, his entire body tense next to hers. Once again she gazed at him. "Don't worry, my love for you is my own problem, not yours. But it's been three weeks since we found that ladder going up to Sammy's room. How long do we continue with this false life we're living? How long are you willing to sacrifice your own life?"

He shrugged. "As long as it takes. I made you a promise, Nicolette. I promised that I'd see you and Sammy through this and I don't intend to break that promise." He sighed. "Maybe it's time to start rotating the other cowboys into the house. Maybe that would at least make things easier on you."

It wasn't what she'd wanted to hear. What she'd hoped for was that by telling him of her love, he'd reciprocate and tell her that he was in love with her, too. She'd somehow hoped that he'd have a startling moment of clarity and confess that he wanted her in his life forever.

"Maybe that would be a good idea," she finally replied, grateful that none of her inner emotions were in her voice. "But let's wait until after tomorrow before doing anything."

"What happens tomorrow?"

"I have a favor to ask you. Could you keep an eye on Sammy while Cassie and I go to lunch in town?"

"You know that's not a problem," he replied easily.

She drew in a deep breath of the night air. "Tomorrow I'm going to tell Cassie that I'm not going back to New York City with her."

Lucas shifted positions next to her in obvious surprise. "What do you mean?"

"I don't want to move back to the city. I also don't want to run a shop. What I want is a nice little ranch house here in Bitterroot with a big yard where Sammy can play. I want to go back to school and get my degree and hopefully get a teaching position here in Bitterroot. I might have been born a city girl, but I want the country to be my home, and now with my inheritance I can follow my dreams and do what I think is best for my son."

He was silent for so long, she wondered if she'd put him to sleep. She looked at him and he stared out at the distance to some undefinable point. "Are you sure this is what you want?" he finally asked.

He focused his gaze back on her. "You've come into a lot of money. You could go anywhere, do anything. A ranch house in the middle of nowhere seems rather humdrum."

Although she'd wished for something different from him, she couldn't help the smile that curved her lips. "It will be anything but humdrum. It will be a ranch filled with love under the beautiful Oklahoma sky."

She pulled her knees up to her chest and wrapped her arms around them. "I've fallen in love with this place. I feel like this is where we belong, that this is home."

"I have a feeling Cassie won't be particularly thrilled with your decision," he replied.

"I know. That's why I want to tell her with just the two of us away from here. But Cassie will be fine no matter what she decides to do with the ranch. It's time I think about my son and my future, and this is where I want it to be. Cassie is a survivor. Eventually she'll be fine with my decision because she'll have to be."

"So, when exactly do you plan to start putting this all into action?" he asked.

She released her hold on her knees and stretched her legs out before her. "I figured I'd start looking for a place right away, although I don't intend to move for a while. Right now I know the safest place for Sammy is here at the ranch with all of you looking over him. But

I also think it's possible that maybe now that the light is shining on Samuel, the danger has passed."

"Are you willing to bet Sammy's safety on that?"

"No, which is why at the moment I don't plan to make any major changes to our living arrangements," she replied. "Besides, it could take me weeks to find exactly what I have in mind here in Bitterroot. I have a vision of the place in my head, and sometimes visions take time to find in reality."

"Nicolette…I'm sorry…"

She held up a hand to stop him from completing his sentence. She didn't want to hear his apology for not loving her. "Please, don't. You don't owe me any apologies or explanations about anything. You've been a gift from fate, a support when I've desperately needed it. You've been a straight shooter from the very beginning and you have nothing to be sorry about."

He got up from the stoop, as if eager to escape a conversation that had gotten far too personal, much too deep. "Are you coming inside?" he asked.

"I'm just going to stay out here a little bit longer," she replied. "Don't worry, I'll make sure and lock up when I come in."

He hesitated at the door, as if reluctant to leave her seated alone in the dark. Finally the screen door creaked and she felt the absence of his presence.

She stared back up at the sky, surprised to see the stars all melted together beneath a mist of tears. She hadn't meant to tell him that she loved him. She'd simply been unable to hold her feelings for him in any longer.

Somehow she'd hoped…foolish hopes, she thought as she swiped the tears that had begun to fall down her cheeks. The past couple of weeks had been a glimpse into a fantasy she'd desperately wanted to claim as fact.

Lucas wasn't just the real kind of cowboy her son loved, but he was the real kind of man who had stolen her heart. It hurt like nothing she'd ever experienced before. Her heartbreak over Samuel had come slowly, ushered in on broken promises and disappointments until she realized she didn't love him at all.

This pain of knowing that Lucas didn't love her was like an arrow piercing through the very center of her. It was going to be difficult to remain here in Bitterroot and see him occasionally and know he would never be anything but a cowboy who'd once made exquisite love to her, a cowboy who had kept her son safe when danger had threatened.

But he would never be the man who loved her. He would never belong in a little ranch house with her and her son. As the stars twinkled overhead and the sweet scent of night surrounded her, she allowed her tears to consume her.

Chapter 15

"I've decided that while you two ladies are enjoying your lunch in town today, a couple of us cowboys are going to get Sammy onto the back of a horse," Lucas said the next morning as they were all seated at the table enjoying coffee.

"It's about time!" Sammy exclaimed.

"Are you sure that's a good idea?" Nicolette asked. It was impossible for her not to remember that the last time they'd planned to put Sammy on a horse, he'd been stolen away by Jeff Bodine.

"It's an excellent idea, Mom," Sammy said. "A real cowboy needs to know how to ride a horse."

"I've already arranged for Dusty and Nick to help," Lucas replied. Nicolette knew that by "help" he meant they would be there with their guns to make sure nobody took off with her son again.

"And then once we have Sammy riding, it will be time to get you on a horse," Lucas said to Nicolette.

She could tell by the twinkle in his eyes that he expected her to protest. "I think I'd like that," she replied. "If I'm going to have a cowboy as a son, then maybe I need to get some of my cowgirl going on."

"Ha, this I've got to see," Cassie said drily. "A woman who has never even owned a dog is going to climb on the back of one of those big beasts."

"It wouldn't hurt for you to learn to ride, too," Nicolette returned. "Instead of riding around in that silly golf cart, you could just saddle up and ride your range."

"I like the golf cart," Cassie replied, her lower lip in a pronounced pout.

"That's just because you can wear your dumb high heels in a cart," Sammy said.

"Maybe I'll fool you all and buy myself a pair of fancy boots while we're in town today," Cassie replied.

"That would be a good start," Lucas observed. "It might give the men a little more confidence in you."

"Then, I'll have to see about that," Cassie agreed easily.

"Are you having lunch at the girlie place or at the café?" Sammy asked.

"I'm treating Cassie to lunch at the café today," Nicolette replied. "And you'll be eating lunch with the men in the bunkhouse."

Sammy frowned at his mother. "Just watch out for that mean Lloyd man."

"Don't you worry," Nicolette assured him. "Lloyd and his friends won't bother us. We're just going for a nice lunch and some girl talk."

Sammy rolled his eyes. "You girl-talk all the time."

Nicolette laughed and told her son to head upstairs to make his bed and get ready for his big day. When he was gone, Lucas and Cassie talked about the plans to take down the shed on Tuesday.

While they spoke, Nicolette found herself only half listening. She was grateful that the morning had held no awkwardness between Lucas and her. Her heartfelt confession of love the night before seemed like nothing more than a dream they hadn't even shared.

She felt as if she'd spoken the words to herself, to the wind, with only the stars overhead to hear, and there was a certain amount of both hurt and relief in the fact that he acted as if nothing was different between them this morning. The truth of the matter was despite her telling him what was in her heart, nothing had changed between them.

But something had changed inside her. She'd awakened this morning with a new resolve to get on with her life, the life that she had decided was best for herself and her son.

Joseph had given her the means to make her own future, and today was the beginning. The first step was letting Cassie know what she had decided.

She hoped their friendship was strong enough to survive Nicolette's choices, but if it wasn't, Nicolette wouldn't be pulled off the path she'd chosen for her son and her.

"I think I'll go check on the bed making," Lucas said. He got up from the table and disappeared from the kitchen.

"So, are you really going to buy some cowboy boots?" Nicolette asked.

"I suppose it does make sense. I'm spending a lot of

time outside these days." Whatever else she was about to say was interrupted by a knock on the front door.

Nicolette's heart leaped. Maybe it was Dillon with some news about the investigation. She and Cassie left the table side by side and met Lucas coming down the stairs, his gun drawn.

He got to the door first and peered outside. "It's Raymond Humes and one of his men." He took a step back so that Cassie could answer.

Cassie opened the door with Nicolette just behind her. She wanted to get a look at the man who had the likes of Lloyd Green in his employ.

"Good morning. Cassie Peterson?" he asked, his voice deep and pleasant. Tall and muscular, with silver hair and lean, hawkish features, Raymond appeared to be in his sixties.

"Yes, I'm Cassie," she replied and then reached back to grab Nicolette's arm. "And this is my friend Nicolette Kendall, and I'm sure you already know Lucas Taylor." Lucas stood to one side, his gun back in his holster. "What can I do for you, Mr. Humes?"

He offered her a smooth smile. "I just thought it was way past time I come by and introduce myself to my new neighbor. Is this a good time for the two of us to have a little chat?"

"Actually, I'm afraid it isn't a good time right now. We have a trip into town planned in a little while." Cassie's voice was also pleasant.

"Then perhaps later this evening," Raymond replied. "I think it's important that neighbors work together and get to know each other."

Cassie finally nodded. "Okay, why don't you come

by for coffee after dinner this evening? Let's say around six-thirty or so."

"Wonderful. I look forward to it." Raymond nodded to Nicolette and Lucas and then smiled at Cassie. "Then I'll see you this evening."

As he and his ranch hand, who hadn't been introduced, left, Cassie closed the door with a frown. "I wonder what that's all about."

"If I was to guess, he wants to get the lay of the land, find out what your intentions might be and how he can profit from them," Lucas said. "I imagine he'd be the first in line with an offer if you decide to sell. He coveted everything Cass had here. Just be careful, Cassie. Raymond Humes is a snake, but he can be a charming one when it benefits him."

Sammy came down the stairs, each boot clomping as if he weighed a thousand pounds. "Mom, when are you and Cassie leaving? Lucas and I have stuff to do and we can't do it until after you're gone." He stood at the bottom of the stairs and looked at them expectantly.

"Okay, I'm off to shower and dress," Cassie said. "I know when I'm not wanted around."

"I'll get ready to go, too," Nicolette said. "If we leave a little early we'll have time to shop for those boots for you."

"Pink. I want pink boots," Cassie said as she climbed the stairs.

Lucas laughed. "Good luck with that, and don't expect any sparkles on any of them either."

It was just before eleven when the two women got into Cass's car and headed toward town. Lucas had assured Nicolette that when she got home she'd find her son no worse for the wear of the horse riding lesson.

"Promise me one thing," Nicolette said once they were on their way.

"What's that?" Cassie asked.

"Please don't sell the ranch to Raymond Humes. I think your aunt would roll over in her grave if you did that. We both know there's bad blood between the two ranches."

Cassie shot her a quick glance. "But we really don't know what started it. Maybe Aunt Cass did something that wasn't so nice that began the bad blood. What am I supposed to do if Humes is the only one who makes a decent offer on the place?"

"You own some of the best pastureland in the state. The Holiday Ranch is more than financially stable. You'll have plenty of offers to choose from. I just know a sale to Humes would ensure that your cowboys would all have to find new places to work."

"They aren't my cowboys," Cassie replied drily. "As Lucas reminded me not too long ago, they're all still Cass's cowboys in their hearts and it's going to take a while for me to earn their respect."

"A pair of cowboy boots might go a long way in starting the process," Nicolette said teasingly.

Cassie laughed. "Enough with the boots. I'll buy me a pair, although I doubt I'll be here long enough to earn the complete trust of any of the men."

The rest of the ride was accomplished in a comfortable silence. True to her word, once they reached town the first store they entered was the boot and cowboy ware shop.

Cassie not only found a pair of denim and black leather boots, but also walked out with a cute denim blouse with pearl buttons and short sleeves.

When they finally headed to the café, Nicolette's nerves pumped up as she thought of the conversation she was about to have with not just her best friend, but her business partner and the woman who had taken her and her son in when they'd had no place to go.

The place was jumping at noon on a Tuesday but Daisy led them to an empty two-top next to the front window. Thankfully it was on the opposite side of the counter and stools where Lloyd and his creepy buddies often ate their lunches.

White blinds were pulled closed to shield diners from the bright midday sunshine, and a centerpiece of fake daisies gave each booth a fresh spring look. Their orders were taken by a cute waitress with a name tag that identified her as Trisha, who promised to return as quickly as possible with their food and drinks.

Cassie settled back in the booth and looked at Nicolette expectantly. "So, tell me what this lunch out is really about."

A nervous laughter escaped Nicolette. "Can't I just take my best friend out to lunch without an ulterior motive?"

"Yes, but you have a son you've been afraid to let out of your sight. You've been on pins and needles waiting to hear from Dillon about the investigation into Samuel. This just doesn't seem like the time you'd invite me out for a leisurely lunch, unless you have an ulterior motive."

The conversation halted as Trisha returned with their glasses of iced tea. "Okay, you're right," Nicolette confessed once Trisha had left their table. "I do have an ulterior motive."

"You want out of the store," Cassie said. "I knew

when you found out about the inheritance from Joseph you'd want out. It was never really your thing to begin with."

"That's part of it," Nicolette agreed. "I certainly don't expect you to buy me out or anything like that. I'll just sign the appropriate paperwork to dissolve the partnership and leave all assets with you."

Once again the conversation was interrupted as Trisha returned with their meals. "A cobb salad for the blonde and a burger and fries for the brunette," she said as she placed each plate before them. "Is there anything else I can get for either of you?"

"I think we're good, thanks," Cassie replied. She forked a bite of her salad and once again focused on Nicolette. "What are you going to do?"

"Go back to school and get my teaching degree. Being a teacher was all I really wanted to do before I met Samuel. I'm reaching for the dreams I'd once set for myself."

"Then I can't be mad at you. You know I love you and just want you to be happy. So, does this mean now that you have the means I'm also losing my roommates?"

Nicolette smiled. "You know that Sammy and I living with you was never supposed to be forever. It's time we find our own place and let you have your apartment back to yourself."

Cassie took a bite of her salad and then chased it with a gulp of iced tea. "I can't say I'm really surprised, although I'll miss having the little monkey underfoot."

Nicolette drew a deep breath. "That's not all I have to tell you."

Cassie leaned back in the booth, her eyes narrowed

slightly as she gazed at Nicolette. "What else could there be?"

"I'm not going back to New York City."

Cassie stared at her as if she'd suddenly spoken a foreign language. "What are you talking about?" She set her fork down as if her appetite had fled. "Of course you're going back to New York with me. That's your home. That's where you belong." Her eyes narrowed once again. "Does this have something to do with Lucas?"

A small burst of sad laughter released from Nicolette. "I wish it had something to do with Lucas. I told him last night I was in love with him."

Cassie's eyes widened. "And what did he say?"

"That he was sorry I felt that way about him. He's told me from the beginning that he has no interest in relationships or building a family. I just couldn't help allowing my emotions to get involved with him."

"Honestly, I would have sworn that he was in love with you. When he looks at you it's with the eyes of a man in love. When the three of you are together you look like a family. I was already worried about the feelings growing between the two of you. Are you sure he isn't in love with you?"

"I think he has desire for me. I know he cares about what happens to me and Sammy, but none of that matters now. He intends to live his life alone and there's no place in it for us." Tears pressed against her eyelids and rose up the back of her throat. She swallowed hard against them, refusing to allow herself to cry another tear for Lucas Taylor.

"Then I don't understand. Why aren't you coming back to the city with me?"

"I've realized over the last couple of weeks that this is where I really belong, that Bitterroot is where I want to live and raise my son."

"I would think with the way you feel about Lucas this would be the last place you'd want to live." Cassie picked up her fork again. "Even though he said he doesn't love you, he's obviously got you under a spell." She took another bite of her salad, and Nicolette knew Cassie wasn't really taking her seriously.

"If I'm under a spell, then it's been cast by Bitterroot and Oklahoma," Nicolette protested. "After weeks of smelling the air, of seeing a canvas of stars at night, I can't imagine going back to the city. I feel it in my heart, in my very soul, that this is where Sammy and I belong. I truly believe both of us will thrive in this small town and find true happiness here with or without Lucas."

Cassie looked at her in dismay. "Now, how can I argue with you when you talk like that? It would be totally selfish of me to want anything for you and Sammy except your true happiness."

"There are planes and trains that go to and from here and New York. It's not like we'd be saying goodbye forever."

"So what exactly do you intend to do? Buy some ranch and learn how to muck out stalls?"

Nicolette laughed. "I don't see me going quite that big, but I would like to find a nice ranch house on a bit of property where Sammy could have a horse if he wanted one."

"Does he know your plans?" Cassie asked.

Nicolette shook her head and picked up a French fry. "I haven't told him yet. I needed to be a hundred percent sure of my decision before sharing it with him."

"He's going to be over the moon and I'll be back in New York crying in my martinis every night."

Nicolette laughed. "You don't even drink martinis."

"But if I did I'd cry and miss you terribly."

"You'll be so busy reinventing the store you won't have time to miss me."

For the next few minutes they ate in a comfortable silence. The conversation had gone far better than Nicolette had ever imagined. She should have known that ultimately Cassie was a good friend who would want only Nicolette's happiness, no matter where that happiness occurred.

"So, when are you planning this next phase of your future?" Cassie asked and pushed her nearly empty salad plate to the side.

"I'd like to stay at your ranch until hopefully we solve the mystery of who is behind the attacks on Sammy, but my plan is to start looking at property in the next couple of days. I figure it will take me a while to find my dream property."

"Nothing new from Dillon?"

"No, nothing. According to the New York detectives working the case, they can't find any way to tie Samuel in to what's been happening here." Nicolette popped the last French fry off her plate into her mouth. "It's just all so frustrating."

For a moment a vision of Lucas filled her head, bringing with it not just frustration, but a piercing ache that she knew she was going to have to learn to live with until it finally faded away.

Right now the wound of Lucas was too fresh, too raw. Instead she focused on how happy Sammy would be to learn that he and Nicolette were not going back to the city, but rather making a home someplace here in Bitterroot.

Granted, he would be upset when he realized Lucas wasn't going to be a part of his everyday life, but once school started Sammy would make new friends and occasionally maybe Lucas would find some time to visit with the kid who had been his little partner for a while.

Trisha returned to their booth. "How about some dessert? I can tell you that the apple dumplings are fresh today and are awesome with a dollop of ice cream on top."

"You sold me," Cassie said. "I'll take one with a cup of coffee."

"Make that two," Nicolette agreed.

"You know, somehow I'm not surprised by your decision to stay here," Cassie said. "You've been happier and more relaxed here than I've ever seen you."

"This feels like home, Cassie. It feels like home in a way that no place ever has before."

"I should have made you stay back in the city manning the store instead of insisting you take the trip out here with me," Cassie said teasingly.

"Honestly, Cassie, you've been the best friend I could ever want. It's important to me that I have your support as I move forward with these new plans."

Cassie waved a hand dismissively. "You know you will always have my complete support. Besides, the two of you can at least fly back to the city during the holidays every year."

Trisha arrived with their desserts, and when she left the table Nicolette's cell phone rang. She hurriedly grappled it from her purse and answered, worried that it might be Lucas telling her Sammy had fallen off a horse and was now in the emergency room.

"Don't say a word," the deep familiar voice said. "I've got Sammy in a car in front of the café. Don't tell Cassie what you're doing, but get up and get out here. We need to talk."

"Okay," she replied calmly, although her heart beat so fast she felt ill.

"Who was that?" Cassie asked.

"Wrong number." Nicolette stood. "I think I need a bit of fresh air. Sit tight and I'll be right back."

She didn't wait for Cassie's reply, but hurried for the front door. Her mind could hold only two thoughts, and both of them scared her to death. The first was how Samuel was here in Bitterroot, and more frightening was wondering how he'd managed to get Sammy away from Lucas.

Chapter 16

"Can we ride more after lunch?" Sammy asked as he, Nick and Lucas entered the dining room, where most of the other cowboys were already seated.

"We thought you three were going to miss lunch altogether," Dusty said when the latecomers had filled their plates and sat at the table next to him.

"We lost track of time while getting Sammy up on Candy's back," Nick said.

"I'm a natural," Sammy announced with pride to anyone who might be listening.

Lucas grinned. The kid was right. He was a natural. Despite his encounter with the big black beast that had carried him away, he'd shown no fear when faced with mounting Candy.

He'd listened to everything Lucas and Nick had told him about equipment, how to sit properly in the seat and how to hold the reins with just the right amount of pressure. By the time they'd knocked off for lunch, Sammy had been riding a small circle area of pasture all by himself.

Lucas had been grateful for the distraction of Nick and Sammy's company, for the last thing he wanted to dwell on was Nicolette's confession of love for him the night before.

Despite his desire to the contrary, as they ate their lunch her words played over and over again in his head. He hadn't wanted her to love him even though he'd seen it happening. He'd watched her growing affection for him and he'd not only allowed it, he'd encouraged it.

He'd thrived in it, fantasized about it, and yet had always known deep in his heart that he would never, could never, allow himself to reciprocate it.

That alone made him a heartless coward.

And worse than that, he knew that Sammy loved him. He knew what childish dreams Sammy held in his heart, that somehow Lucas would wind up being his father. While he hadn't encouraged Sammy, he'd certainly done little to discourage him.

If he was true to himself, he'd recognize that he'd wanted them to love him. He liked feeling special in their lives. He'd allowed himself to wallow in being loved for the first time in his life. It had been an incredibly selfish thing for him to do, and now he didn't know how to fix things.

If he could go back in time, he'd be that spitting, cow-dung-smelling, half-civilized hick that Nicolette had assumed he'd be. But, the genie was out of the box now and her confession of love rang in his head, piercing him with sadness as he realized he wasn't the man

Cass had wanted him to be, and he wasn't half the man he thought he'd become.

"Won't Mom be surprised when she gets home and sees that I can ride a horse all by myself?" Thankfully Sammy's voice pulled Lucas from his thoughts.

"Our next job is going to be to get her behind in a saddle," Lucas replied.

Sammy giggled. "She'll make up all kinds of excuses, but sooner or later she'll ride, too. She won't want to be left out when you and I go riding the range together."

Riding the range together. But he'd already told her he rode alone, and despite all his warnings, she'd somehow convinced herself she was in love with him.

Before, he'd been able to tell himself that everything between them would come to a halt when she left to return to the city, but now she didn't intend to leave Bitterroot.

He didn't doubt her plans to remain here. He'd watched her fall in love with the country. He'd seen her drawing deep breaths of the sweet air, looking up at the big blue sky overhead and watching the stars at night.

He'd judged her as a city girl, but now realized she was a country girl at heart, low maintenance and happy with simple pleasures.

Cassie hadn't shown any indication that she'd shed her love of the city, that she might stick around here and learn to love ranching and the small-town community of Bitterroot.

Friday they would begin the takedown of the damaged shed. Lucas figured it would take two to three weeks to get a new one up, depending on the weather. That shed was the final piece in Cassie's plan. All the other storm damage had been taken care of and with the new shed in place the ranch would be in perfect order to go on the market to sell.

It was ironic that as Nicolette began to build a future here, he was going to, in all probability, lose his. He looked around the table at the men who remained. They shared friendships forged in youth and shared pain.

If the ranch sold, unless the new owner decided to keep them all on, then they would all go different directions, seeking work, seeking new lives wherever they could be found.

Maybe it was time for Lucas to pick up and leave Bitterroot altogether. He could always find work on some ranch in Texas or maybe head to Wyoming.

Certainly life would be easier on Nicolette and Sammy if they didn't have the chance to run into him. His absence from town would probably make life better, easier for them.

"Hey Lucas, do you think I could pretend that Candy is my horse for as long as we stay here?" Sammy asked, thankfully pulling Lucas from his maudlin thoughts.

"I think Cass would have been happy if you pretended Candy was your horse," Nick replied.

"She'd definitely want that horse to be loved by somebody," Lucas replied. "And I can't think of a finer cowboy than you for the job."

"Good, because I already love Candy," Sammy replied.

Before Sammy could continue, Lucas's cell phone rang from his pocket. "That's probably your mother calling to make sure you haven't bounced off the back of a horse and onto your pointy little head."

Sammy giggled as Lucas answered, surprised to hear Cassie's voice. "Lucas, something weird just happened."

He sat up straighter as he heard the edge of panic in her voice. "What?"

"Nicolette and I were just about to have dessert when she got a phone call. She immediately got up from the table and left the café. I peeked out the blinds and I saw her get into the passenger door of a dark sedan. Lucas, Samuel was driving that car."

Shock sizzled through him. "I'll be right there," he said, and disconnected at the same time he got up from the table. "Nick, can Sammy hang with you for the rest of the afternoon?"

"Problem?"

"I think so. I'll be in touch." He gave Sammy a squeeze on his shoulder. "Be good for Nick and I'll see you later."

He hit the dining room door at a run, his heart pounding unnaturally as he raced for his truck in the large garage in the distance.

Although there might be many reasons a divorced couple with a child might meet, this felt wrong...so very wrong on so many levels.

What was Samuel doing here in town? Why couldn't he have spoken to Nicolette in the café? Nicolette had been suspicious of him. What on earth could have made her decide to get into a car with him?

Lucas jumped into his truck and roared down the lane and out onto the road that would take him to Bitterroot. It just didn't make sense that Nicolette would go anywhere with her ex-husband for any reason.

He ripped up the road, ignoring the posted speed limit. Why would Samuel show up here for a meeting with Nicolette? There was only one reason, and that had to be money. Somehow, some way, Samuel wanted the money that had been left to his son. In his heart he knew that Nicolette was in danger.

He punched the button on his steering wheel that would allow him to make a phone call hands-free. "Call Dillon," he said out loud and was grateful when the lawman answered on the second ring.

"Samuel Kendall is here in town and he lured Nicolette out of the café, where she was having lunch with Cassie."

"What do you mean he lured her out?"

"I don't know. He called her and Cassie said she immediately got up and left the café and got into a dark sedan with him. My gut tells me she's in trouble, Dillon. We need to find them before something bad happens."

"Cassie didn't get a specific make or model of the car?"

"She just said a dark sedan."

"There are only two roads into Bitterroot. I'll get some men to set up roadblocks on both places. We won't let them get out of town."

"Thanks, Dillon. I'm almost to the café now," Lucas replied, and then hung up.

He spied Cassie standing on the sidewalk and she waved to him as he pulled to the curb. He rolled down his window. "Which way were they going?"

"That way." She pointed down the street to the left. "Find them, Lucas. I'm afraid for her."

He nodded and stepped on the gas, unable to hear anything but his own heartbeat banging wildly in his chest, echoing in his head.

First the kidnapping attempts on Sammy and now

a sudden, unexpected encounter for Nicolette with her ex-husband, the man she had come to believe had been behind the attempts to grab Sammy.

A cold rush of wind blew through him as a sudden thought popped into his mind. What if something happened to Nicolette? Custody of Sammy would automatically go to his father, and with custody of Sammy, Samuel would have access to the millions of dollars that had been left to his son.

There had been many times in the past when Lucas had smelled the odor of evil, and right now the smell was rife in the air. If he didn't find Nicolette as soon as possible, she'd never realize her dreams of becoming a teacher and living a wonderful life in Bitterroot with her son.

Nicolette recognized her mistake the moment she closed the passenger door. Sammy wasn't in the car, and if she would have reacted intelligently rather than emotionally she would have known that there was no way Lucas would allow Samuel to take Sammy anywhere away from him and the ranch.

"You lied to me. You don't have Sammy," she said. She turned to open the passenger door and leave only to realize in horror that the door handle had been removed.

Samuel stepped on the gas as she stared at him in horror. "What are you doing, Samuel? Why are you here?" Her heartbeat raced as she stared at the man she'd once been married to.

Although it had been only two years since she'd seen him, he hadn't aged well. His lifestyle had begun to catch up with him, giving him the beginnings of jowls, small broken blood vessels across his nose and the bleary eyes of a man who had seen it all, done it all.

"I told you we need to talk," he said.

"We could have done that by phone," she replied as she tried to tamp down a sense of panic that threatened to consume her. "But now that I'm here, what do we have to discuss? Certainly you can't want to know about Sammy. You haven't asked a single question about him or wanted to talk to him since I left you."

Fear crept up the back of her throat as he turned off Main Street and onto a residential street. "You know, I went about this all wrong from the very beginning," he said, his voice pleasantly conversational.

"Stop the car and let me out," Nicolette said, trying to keep the panic from her voice as he turned again on another road, this one leading to the road that would take them out of town.

"I'm afraid I can't do that, and in any case I was in the middle of telling you something. It would be rude for you not to listen to me." There was a touch of self-righteous narcissism in his voice, as if he just assumed she would want to hear anything and everything he might have to say to her.

"Tell me what you think I need to hear and then let me out of this car." She would have used her cell phone, but she'd raced out of the café so fast she'd left it and her purse at the booth.

She glanced to the backseat and noted that both of the handles on the doors had also been removed, making it impossible for her to climb over the seat and make an escape.

"I was starting to tell you that I went about this wrong way from the very beginning. Initially, I figured if I had Sammy in my physical custody, then I could use some friends of mine in the New York court system to get legal custody of him."

Even though she'd suspected as much, she stared at him in horror. "So, you were behind the kidnapping attempts."

"I know, pretty stupid, but I wasn't thinking clearly at the time." He took a sudden turn off the road into a field, the car bumping and rocking over the rough terrain as he headed for a stand of trees in the distance.

Every muscle in her body tensed as he pulled up near the trees and then cut the engine. He unbuckled his seat belt and turned to face her. "This all would have been so much easier if you'd still been in the city. You have no idea how much it's costing me to be here now, all the people who had to be paid off to provide an alibi."

Her heart beat hard and fast. "Why would you need an alibi to come out here and visit your ex-wife and son?"

"When I heard about my father's will and realized the bastard had left me virtually nothing and instead had left you and Sammy almost everything, I have to admit that I was filled with a mindless rage. My first thought was just to get Sammy. Once I gained custody of him then I'd have access to his inheritance. Unfortunately that didn't work out. So, here we are and I have a new plan, one that is virtually foolproof."

Nicolette shrank against the door as he pulled a gun from his pocket. "Samuel, this is crazy."

"Unfortunately, you are the only thing standing between me and millions of dollars. Once you're out of the way, Sammy and his money will be mine. Over the last year or so my monthly allowance hasn't been enough to keep me in the lifestyle I need. Now I'm going to get out of the car and let you out, too."

She wanted to scream, but knew the odds of anyone hearing her in this vast field were minimal. "Samuel, surely we can work this out. You can't do this. If you kill me, then you'll be the first person they look at as a suspect."

"They can look all they want, but they'll never be able to tie me to a crime here in Bitterroot. I used a friend's private plane to get to Oklahoma City. I'm not listed on the passenger manifesto. This car is stolen and can't be traced back to me, and I have half a dozen men who will swear I spent the day skeet shooting with them and then having drinks at one of their sport lodges in upstate New York."

He got out of the car and slammed the driver door. As she watched him stride around the front of the car, her mind raced with a million thoughts.

Had Cassie seen where she'd gone? Who had been at the wheel of the car? It was possible she hadn't even looked out of the window blinds when Nicolette had run out of the café.

But was it possible Cassie had seen Samuel and had then called Lucas? That Lucas had contacted Dillon and his men and they were all searching for her now? Oh, please let it be so.

Samuel reached the passenger door and Nicolette pulled her legs up to her chest, knowing she couldn't depend on any rescue from anyone else. She had to do whatever she could to save herself.

He opened the door and she kicked her legs, striking him midcenter. He grunted and stumbled backward and she flew out of the car, intent on running as fast as she could for the cover of the trees.

He might eventually kill her, but she didn't intend to make it easy for him. She had taken only a few steps when he grabbed her hair from the back and pulled her to the ground.

She scrambled back to her feet, facing the man she'd once believed she loved, the man who had fathered her beautiful son. Sammy. Her heart cried for her child, who would be lost and alone in the custody of his cold, heartless father.

"I'll give you the money," she said and tried to ignore the gun that once again he pointed at her center. "I'll sign whatever paperwork needs to be signed to make sure you get the money."

"It's too late for that now. Besides, I'm not going to spend the rest of my life looking over my shoulder for you to come after me. It ends here, Nicolette. You can blame my father for this. If he hadn't been such a self-righteous bastard and done the right thing by naming me beneficiary, then we wouldn't be here now."

They both turned at the sound of an approaching vehicle. The familiar black pickup appeared to drive erratically across the field and came to a stop some distance from where Samuel had pulled Nicolette up next to him, the gun pressed tightly against her side.

Lucas! Her heart leaped with both hope and fear for him.

He opened his truck door and wobbled out, a goofy smile on his face. "Hey, Nikki, what's happening? What are you doing out here in the middle of Miller's Field?"

His words slurred together and he leaned heavily against the open door. Nicolette's mind raced. He appeared to be drunk as a skunk, but she knew he rarely drank and he'd never be here now drunk. He was playing a game and she knew that it was important that she play along.

"Get rid of him," Samuel whispered harshly, the gun stabbing her in the side.

"Lucas, you're drunk. Go home and sleep it off," she shouted to him.

"I just knocked back a few at the Watering Hole. Who is your friend?" Lucas left the truck and took two steps forward.

"I'll kill him right before I kill you," Samuel whispered in her ear. "I said get rid of him now."

"This is my ex-husband and we're in the middle of something here. Just leave us alone, Lucas. Go back to the ranch and get some hot coffee or some sleep."

"So, this is like a little family reunion," he replied, again a loopy smile curving his lips. "So, is Sammy here, too?"

"He's back at the ranch. I'll be home soon, and Cassie is going to be angry with you if you don't get back there right now."

"Okay, okay. It was nice meeting you, ex-husband." Lucas stumbled back to his truck door and got inside.

Nicolette watched in horror as he started the engine, pulled a U-turn and left the field, leaving her alone with a man who intended to kill her.

Chapter 17

Lucas drove down the road a short distance and then cut his engine and jumped out of the truck. With his gun in hand, he raced back toward the wooded area near where Samuel and Nicolette were, his heart pounding so hard he could scarcely breathe.

After speaking with Dillon and being assured that any dark sedan would be stopped before leaving town, Lucas had tried to crawl into Samuel's mind.

He'd realized that if he were Samuel, he wouldn't want Nicolette taken out of town. If he intended her harm, he'd want that to happen here in and around Bitterroot, where a local investigation would occur.

Lucas figured Samuel would want to get Nicolette into an isolated area, and a farmer's field with no fences would be just what he'd look for. It had been by sheer luck that he'd spied the car in the distance on the Miller property.

The first thing he'd needed to do was check out the situation, and thankfully it appeared that Samuel had fallen for his drunken cowboy act.

But Lucas had seen the glint of silver of the gun in Samuel's hand and he knew the situation was dire. Samuel had no interest in allowing Nicolette to leave that field alive. He had millions of reasons to ensure she never left that field.

Lucas now approached the trees from the opposite side, grateful that he hadn't heard a gunshot yet. If only Nicolette could stall long enough for him to get into position, then hopefully he could take out Samuel before Nicolette got hurt.

He'd never seen this coming. They'd all been so focused on protecting Sammy, they'd never realized that Nicolette could be a target. He silently cursed his oversight now as he entered the woods.

He was grateful that the tree branches were spring supple, and he made little noise as he stealthily maneuvered in the direction where he'd seen Samuel and Nicolette standing.

He heard them before he got a visual of them.

"Just let me go, Samuel," Nicolette said. "I won't tell anyone you were here. I'll sign whatever you want me to sign. Sammy and I were doing fine without your father's money."

"You say that now, but that's because I've got the gun and you don't," Samuel replied. "I'd say you'd be able to claim a case of signing papers under duress. Now, move away from the car."

Lucas stepped behind a tree that gave him a perfect vantage point. Nicolette stood by the front of the car as if knowing that if he shot her there the possibility of damage to the engine might occur.

Smart woman, he thought, even as his blood ran cold in his veins. The standoff was seconds from ending, and he could smell Samuel's frustration.

There were two ways this could end…Samuel could shoot Nicolette and then Lucas would shoot Samuel. That scenario was absolutely unacceptable. The only other way to bring this to an end and ensure Nicolette's safety was for him to become Samuel's target.

He had to hope that luck would be on his side, that he could draw Samuel's attention and get off a shot before the man shot him.

As he thought about Sammy not having his mother, as he thought of the world not having Nicolette in it, he stepped out from behind the tree where he'd been hidden.

"Hey, Samuel," Lucas yelled.

Samuel swung to face him and Lucas fired his gun. At the same time he heard the sharp bang of Samuel's weapon and felt a piercing pain in his shoulder.

Nicolette stared in shock as Samuel fell to the ground, clutching his thigh and screaming in agony. She released a sob and quickly kicked Samuel's gun well out of his reach and then ran to Lucas.

With tears streaming down her face, she wrapped her arms around his neck and held tight. She sobbed, talking incoherently between gasps. "He was going to kill me to get custody of Sammy. He just wants the money. He told me Sammy was in the car. I wasn't thinking straight when I saw him."

"It's all right now," Lucas said as he held her tight. He breathed in the scent of her hair, felt the warmth of

her body even as his own ebbed away. "I kept my promise. You and Sammy are safe now."

He was vaguely aware of Samuel's groans of pain,
but they seemed to be coming from farther and farther away. He finally disentangled from her, and as she
stepped back from him she gasped.

"Oh my God, Lucas, you're hurt." Tears began to
race down her face again.

"Just a little flesh wound," he replied, his own voice
sounding funny to his ears. It took an enormous amount
of effort for him to get his cell phone from his pocket.
He held it out to her. "Call Dillon. Tell him we're in
Miller's Field. I think I need to sit down for a minute."

He slid to sit on the ground next to his truck and
leaned back. Cold. He was so cold. He was grateful that
Samuel had gone quiet, and sweet relief rushed through
him as he heard Nicolette make the call to Dillon.

Safe. She was safe now. Sammy would be safe now,
as well. He'd done his job. He'd kept his promise. This
thought comforted him as he slid into a peaceful, em-
bracing darkness.

Blood. There was so much blood. Lucas's entire
shoulder and chest were soaked in it. Afraid to look
at his wound, fearing that even moving his shirt away
might do more damage, Nicolette sat beside him and
wept as she held his cold, lifeless hand.

"Don't you die on me, Lucas Taylor," she cried. "You
don't have to love me, but you can't die." Not like this…
not for her. He'd sacrificed his own safety by calling
out to Samuel, by drawing his attention away from her.

Lucas had shot to wound, but Samuel had shot to

kill. She glanced over to where Samuel remained on the ground, obviously unconscious.

He'd tried to steal his son away. He'd intended to kill her, all for the love of money. Even with the trust fund, Samuel would never have had enough.

She squeezed Lucas's hand as she continued to cry. "Hang on, Lucas. Please hang on."

Sirens sounded in the distance, indicating help was on the way. Within minutes emergency vehicles were racing toward her. She motioned the ambulance to where Lucas was slumped against his truck.

Dillon rushed to her side as the paramedics bent over Lucas and then began to load him on a gurney. "It was Samuel," Nicolette said, and pointed to where he remained on the ground.

Dillon shouted for another gurney and sent several deputies to see to Samuel. "Samuel brought me out here to kill me and somehow Lucas found us and he saved me. He shot Samuel and Samuel shot him. Lucas took the bullet that was meant for me."

She looked at the ambulance where they had loaded Lucas and were now wheeling Samuel on a gurney to also be loaded. "He can't die." She grabbed hold of Dillon's hand. "Please don't let Lucas die."

Dillon squeezed her hand reassuringly. "He's a tough guy. I imagine it will take more than a single bullet from a city slicker to put him down. Come on, I'll take you to the hospital and we can talk more on the way."

By that time the ambulance had left with a wail of the siren and swirling lights. Dillon led Nicolette to his car, and while they drove to the hospital he questioned her about everything that had happened that had brought her to the field with Samuel.

She told him everything that Samuel had told her, about initially acting impulsively and just wanting to grab Sammy and then realizing the easiest way to get to the money was to get rid of her.

She wrapped her arms around her shoulders, chilled despite the warmth of the day. Was Lucas still alive? It didn't matter that he couldn't give her his love. He'd given her life, but she didn't want the price of that to be his own.

While he drove, Dillon continued to ask questions and promised to coordinate with the New York detectives to see that Samuel lived a very different kind of lifestyle from what he was accustomed to…one behind bars.

By the time they reached the small Bitterroot hospital, both Lucas and Samuel were in the emergency room and Nicolette was relegated to a chair in the small waiting room.

Dillon eased down next to her. "Could I use your phone?" she asked. "I left mine in my purse at the café and I don't know where Sammy is."

"I imagine he's with Cassie. I sent a deputy to the café after Lucas called me to tell her to gather your things and go home." Dillon handed her his phone.

Cassie answered on the first ring, and when she heard Nicolette's voice she burst into tears. "Thank God you're okay."

"I'm fine. How's Sammy?"

"He's been stuck like glue to Nick's side since Lucas left. I haven't told him anything about what happened. I just told him you had some extra errands to run in town and would be home later. Where are you now?"

"I'm at the hospital. Lucas was shot." Nicolette swallowed against the sob that rose up inside her.

"How did that happen?" Cassie asked with a gasp.

"I'll explain it all when I get home. I just need to wait here until I know for sure that Lucas is okay."

"Don't you worry about things here. Sammy is fine. We're all fine. You just do what you need to do and we'll be waiting for you when you get home."

Nicolette hung up and handed the phone back to Dillon. Now that she knew Sammy was well taken care of, all her thoughts went to the man she loved, the man who had saved her life.

He had to be okay. He'd already overcome so much in his life. She couldn't stand the thought that she might be responsible for his death.

It felt like forever before a young man in scrubs came out and introduced himself as Dr. Frank Neilson. Both Nicolette and Dillon stood to greet him.

"Is he okay?" Nicolette asked, her heart thumping wildly.

"The bullet shattered his femur bone and so he's undergoing surgery to put pins and rods in place," Dr. Neilson said.

Nicolette stared at him in confusion and then realized the doctor had assumed she was asking about her ex-husband's condition. "Not him. I don't care about him. What about Lucas? Is he okay?"

"The bullet entered and exited the fleshy portion of his upper arm. He lost a lot of blood and has required a transfusion, but other than being sore for a while, he'll be just fine."

Nicolette sagged against Dillon with relief. He'll be just fine. That's all she'd needed to hear.

"We're going to keep him here overnight, but he should be ready to go home tomorrow," Dr. Neilson continued. "As far as Samuel is concerned, he will be our guest for several days."

"And once he's on his feet, so to speak, he'll be my guest for a while," Dillon said.

"Can I see him?" Nicolette asked.

Dr. Neilson didn't make the same mistake. He obviously knew exactly whom she wanted to see. "I'll warn you he's conscious, but he's pretty drugged up right now."

"That's okay. I just need to see him," Nicolette replied.

"He's in room 112."

She was vaguely aware of Neilson and Dillon continuing to talk together as she left them and hurried down the hallway in the direction of Lucas's room.

Her heart squeezed at the sight of him in the pristine white bed, his eyes closed and his left shoulder heavily bandaged. So close. If the bullet had struck him an inch or two to the right, she wouldn't be seeing him right now.

He'd be dead.

She had no intention of bothering him, but as she stood silently in the doorway, his eyes opened and he turned his head toward her.

"I knew it was you. I could smell your perfume." He sounded as drunk as he'd pretended when he'd first shown up in the field.

"Oh, Lucas, you crazy man, you could have been killed." She moved from the doorway to sit in the chair next to his bed.

"It was nothing," he replied, his eyes slightly glazed from the pain medication he'd been given. "What about Samuel?"

"The bullet shattered his femur. He's in surgery now and once he gets well he'll go to jail." She wanted so badly to touch him, to curl up next to him in the bed, to place her hand over his heart to assure herself it beat strong and with life.

"He's going away for a long time. You and Sammy will never have to worry again." He gave her another loopy smile. "It's over, Nicolette. The danger is finally gone." His eyes slowly drifted closed.

Nicolette sat for several long moments, just gazing at him, just loving him. Finally she stood to leave, but before going she leaned over him and gently swept a strand of his shaggy dark hair away from his forehead.

His eyes opened once again and his gaze held hers. "I couldn't let him kill you because I love you." His voice was a mere whisper and then his eyes closed once again.

She stood frozen in place, waiting for him to wake up again, wanting him to repeat what he'd just said to her. But he remained asleep and finally she crept out of the room.

Dillon stood in the waiting room. "I told you he was tough," he said. "Come on and I'll take you home."

I love you. He'd said the words. She hadn't imagined them, she thought as they left the hospital. But he was drugged and probably wouldn't even remember he'd spoken the words out loud. He possibly hadn't even meant them.

Still, they rang in her ears, sweet with promise and bringing a fool's hope that she knew better than to entertain. The man had been practically unconscious. She'd be crazy to seriously consider anything he'd said to her.

Chapter 18

Lucas was released from the hospital Wednesday afternoon. Nick drove in to pick him up, and although Lucas felt weak and his shoulder burned like fire, he was more than ready to leave the hospital behind.

Knowing he wouldn't be worth anything for a few days, he had Nick take him directly to his bunk. There was no reason for him to go to the main house. The danger had passed and his job as bodyguard was finished.

"Are you sure you don't need anything?" Nick asked as he and Lucas got out of his truck in front of Lucas's place.

"I've got my pain pills and really all I need is some extra sleep and time to rest. I'll be fine," Lucas assured his friend.

"If the weather forecast holds true, the takedown of the old shed may be pushed back from Friday. We're supposed to have some storms in the area tomorrow and Friday."

"Just keep me posted. I doubt I'll be much help when it happens, but I'd like to at least be there when the old place comes down."

"I'll let you know if and when plans change," Nick assured him, then with quick goodbyes, Lucas entered his bunk and Nick drove away.

Lucas immediately took two pain pills and then stretched out on his bed. It felt as if it had been forever since he'd been here...here where there was no scent of Nicolette, no scampering footsteps of Sammy.

Isn't this what he'd wanted? Peace and quiet, without distractions from Nicolette or Sammy? Hadn't he believed himself more than ready to distance himself from the woman and young boy who had made him think of foolish fantasies he would never embrace?

This was where he belonged, in the room that Cass had assigned him when he'd been seventeen years old and streetwise but life stupid.

He closed his eyes, trying not to think about Nicolette and Sammy. He snoozed off and on, awakened regularly by his fellow cowboys who stopped in to check on him.

They were his family, he reminded himself. All he needed to live a peaceful, fulfilling life was right here on this ranch. He didn't even want to contemplate the future if Cassie decided to sell the place. For now he was where he belonged.

It was early evening when a soft knock fell on his door. Instinctively he knew it was Nicolette and Sammy. Steeling himself for the emotional stress of seeing them, he yelled for them to come in.

Sammy barreled through the door first, halting in his tracks as he stared at the bandage on Lucas's shoulder.

"It's okay, Sammy. I'm fine," Lucas said as he saw tears welling up in Sammy's eyes. He patted the edge of the bed, inviting Sammy to sit.

"Mom said you were okay, but I had to see for myself," Sammy said, his voice trembling slightly as he eased down next to Lucas on the bed.

Lucas looked at Nicolette, who hovered in the doorway. "Come in and close the door," he said. "We don't want to let the bugs in."

She stepped inside and closed the door behind her. Instantly the room filled with the fragrance that would always evoke memories of her in his mind. "I couldn't keep him away," she said.

"Us cowboys got to stick together," Sammy replied. "Mom told me that you're a hero. You saved her life."

"I had to shoot your dad," Lucas said, hoping that Nicolette had already told Sammy that piece of information.

"He wasn't a nice man. You're a good guy and he wasn't," Sammy said. "He was going to hurt my mom and you had to stop him. I'm glad you saved my mom and I'm glad you're okay. But that looks like a big boo-boo."

"It's mostly bandage. I'll be back to work in a day or two."

"Good, 'cause we have to show Mom how I can ride Candy, and we need to get her up on a horse, too. We've got lots of stuff to do when you get better," Sammy said.

"Sammy, Lucas will be back to his regular work when he gets better," Nicolette said. "He won't have time to spend with us anymore."

Sammy leaned against Lucas's side and smiled up at him with confidence. "He'll make time for us, Mom."

"Come on, let's leave Lucas to rest. You've seen that he's okay now," Nicolette said.

Sammy got up from the bed and moved toward the door, where Nicolette stood. "I'll come and visit you tomorrow, okay Lucas?"

"We'll see," Nicolette said before Lucas could reply. And then they were gone, leaving behind the scent of loving little boy and Nicolette's haunting perfume.

In all his years on earth, Lucas had never felt so alone. How on earth had a pint-size wannabe cowboy and his city slicker mother managed to get so deeply beneath his skin?

Somehow, someway, he had to pick them out like ticks, pull them off his skin and out of his heart. The problem was he had a feeling they'd already burrowed in too deep.

True to the weather forecast, it rained Thursday and Friday, postponing the teardown of the shed. Cassie had set the new date for the following Thursday, hoping the ground would be dry enough by then to get in some equipment.

Tuesday morning Nicolette awakened to the sun shining through her bedroom window. She rolled over on her side and stared out, thinking of the past two days.

She hadn't seen Lucas, although yesterday morning Nick had appeared to take Sammy to visit with him and yesterday evening Dusty had come by to take Sammy to see Lucas again.

Last night she'd told Sammy that they weren't going

to leave Bitterroot, that she intended to find them a nice house so they could stay here forever.

Sammy was over the moon at the news that they weren't returning to the city. He'd spent the evening drawing different pictures of houses he'd like to live in, of a horse that looked suspiciously like Candy, whom he would keep in a stable that was drawn next to the house.

With the danger to Sammy and herself finally over, Nicolette was more certain than ever of what she wanted her future to look like.

She'd gotten on her computer and contacted the University of Oklahoma in Oklahoma City to get information about continuing her education beginning in September. Today she intended to take Sammy and do a little house shopping and get an idea of what was available.

Everything was falling into place. Except Lucas. Despite his words of love in the hospital, he'd done nothing in the past couple of days to follow up on them. While he'd visited with Sammy, he hadn't asked to see or speak to her.

If she'd had any doubts as to whether his dopey words of love had meant anything, the past two days had given her the answer.

Still, she didn't intend her heartache over Lucas Taylor to put a damper on a day of house hunting with her son. It was going to be a day of future possibilities, of joy and laughter, as she and her best man decided on their future forever home.

As if summoned by her thoughts alone, Sammy appeared in her doorway. Seeing that she was awake, he jumped into her bed and bounced up and down with excitement.

"We're going to find our home today. We're going to find our home today," he said in a singsong fashion. "Get up. Get out of bed, lazy head. We have to find the perfect house for us."

Nicolette laughed. "There's no guarantee we'll find our new home today, but at least we'll get some ideas. First we need some breakfast and we need to get dressed. We can't meet our new home in our pajamas."

Sammy giggled and then squealed as Nicolette tickled him. "Stop!" he said with a laugh.

She finally stopped, loving the sound of laughter, the knowledge that she no longer had to be afraid. Samuel was still in the hospital under arrest and with a guard at the door. Once he was well enough he'd face enough charges that she'd never have to look over her shoulder for him again.

"Let's go make breakfast so we can get dressed and go," Sammy exclaimed.

As he raced from the room, Nicolette got out of bed and pulled a robe around her nightgown. She didn't bother brushing her hair as she'd done before each morning when Lucas had been in the house.

She met Cassie in the hallway, also clad in her pajamas and a robe and still looking half-asleep. "I miss having a man in the house to get up early and make the coffee," she grumbled as the two of them headed down the stairs.

"Where's Adam this morning? He is usually here fairly early with the coffee on."

"He and Flint left last night to go into Oklahoma City for an early morning meeting with the meat-packaging company." Cassie flung herself into a chair at the kitchen table.

"And you shouldn't have gone?" Nicolette asked as she set about making a pot of coffee.

"I probably should have, but I didn't want to. I told Adam to take care of things. Besides, with the shed coming down tomorrow, I imagine in less than a month I'll be out of here and back home."

"We're going to find our new home today," Sammy said as he came into the kitchen. He sat down next to Cassie. "I wish you'd just stay here, too. It would be nice if we could all be together in the same town."

Cassie reached over and gave Sammy's dark hair a tousle. "That would be nice, but I'm just not a country girl. Though this has been a nice break, I'm ready to get back to the city."

"And I'm ready for some bacon and eggs," Sammy replied. "We have to fuel up for our house hunt, right?"

"Right," Nicolette replied. Once the coffee was dripping into the carafe, she pulled out a skillet and got to work frying bacon.

As she made breakfast, Sammy filled Cassie's ears with everything he was looking for in a house. "It has to have a front porch because Mom likes to sit on the porch in the evenings," he said. "And a big yard, big enough to have a horse for me and maybe a dog." He slid a glance at Nicolette. "We'll have to see about the dog," he added when Nicolette didn't bite.

"And how many bedrooms will this mansion of yours have?" Cassie asked.

"Three. One for me, one for visitors and one for Mom and Lucas."

Nicolette gasped and turned from the stove. "Honey, Lucas isn't going to live with us."

"I think he would if you'd ask him. He loves us,

Mom, and he doesn't have any family of his own. We could be his family and I think he'd be real happy."

"It's much more complicated than that, Sammy." Nicolette turned back to the stove to remove the scrambled eggs from the skillet.

"I don't know why it's gotta be complicated. He loves us and we love him and that's that," Sammy exclaimed.

If only things were so easy in real life, Nicolette thought later as she got dressed for the day's excursion. But real life was rarely easy and there was no way to effectively explain to a six-year-old the ins and outs of adult relationships.

May had gone and June had ushered in the past couple of days of rain. But with the sun shining brightly, Nicolette chose a pair of jeans and her boots and topped it with a sleeveless red cotton blouse that would be comfortable if the afternoon got unusually warm.

She'd checked the real estate section of the morning paper and had several addresses to look at. She hadn't contacted a real estate agent yet. She preferred this be an adventure for herself and Sammy. There would be time enough for a real estate professional when they found something they were really interested in.

It was just after nine when she and Sammy stepped out of the back door and headed toward the garage where Cass's car was stored.

They were halfway there when she saw Lucas approaching from the bunkhouse. She couldn't help the way her heart swelled at the sight of him clad in a pair of worn, tight jeans and a black T-shirt that showed that his bulky bandage was gone and only a band of gauze showed beneath the short sleeve of his shirt.

"Lucas!" Sammy shouted and ran ahead to meet him.

Nicolette made it to the garage and paused outside the door as the two males caught up with her.

"How are you feeling?" she asked.

"Better each day," he replied. "I heard through the grapevine that you were going house hunting today."

"Always nice to know that the grapevine is alive and well," she replied lightly.

"I think you should go with us," Sammy said. "I think you should help us find a house where the three of us could live and be happy together."

It was as if Sammy had become a wind-up toy and somebody had turned the key too tightly. "You could be our family, Lucas, and we could be yours. I know you love us and we love you."

Sammy grabbed Lucas's hand and Nicolette knew she should stop her son, but at the moment he appeared to be a seething little bundle of raw emotion.

"I know you love us, Lucas. Don't you want to be my dad? Don't you want to marry my mom and be happy for the rest of your life?"

Lucas's features tautened and he gazed at Nicolette, as if seeking some kind of help, but he was on his own as far as she was concerned.

He'd told her he loved her while in the hospital. She knew that he loved her son. She could see the depth of love for them shining from his eyes. Happiness was within his reach, but he had to be the one to stretch out his hand and take it.

"Lucas?" Sammy dropped Lucas's hand and took a step back from him. His little face held such hope, such certainty that his dream of a new home and a full family would come true.

"Sammy, I do love you and I love your mom, but I

never told you that we would all move in together and be a family. I always thought you and your mom would be going back to New York City."

"But now we're not. We're staying here, Lucas, so we could be a family." Sammy's heart was in his trembling voice and Nicolette could stand it no longer.

"Come on, Sammy. We're going to find the best house ever for you and me to live," she said. "Go on and get in the car."

Sammy headed for the garage and Nicolette turned to gaze at Lucas.

"I think you do love us, Lucas, and I believe we could have had a wonderful future together, but I think you're afraid to trust in that love." She took a step back from him, her heart breaking all over again as she saw the dark torment in his eyes.

"Afraid?" Sammy appeared at her side once again. "Cowboys aren't afraid. Real cowboys face their fears and Lucas is a real cowboy, right?"

"Not this time, buddy," Lucas said, his words strangled as they left him. He half turned to leave, but paused as Sammy cried out his name.

"You lied to me." Sammy pulled his hat from his head and threw it on the ground. "If you're a real cowboy, then I don't want to be one anymore." He stepped in the center of his hat and then ran back to the garage.

The sound of the slam of the car door made Lucas visibly jump. "I'm sorry," he said.

"Don't be sorry for us. We're going to be just fine. You're the one who is choosing a life alone." She turned and hurried into the garage and got into the car, where Sammy was slumped against the passenger seat, tears seeping from his eyes.

"Sammy, I know you're hurt right now. But we're going to be just fine." She started the car engine and cursed herself for allowing her son to get so close to Lucas.

She should have halted their relationship the moment it had begun, but she'd been caught up in her own emotions where Lucas was concerned.

She pulled out of the garage, grateful that there was no sign of Lucas in the area. It took plenty of talking during the drive to town before Sammy straightened up and appeared to put his sadness about Lucas behind him.

To be as resilient as a child, she thought as she tightened her fingers around the steering wheel. Oh, she knew Sammy's heartbreak over Lucas wasn't over, but her son had the tremendous ability to compartmentalize and right now he appeared to embrace the excitement of finding a home.

"Why don't we start just by driving up and down streets and seeing if we find for-sale signs on houses," Nicolette suggested. "You can write down the addresses for me and then we can make arrangements to look at any that interest us."

She pulled a small notepad from her purse, along with a pen, and handed them to Sammy. "I'd like to find a place where I could keep a horse," he said. A frown tugged his lips downward. "Even if I'm not going to be a real cowboy anymore, I could still have a horse, right?"

"We'll see what we find in town and then we'll work our way out a little bit to find a place with more land. Maybe a dog would be easier to keep than a horse," she suggested.

"If I'm not going to have a dad, then a dog might be good," Sammy replied.

"And you're going to meet so many new friends and be busy doing fun new things." She slowed the car as they reached the city limits. "We're going to have a wonderful life here, Sammy."

"I know. I just think it would have been so much better if Cowboy Lucas could be with us."

Sammy's wistful words squeezed her heart tight. Still, she knew there was no way she could make Lucas love more than he feared. She couldn't love him enough to help him overcome whatever barriers stood in his way of opening himself up completely to love.

All she could do was find her own little piece of heaven here in Bitterroot and build a happy life for herself and her son.

Chapter 19

It was the longest day of Lucas's life. No matter what work he tried to lose himself in, his head was filled with Sammy's utter heartbreak and Nicolette's sad eyes.

He tried not to think about how it would be, to let himself go, to get past the fear that he hadn't even realized had been a constant companion to him since the day his mother had abandoned him.

What if he allowed himself to fully embrace Sammy and Nicolette in his heart, in his life, and they wound up finding him inadequate, not worthy to keep, and walked away from him?

Alone. He was meant to go through life alone, depending only on himself as he had done since he was fifteen. Nicolette and Sammy had been a tantalizing glimpse into a fantasy he didn't believe could come true.

It was just after dinner and still the house hunters

hadn't arrived home. Lucas found himself at Cass's gravesite in the small cemetery, picking weeds that had sprung up around the granite stone with the recent rain.

"Chasing ghosts?"

Lucas looked up to see Nick standing nearby. "Chasing weeds," he replied. He straightened and Nick gestured for him to join him on a concrete bench that Cass had placed in the cemetery when her husband had died.

Lucas sat next to Nick and gazed toward the house. "Unfortunately, I was just around the corner of the garage when Nicolette and Sammy left this morning," Nick said. "The little buckaroo had a bit of a meltdown."

"Yeah, he'd gotten it into his head that I was going to marry Nicolette and be his daddy and we'd find a new place to live happily ever after as a family."

"And you aren't in love with Nicolette?" Nick asked.

Lucas wanted to say no. He wanted to distance himself from the emotions the beautiful brunette stirred inside him, but he couldn't lie. "I'm in love with her and I love Sammy, too."

"So, what's the problem?" Nick eyed him from beneath the brim of his cowboy hat.

Lucas released a tortured sigh. "After all these years together, you should know that we're all bad bets for relationships. None of us have ever had a meaningful relationship since we've been here. That should tell you something."

"Yeah, it tells me you're one lucky guy to find somebody you love, somebody who loves you back. None of us has been so lucky, but that doesn't mean it isn't something we all want," Nick replied. "You've got a chance to be more than just one of Cass's cowboys. You have a chance to be a husband and a father."

Nick stood. "You know I love you as a brother, Lucas. I don't want to tell you what to do, but I also don't want to see you just walk away from true happiness. Cass is gone and who knows what's going to happen around here. Nicolette isn't your mother, Lucas."

"I know that," Lucas replied, also rising from the bench. Rationally he knew that everything Nick said was right, but it was done...over.

Sammy would get over it and eventually so would Nicolette. She was a strong woman who would build her life on her terms, with or without him in it.

And he couldn't help but think this was what was best for her. Eventually she'd find a good man who would fulfill her dreams for herself and Sammy. He'd just reached the bunkhouse when he heard the car pull in and head toward the garage. He didn't look back but instead opened his unit door and disappeared inside.

It was long after dark, after Sammy had gone to bed and Cassie had retired to her room, that Nicolette sat on the back porch and thought about the day.

It had taken a little while to get both herself and her son into a festive mood after the encounter with Lucas, but eventually they had managed to put the sadness behind them and get on with the day.

They had started on the south side of town and found two houses with for-sale signs in the yard before lunch. The first they'd both agreed was too small and the second didn't have a porch that Sammy insisted they needed.

They'd stopped for lunch at the café, where Daisy had told them about a couple more houses for sale north of Main Street. The waitress had seemed genuinely pleased that the two of them intended to make Bitter-root their permanent home.

She'd talked to Sammy about some of the local boys his age and the after-school programs that would be available for him to enjoy.

For the first time since arriving in town, Nicolette felt a sense of community that she knew would only grow as she and Sammy immersed themselves in their new lives.

They'd happily taken off after lunch to check out the new places Daisy had told them about and found one that held enough potential that she intended to check with the real estate office the next day to set up an appointment to see the inside.

"Did you find what you were looking for today?"

The deep voice came out of the darkness of the night to her left and not only sent a shaft of pain sweeping through her but also a touch of anger. If he didn't want them, if he didn't want to be a part of their life, then he needed to just leave them alone.

She drew in a deep breath and released it slowly as he stepped into view, Sammy's cowboy hat in his hand. "I looked for that when we got home, but I thought the wind must have blown it away," she said.

"I know he was mad at me, but I also knew he'd probably eventually want it back." He held it out to her. She took it and set it on the porch next to her.

"Thank you," she replied and wished he would just go away.

"So, you never answered me. Did you find any places today that caught your interest?" he asked, and as if to further her irritation, he moved Sammy's hat and sat down next to her.

"What difference does it make to you, Lucas? You've made it clear that you ride alone, that you have no desire to build a life with me and my son, so why do you care whether we found something interesting today or not?"

His features were visible by the light that spilled out of the kitchen windows, and she wished the lights were off and the moon wasn't quite so bright.

"I was just trying to break the ice before I got to the real reason I wanted to talk to you. I realized something this evening while I was cleaning off Sammy's hat." He didn't look at her but rather stared out toward the lunar-lit pasture.

"And what did you realize?" she asked, trying to control the sudden quick acceleration of her heartbeat.

"I love that kid like he's my own, and breaking his heart today shattered pieces of my own I didn't even know I possessed."

"He'll get over it," she replied.

"But I don't know if I will. I don't know if I'll ever get over loving you and being foolish enough to let you go." He turned to face her, his eyes glittering in the light. "I've had my eye on a place just outside of town for the last couple of months. It's not as big a spread as this one, but it is enough land that I could make a living raising cattle and horses. It's got a nice three-bedroom house on it and the house even has a front and back porch."

"So, why haven't you bought it?" What was he doing? Torturing her on purpose? Talking about his potential future plans for his own happiness?

"I think I knew the moment I saw the place that it was meant for a family, not for a man who rides alone. And then I realized this evening that I haven't ridden alone for the last month and I've never been as happy as I've been this past month."

Once again Nicolette's heart began to dance an unsteady rhythm. He reached out and took one of her hands in his. She wanted to pull away, but couldn't as crazy, wild hope soared through her.

"I feel like I'm at a crossroads in my life. I can continue to be the poor, scared kid who was abandoned by my mother, or I can be the man I was meant to be, the man who Cass believed me to be, and reach out for love. I need you, Nicolette. I need you and Sammy. I thought I could let you go, but I can't. I don't want to ride alone anymore. I want you and Sammy in my life forever."

He stood and took her hand to pull her up from the porch. "So, what do you think?" His moonlit gaze held a vulnerability she'd never seen before.

She wrapped her arms around his neck. "Forever sounds wonderful to me."

His lips took hers and tears of happiness slid from her eyes as she tasted his love, her future in his kiss. This was her home. This was where she belonged, with Lucas through the rest of their lives.

When the kiss finally ended, he gazed at her with eyes that appeared to be lit from within. "I promise you, Nicolette, I am going to love you and Sammy forever, and you know that a real cowboy never breaks his promise."

As they kissed again, Nicolette knew that all her dreams were coming true in a dusty Oklahoma town called Bitterroot. She'd found herself here, she'd rediscovered dreams for herself and her son and she'd found the man who would add his love to her happily-ever-after.

Epilogue

Thursday morning at nine all of the cowboys were in the pasture next to the shed that was about to be taken down. A backhoe had been brought in, along with several huge Dumpster containers that would be filled with refuse and then taken away.

Once that was done, the cowboys would move in to pull up whatever was left of the old wooden flooring so a new shed could be built from the ground up.

Cassie stood talking to the backhoe driver while Lucas, Nicolette and Sammy stood some distance away. Yesterday Lucas had taken them to show them the house and property he'd had his eye on for a while.

It had been perfect. A three-bedroom ranch house with a large, airy kitchen and a living room Nicolette could instantly envision as their own.

The front porch led to a large yard perfect for catching fireflies and the back porch had a view of a barn, stables and lush green pasture complete with a pond.

The place had been empty for almost a year and needed some work to get it into move-in condition, but before the day was over Lucas had put up earnest money and signed contracts to buy.

Sammy's feet hadn't touched the ground since they'd told him that the three of them were going to be a family and live in the house that not only had enough property for horses, but also maybe a dog and eventually a new brother or sister.

Cassie stepped away from the backhoe and the driver started the engine. Cassie joined Nicolette, Lucas and Sammy, and in surprisingly short order the destroyed building was taken down to the ground.

As the backhoe began to scoop and fill the Dumpster containers, Nicolette couldn't help but wonder what would happen to the eleven of Cass's cowboys left when Cassie sold the ranch.

Raymond Humes and several of his men were visible on horseback along the property line. Cassie's meeting with the man had been put off by the events of the day that Samuel had taken Nicolette from the café. At the moment he and his men reminded Nicolette of circling vultures. She looked away from them.

Several of the cowboys got to work pulling up the wooden flooring that still remained. Lucas was just about to leave their side to join in the work when all hell broke loose.

Forest pulled up a large piece of wood from the ground and reeled backward, his cry of surprise even louder than the roar of the backhoe. He scrambled to his feet and raced a finger across his neck to get the back-hoe driver to shut down. Lucas ran forward.

"I wonder what's going on," Cassie said worriedly.

"Maybe he found some buried treasure," Sammy replied.

Several of the other men walked over to see what Forest had uncovered and reeled back in obvious shock. "Call Chief Bowie," Mac yelled to Cassie. "He needs to get out here right away."

Lucas raced back toward them, his face set in grim lines. "Sammy, why don't you run ahead and say hello to Candy in the stables."

"Okay," he agreed, and as he took off running Cassie and Nicolette stopped walking and looked at Lucas expectantly.

"I think we just found Wendy Bailey."

Cassie gasped as Nicolette reached for Lucas's hand. "The waitress who has been missing?" Cassie asked.

Lucas nodded. "We need to get Bowie out here because that's not all. I also saw a skeleton next to Wendy's body."

Cassie fumbled her cell phone out of her pocket and stepped away from Lucas and Nicolette to call the police chief. Nicolette squeezed Lucas's hand. "Who could be responsible for this?"

"I don't know, but why don't you take Sammy into the house. I don't want either of you to be out here when Dillon arrives. This isn't something either of you need to see."

Nicolette definitely agreed. Lucas headed back to where the other cowboys now stood in a group some distance from the fallen structure while she headed to the stables to get Sammy.

She found him in front of Candy's stall, stroking Candy's nose while sweet-talking her. He turned at the sound of her approach, but no smile lit his face. "Something bad has happened, hasn't it?" he asked.

Nicolette hesitated a moment and then nodded. "Yes, but it doesn't have anything to do with you or me or Lucas. Why don't you come inside the house with me and you can draw and color a picture of what you want your room to look like in the new house."

"Okay," Sammy agreed. "I think I want bunk beds for when I meet all my new friends and sometimes somebody comes over to spend the night."

"That sounds like a plan." She hurried him into the house as she heard a siren piercing the air.

She got Sammy settled at the kitchen table with paper and crayons, and she stood at the back door and watched as Chief Bowie's patrol car zoomed by the house and directly toward the shed site in the distance.

Within an hour there were half a dozen patrol cars along with the coroner's vehicle parked by the shed. Adam stood nearby with his arm around Cassie, and the rest of the men gathered in a group by Nick, who even from this distance she could tell was distraught.

Sammy finished his picture of his dream room and then moved on to drawing the front yard of the new house with Nicolette and Lucas seated on the porch and Sammy playing with a shaggy-haired dog.

A body bag was loaded into the coroner's van and drove away. She assumed Wendy's body was in the back and her heart squeezed tight with grief for the young woman she'd never met, a woman she would now never meet.

Her stomach twisted in knots as Lucas approached

the house, his features grim. He walked into the back door and instantly placed a smile on his face as Sammy showed him the pictures he'd drawn.

"I need to talk to your mother in the living room," he said. "Why don't you draw a picture of Candy in our stable at the new house because I have a feeling if your mother talked to Cassie we could manage to get her to let us take Candy with us when we move."

"That would be awesome!" Sammy grabbed for a fresh piece of paper while Lucas took Nicolette's hand and led her into the formal living room.

Only then did he look both grim and horrified as he faced her. "It's bad. It's really bad."

"What could be worse than Wendy's body found and a skeleton next to her?" Nicolette asked as she moved closer to him.

He stared at her hollowly. "Six more skeletons."

Nicolette gasped and reached for his hands. "My God, Lucas."

He squeezed her hands tightly. "It appears that somebody has been using the space under the flooring in the shed as a burial ground for years."

"So, what happens now?"

"An investigation will begin first in the case of Wendy's murder. As far as the skeletons are concerned, Bowie intends to call in a forensic anthropologist from Oklahoma City. Her first job will be to help identify the remains. Unfortunately Cassie isn't going to get her wish to sell this place anytime soon. It's now a crime scene and I have a feeling it's going to be quite a while before things are cleared up."

"She'll get through it. She's stronger than you all give her credit for," Nicolette replied.

He nodded. "I imagine all of us who have worked here for so long will be potential suspects, but I can't imagine any of them having anything to do with this."

He pulled her into an embrace. "This has nothing to do with us. We're going to work together to get that house ready for move-in and then the three of us are going to have a wonderful life together."

His words warmed her, excited her, but her excitement was tempered slightly by the question of what evil existed at the Holiday Ranch.

* * * * *

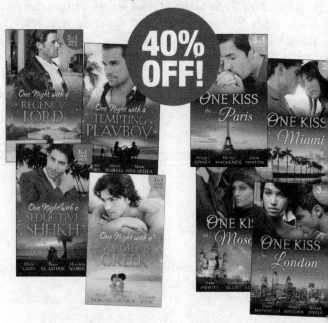

MILLS & BOON®

The Chatsfield Collection!

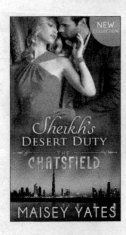

Style, spectacle, scandal…!

With the eight Chatsfield siblings happily married and settling down, it's time for a new generation of Chatsfields to shine, in this brand-new 8-book collection! The prospect of a merger with the Harrington family's boutique hotels will shape the future forever. But who will come out on top?

Find out at
www.millsandboon.co.uk/TheChatsfield2

SFIELD_PROMO_BK

ST_9

MILLS & BOON®
INTRIGUE
Romantic Suspense

A SEDUCTIVE COMBINATION OF DANGER AND DESIRE

A sneak peek at next month's titles...

In stores from 20th March 2015:

- **Reining in Justice** – Delores Fossen
  and **Agent Undercover** – Lisa Childs

- **Kansas City Cover-Up** – Julie Miller
  and **Manhunt** – Tyler Anne Snell

- **SWAT Secret Admirer** – Elizabeth Heiter
  and **Killshadow Road** – Paula Graves

Romantic Suspense
- **Cavanaugh Fortune** – Marie Ferrarella
- **Secret Agent Boyfriend** – Addison Fox

0315/46

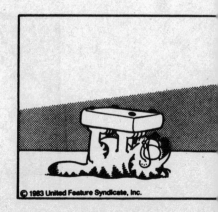

GARFIELD, I KNOW YOU'RE IN MY FERN. I CAN SEE YOUR TAIL

WHAT DO YOU HAVE TO SAY FOR YOURSELF?

© 1983 United Feature Syndicate, Inc.

IF YOU MUST KNOW, I AM A RARE CARNIVOROUS FERN, AND IF YOU DON'T MIND, I'D LIKE TO FINISH EATING YOUR CAT IN PEACE

JIM DAVIS

8-1

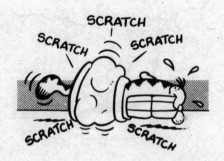

THERE IS ONE
THING I LIKE
ABOUT THIS
SWEATER

JPM DAVPS   3-10

© 1983 United Feature Syndicate, Inc.

HAPPY DIET, GARFIELD.
HERE'S A BANANA
FOR BREAKFAST

8-17   JIM DAVIS

BANG!

© 1983 United Feature Syndicate, Inc.

© 1983 United Feature Syndicate, Inc. 1-27

1-28

OH, A HEAT VENT

THE NEXT BEST TO MY SUNBEAM.

© 1983 United Feature Syndicate, Inc.

GEE...UH, THANKS, ODIE

CLUNK!

WHAT IS IT, GARFIELD?

I'D WAGER IT WOULD HAVE BEEN EASIER TO RECOGNIZE BEFORE IT WANDERED INTO TRAFFIC

© 1983 United Feature Syndicate, Inc.

© 1983 United Feature Syndicate, Inc.

JIM DAVIS   7-1

© 1983 United Feature Syndicate, Inc.

© 1983 United Feature Syndicate, Inc.

SILLY ME HAD TO FALL INTO THE HEATING VENT. NOW HERE AM, RESIDING DEEP WITHIN THE BOWELS OF MY HOME

9-6

FORCED TO SPEND MY REMAINING DAYS FENDING FOR MYSELF IN THE TIN TUNNELS OF THE DUCT WORK, THE SOLENOID JUNGLE OF THE WIRING SYSTEM AND THE POLYVINYL CHLORIDE PLAYGROUND IN THE CRAWL SPACE

HEY! I THINK THERE'S A BOOK HERE SOMEWHERE

© 1983 United Feature Syndicate, Inc.

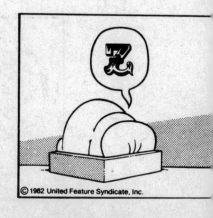

© 1983 United Feature Syndicate, Inc.

5-5   © 1983 United Feature Syndicate, Inc.

JOGGING IS MUCH MORE ENJOYABLE IF YOU HAVE THE PROPER MOTIVATION

THINK ABOUT
A BIG, JUICY
BONE, ODIE

DON'T MAKE FUN OF ODIE, GARFIELD. THAT'S NOT NICE

© 1983 United Feature Syndicate, Inc.

THAT'S EVEN LESS NICE

© 1983 United Feature Syndicate, Inc.

© 1983 United Feature Syndicate, Inc.

OTHER GARFIELD BOOKS AVAILABLE

Pocket Books	Price	ISBN
Bon Appetit	£3.50	1 84161 038 0
Byte Me	£3.50	1 84161 009 7
Double Trouble	£3.50	1 84161 008 9
A Gift For You	£3.50	1 85304 190 4
The Gladiator	£3.50	1 85304 941 7
Gooooooal!	£3.50	1 84161 037 2
Great Impressions	£3.50	1 85304 191 2
Hangs On	£2.99	1 85304 784 8
Here We Go Again	£2.99	0 948456 10 8
In Training	£3.50	1 85304 785 6
The Irresistible	£3.50	1 85304 940 9
Le Magnifique!	£3.50	1 85304 243 9
Let's Party	£3.50	1 85304 906 9
Light Of My Life	£3.50	1 85304 353 2
On The Right Track	£3.50	1 85304 907 7
Pick Of The Bunch	£2.99	1 85304 258 7
Says It With Flowers	£2.99	1 85304 316 8
Shove At First Sight	£3.50	1 85304 990 5
To Eat Or Not To Eat?	£3.50	1 85304 991 3
Wave Rebel	£3.50	1 85304 317 6
With Love From Me To You	£3.50	1 85304 392 3

new titles available Feb 2002:

No. 43 - Fun in the Sun	£3.50	1 84161 097 6
No. 44 - Eat My Dust	£3.50	1 84161 098 4

Theme Books		
Guide to Behaving Badly	£4.50	1 85304 892 5
Guide to Being a Couch Potato	£3.99	1 84161 039 9
Guide to Creatures Great & Small	£3.99	1 85304 998 0
Guide to Friends	£3.99	1 84161 040 2
Guide to Healthy Living	£3.99	1 85304 972 7
Guide to Insults	£3.99	1 85304 895 X
Guide to Pigging Out	£4.50	1 85304 893 3
Guide to Romance	£3.99	1 85304 894 1
Guide to The Seasons	£3.99	1 85304 999 9
Guide to Successful Living	£3.99	1 85304 973 5

new titles now available:

Guide to Coffee Mornings	£4.50	1 84161 086 0
Guide to Cat Napping	£4.50	1 84161 087 9

All Garfield books are available at your local bookshop or from the address below. Just tick the titles required and send the form with your payment to:-

BBCS, P O Box 941, Kingston upon Hull HU1 3YQ
24-hour telephone credit card line 01482 224626
Prices and availability are subject to change without notice.
Please enclose a cheque or postal order made payable to BBCS to the value of the cover price of the book and allow the following for postage and packing:

UK & BFPO:	£1.95 (weight up to 1kg)		3-day delivery
	£2.95 (weight over 1kg up to 20kg)		3-day delivery
	£4.95 (weight up to 20kg)		next day delivery

EU & Eire:	Surface Mail	£2.50 for first book & £1.50 for subsequent books
	Airmail	£4.00 for first book & £2.50 for subsequent books
USA:	Surface Mail	£4.50 for first book & £2.50 for subsequent books
	Airmail	£7.50 for first book & £3.50 for subsequent books
Rest of the World:	Surface Mail	£6.00 for first book & £3.50 for subsequent books
	Airmail	£10.00 for first book & £4.50 for subsequent books

Name ....

Address ....

....

....

Cards accepted: Visa, Mastercard, Switch, Delta, American Express

Expiry Date........................Signature ....